RAGING SEA

RAGIN

THE SECOND UNDERTOW NOVEL

G SEA

MICHAEL BUCKLEY

HOUGHTON MIFFLIN HARCOURT

BOSTON   NEW YORK

All rights reserved. For information about permission to reproduce
selections from this book, write to trade.permissions@hmhco.com
or to Permissions, Houghton Mifflin Harcourt Publishing Company,
3 Park Avenue, 19th floor, New York, New York 10016.

www.hmhco.com

The text was set in Dante MT Std.
Book design by Lisa Vega

Library of Congress Cataloging-in-Publication Data is available.
ISBN: 978-0-544-34844-8

Manufactured in the United States of America
DOC 10 9 8 7 6 5 4 3 2 1
4500575523

For Sarah Landis, who guides this ship

ALLEGED CONEY ISLAND TERRORIST, LYRIC WALKER, STILL AT LARGE

BY VIDA FARGIS, *NEW YORK TIMES* REPORTER

CONEY ISLAND, NY – LYRIC WALKER, THE SEVENTEEN-YEAR-OLD SO-CALLED CONEY ISLAND TERRORIST, IS STILL AT LARGE AND CONTINUES TO ELUDE FEDERAL MARSHALS AND LOCAL POLICE DEPARTMENTS. THE FBI ONCE AGAIN HAS CALLED FOR THE PUBLIC'S ASSISTANCE IN TRACKING WALKER DOWN, DOUBLING ITS REWARD TO FIVE MILLION DOLLARS FOR ANY INFORMATION LEADING TO HER CAPTURE AND ARREST. TODAY THE AGENCY REASSERTED ITS CLAIM THAT IT IS EAGERLY PURSUING EVERY LEAD.

"[Walker] is allegedly tied to the deaths of nearly fifteen thousand people, as well as the disappearance of another four thousand. Bringing her to justice is the agency's top priority," FBI director David Winslow explained. He said the search has been hampered by the fact that the department is "working in a vacuum." "We know she's out there, but we need everyone's help to find her," Winslow stated.

Winslow pointed to the FBI's twenty-four-hour tip line and website. He also stated that every police precinct in the United States is on heightened alert for Walker because of her alleged involvement in the destruction of the Coney Island neighborhood of Brooklyn, New York. Two weeks ago a massive tidal wave slammed into the community, causing countless deaths and billions of dollars in property damage, shortly after local police attempted to arrest Walker and her parents, Leonard and Summer Walker, on suspicion of espionage as Alpha terrorists. Credible evidence suggests that the wave was not an act of nature but the result of a weapon created by Alpha scientists.

A high-ranking official in the State Department who was not authorized to speak on behalf of the president complained that the failure to locate Ms. Walker is making law enforcement officials look incompetent.

"This girl has no family outside New York City. She has no credit cards and, as far as we can tell, no cash. Yet she's somehow managing to stay off our radar," he said. "We've gotten tips from New York all the way to Texas, but the police can't make an arrest."

Some reports allege Walker is traveling with a friend named Rebecca Conrad and an Alpha female who goes by the name Arcade and is rumored to be a member of the Triton clan.

"How hard is it to find three teenage girls, one of whom happens to be from a completely different species?" the source continued. "I won't lie. This is frustrating. I know the American public is frustrated." The source added that the young women "are making us look like fools."

Recently appointed NYPD chief Albert Hand says his department has officers working overtime with military officials, sifting through surveillance-camera footage from the city and surrounding states.

"We're going through video from banks, ATMs, convenience stores, libraries, anywhere there's a camera." Chief Hand says it's "possible, though unlikely" that Walker remains here in New York. "We believe she is headed to the Southwest and has eluded the roadblocks that many states have constructed to keep out East Coast refugees. We've been working hand in hand with departments in New Jersey, Connecticut and Pennsylvania to find her. People need to be patient. We'll catch her. It's impossible to hide in modern America."

CHAPTER ONE

SHE SITS AMONG THE CACTUS AND STONES AS THE RISING Texas sun ignites the edges of her silhouette. Her eyes are closed, her legs crossed, as if she is meditating. But the only higher plane she's trying to reach involves killing and maiming her enemies. She barks at her fish god, the one she calls the Great Abyss, repeating an endless diatribe that deals with ripping out entrails, and severing heads from necks. This is how Arcade prays, and it can take hours. I was out here waiting when the temperature dropped and my bones froze stiff. Now the sun is rising and the air is broiling and I have run out of patience. We're supposed to be training. We're supposed to be getting ready for Tempest, but nothing happens until the Great Abyss gets an earful.

I kick a stone, a passive-aggressive reminder to her that I am still here.

I kick another.

"Come on!" I growl, giving up on the passive.

She opens her sharp blue eyes and stares at me. They form narrow slits that I'm sure would shoot lasers if they could. I have broken her unspoken rule—no talking when she's doing her fiery-religion thing.

"The Great Abyss is owed praise for his favors," she says. "He is the giver and the taker, the creator of all things, the beginning and the end of this world, and it would be wise for you to kneel and prostrate yourself before him."

"I don't believe in the Great Abyss."

"The Great Abyss does not need you to believe in him. He is, whether you accept his existence or not. Dismiss him at your own peril."

"Thanks for the warning."

"Do humans not have a god of their own you could speak to?"

"We've got hundreds of them, but the one I picked isn't much of a talker," I say as I raise my hand into the sky. My palm is encased in a thick metal glove that wraps around my wrist and exposes the fingers. With just a thought, it explodes with power and energy, turning my whole arm into a supernova of bright blue light. I smile. It wasn't so long ago that I was terrified of this thing, but now I'm digging it—a lot. Wearing it makes me feel intimidating, like I'm an Amazonian warrior. I feel dangerous, gigantic, and five hundred feet tall. "We're wasting time! If I don't break something, I'm going to go crazy."

"You want to break something, little minnow? Then break me," Arcade says as she climbs to her feet. Once there, she ignites her own glove, and without warning, the ground heaves, first left, then right, bucking me like I'm a pesky flea it wants to shake off its hide. A crevice opens beneath me, and mud, silt, and water belch through it, rocketing high into the sky and knocking me to the ground.

I should have seen that coming.

I bear down on my thoughts, turning Arcade's geyser into a baseball bat as big as a man. I fill it with sand and stones, and then I swing for the fences, right into her rib cage. The impact knocks her off her feet and sends her flailing across the dusty field. She lands with a bone-crunching thud that would kill a normal person. Arcade is made of tougher stuff. She is a Triton, a warrior from an undersea empire flung to the surface by war and horror. Before she set foot on land, she lived her whole life in an inhospitable environment that made her stronger and faster and meaner. My attack was no more than a swat in a pillow fight. She runs toward me, roaring in my ears, with her glove leaving a comet's trail behind her. It's her turn to clobber me.

Two weeks ago, I would never have stood my ground like I do now. When Arcade agreed to train me to fight, I was still clinging to the quiet little girl I had been for so long. When she demanded that I think of myself as a weapon, I just couldn't do it, even though I knew it was confidence and passion that fueled the crazy weapon on my hand. Don't ask me how it works. All I know is the more badass I feel, the more damage I can do. But getting over years of invisibility wasn't easy, and my cowardice held me back. Now that wall I built around me is falling down. Now I'm feeling like the wild thing I was always meant to be. Which is convenient, because now we're in Texas, where Tempest is, where they are keeping my family. Anyone who gets in my way has a big frickin' problem on their hands. Even Arcade.

Oh, wait—here she comes.

A huge watery fist materializes before me and catches me in the face. I flail backwards, end over end, like a pickup truck just hit me in the mouth. I crash onto my back, hard. Pain stampedes through my hips, neck, and chin. I see stars, and I'm suddenly not sure where I am.

Arcade stands over me, impatient and unsympathetic.

"Get up!" she demands. "Do you think the soldiers at Tempest will give you a chance to recover? They will shoot you where you lie, half-breed."

I hate when she calls me that word, which is exactly why she does it. She knows it sets me off. She's asking for it, so I wrap water around a nearby boulder, one that would take ten men to heft an inch, and use the liquid to wrench it free from the soil. It hovers between the teacher and the student. I want Arcade to see what I've learned, let her think I will fling it at her if she doesn't stop insulting me, but her eyes are full of smiles. She's calling my bluff.

Furious, I send it sailing in her direction. It's too fast to dodge, and it slams into her with all the power of a subway train. Her body is flung fifty feet away, narrowly missing a patch of wild cacti when she lands. I'm sure I've killed her this time. I scamper to my feet in a panic and rush to her side.

"You are the only person in the world who bleeds when she attacks someone else," she says.

I reach up and touch my nose. It's wet, and when I look at my fingers, they are smeared in red. I'm not sure why this keeps happening. It seems if I go overboard with the glove, it breaks something inside my head. It's probably killing me.

"Maybe I need a break," I confess.

"A break?" she scoffs. "An Alpha does not need a break. Your mother's blood runs through you, Lyric Walker. Can't you hear its call for war?"

"My mother was a yoga teacher!"

"Your mother is a Daughter of Sirena. She fought off a pack of barracudas when she could barely lift her own head. Her father was Lan, hero of the Trill campaigns. There are songs about him that will be sung for generations. Your grandmother Shar was also known throughout the hunting grounds for her bloodthirstiness. She once defeated an Orlandi chieftain in hand-to-hand combat, all with a broken arm."

"Trill? Orlandi? Are they Alpha clans?"

She shakes her head. "There are other empires, Lyric Walker. Did your mother teach you nothing?"

"I didn't want to know," I confess. When I found out my mother wasn't a human being, I avoided everything about her past. I didn't want Summer Walker the Underwater Barbarian.

I wanted Summer Walker wearer of cutoff jean shorts and flip-flops.

"There are many things in the sea, Lyric Walker. Be thankful that you have only seen a small number of them."

I shudder. I've seen enough to give me nightmares for the rest of my life.

"So you knew my family?" I ask. "All my mother really told me is that they were important figures in the Alpha government. I didn't know they were famous."

"As counselors and consorts, they were widely regarded, but it was their warrior instincts that earned them respect. You dishonor them with your halfhearted efforts."

"I'm getting better!" I argue.

Water ruptures from the soil and curls around my neck like an anaconda. It jerks me off the ground nearly ten feet. I dangle and kick for freedom. She could kill me right here. She just might.

"Better is not good enough, Lyric Walker," she says casually, as if she's not strangling the life out of me. "We march to Tempest to free our people. Your pathetic efforts will intimidate no one. Is there no ferocity in you?"

The air slowly leaves my lungs. My legs search for land that isn't there.

"Your city has been demolished. Your friends are dead and gone. Enemies roam your lands. Soldiers have taken your people, torn them from the arms of their mothers, all to cut them open and see how they work! Does none of this burn your passions? Where is your fury?"

"I can't breathe!" I croak.

She frowns, and just like that, the water releases me. It rains to the ground, taking me along with it, and I land in the sand, gasping for oxygen. She stands over me with the sun behind her, so I cannot see her expression, but I don't need to see it to know it is full of disgust.

"I have fury." I choke.

"Then why don't I fear you? Do you know why I am so much stronger than you with this glove? It's because, as the humans say, I have scores to settle. My people were obliterated, reduced from millions to thousands. We suffered the indignation of living like rats in your surface world, to be spied on and attacked by human filth. We humiliated ourselves, cowering on your beach, and it was all for nothing! The Rusalka found us. We were easy targets. They slaughtered even more of our people, taking us from thousands to hundreds, and among those broken souls was my selfsame. Fathom's death will not have been in vain. This weapon I wear burns bright with revenge, and I will use it to crush those responsible — the Rusalka, the prime, and the people at Tempest."

Fathom. Hearing his name is a punch in the belly. In the two weeks that Arcade and I have traveled together, she has never mentioned him once, not in passing, nothing. I've been smart enough to keep my mouth shut too. After all, we're both in love with him. I suddenly suspect that all this training is an excuse to get me out into the middle of nowhere so she can kill me. She would be justified, I suppose.

"He's not dead," I croak.

"Of course he is," she says, watching me like I've said something crazy. "The prime and his consort cut him down in the water. If the Rusalka didn't track him and feed on his body, then the sharks devoured him for sure. No, he did not survive. He has gone on to join the Great Abyss."

I'm incensed by her certainty that the boy we both love did not survive. I saw the wound on his side and the blood that leaked from it, and I saw the goodbye in his eyes when he kissed me and swam away, but I can't give up hope. I cannot accept a world in which he's not alive.

The glove glows brighter on my hand. Yes, I do have something that fuels it. It's regret for not holding on to him tighter. I should have held him and never let him go. I was a fool to respect their relationship. She didn't . . . doesn't love him. When you love a person, you don't shrug your shoulders at their loss. You don't just move on.

A funnel of water shoots out of the ground and catches Arcade, catapulting her into the sky. I wrap her in silt and mud and bring her down to the ground like a pile driver. This time I don't hold back, so when she hits, there's a bang I'm sure can be heard for miles.

I walk over to her limp body as she recovers. Instead of a fiery anger, I see the faintest hint of a smile.

"There is a fighter inside you, Lyric Walker," Arcade says. "Tempest may tremble before you after all."

I hear someone clear her throat behind us. When I turn, I find Bex standing a few yards away, holding my empty back-pack. She's wearing a miniskirt, a Superman T-shirt, and a pair of Mary Janes that add two inches to her already-tall frame. She'd look hot if it weren't for the impatient crease between her eyes.

"We're out of food," she says. "If you're done killing each other, we need to go shopping."

CHAPTER TWO

I KNOW IT'S NOT SOMETHING I SHOULD BRAG ABOUT, BUT I'M really good at shoplifting.

Of course, I had to learn the hard way. My first attempts were embarrassing. I was too nervous, fumbling with my backpack and looking around suspiciously. I got caught six times in a row! On one of my first tries, the Korean owner of a convenience store chased Bex and me into the woods with a shotgun. We had to hide in a wetland all night while he shouted Korean profanities and mosquitoes dined on our skin.

Anyway, I learned some things from those experiences, like to avoid stores where the guy behind the counter is also the guy who owns the shop. This is how he pays his bills, and it means a lot to him. Big chain stores like 7-Eleven and Wawa don't pay their employees enough to care if you walk out with a case of Slim Jims, so they don't when you do.

Making a list is also helpful. My mom used to make them when we went for groceries at C-Town. She said it helped her stay focused. She was right. The stores I'm ripping off have a rainbow of colorful distractions and can hypnotize you with their endless varieties of corn-syrup-soaked foodlike products. When I go in, I know what I want to take, and if it isn't on the list, then it stays on the shelf.

But the real secret to my success is what I call the four simple steps:

1. Find a store with a male cashier, somewhere between the ages of nineteen and fifty-five.
2. Dress Bex in some hoochie clothes.
3. While the cashier/pervert is drooling over her, fill up the backpack with necessities.
4. Run like maniacs.

For the most part, the four simple steps are foolproof, just so long as Bex has Cashier Boy's attention. Unfortunately, today's "shopping trip" has a bit of a snag in it. Bex is in a mood and not talking to me.

"It's nothing," Bex says as she applies a thick layer of eyeliner in the side-view mirror of our Dodge Caravan.

"It's something," I mutter. The tension between us grows like weeds these days. I assumed it was due to sleeping in construction sites and wearing the same clothes for days on end. Or maybe that's what I wanted to think. My friend is an enigma, the queen of the emotional stiff-arm, and few can see the trouble behind her happy eyes. I've learned ways to get around it, but nothing seems to work now. All I know for certain is that "nothing" is about me.

"Forget it, Lyric," she whispers as she touches up her lip gloss, then steps back to get a better look at herself in the tiny mirror. She looks like she just stepped out of *Lolita*. When you combine all the tiny clothing, makeup, and her natural sun-kissed California-girl face, she's impossible not to notice and, we hope, impossible to resist.

"How is it that we have both been washing our hair in park fountains, eating the same diet of Snapple and Swedish Fish, and yet you look like you're ready for the runway, while I look like that thing that lives in the folds of Jabba the Hutt's skin?"

"Let's get this over with, all right?" she says, then walks across the empty street.

"I do not approve of this behavior," Arcade seethes. She sits on the hood of the Dodge, staring at our target, the Piggly Wiggly across the street. Unlike Bex, Arcade's stiff-arms are not so emotional. They're more like angry uppercuts. There's no beating around the bush with her feelings. Right now she's looking at me like I'm something on the bottom of her boot.

"We've been through this a hundred times, Arcade. We've got to eat," I explain, reaching into the back of the Caravan for my water bottle. I eyeball it to make sure it's full, then slip it into my backpack.

"There is honor in hunger."

"If we starve to death before we get to Tempest, that would be disappointing."

She grunts.

"In the hunting grounds, my people threw thieves into the black chasm to feed the Leviathan."

"Leviathan?"

"A mammoth beast as big as a ship with a thousand teeth and a taste for brains," she says matter-of-factly.

"Is there anything where you're from that's not gross?"

She doesn't answer. Instead she turns her disapproving gaze back toward the store. Out front is a sign featuring a cartoon pig with a big "Come on in, folks!" grin on his fat pink face. I don't think he'd be smiling if he knew what I'm planning.

"Stay in the car and try to stay out of sight," I beg her. Like Bex, Arcade is a beauty, but there is something slightly nonhuman about her appearance that draws a lot of attention.

"A Daughter of Triton does not hide," she barks.

There's no point in arguing with her, so I hurry to catch up with Bex.

I find her out front peering through the store's big windows. A large NO COASTERS! sign is taped to the glass.

"He's perfect," she says.

I take a peek. The cashier inside is watching a football game on a tiny TV set he's propped up on the counter. He's in his late twenties, chubby, balding, and pink, not unlike the pig on the sign. He's exactly what we hope for when we do this. Teenage boys are nervous as pigeons around Bex; same with the sad forty-year-olds we sometimes come across. The mid-twenties guy is our sweet spot. He's trapped in a dead-end job, insecure about it, and desperate for some attention from a pretty girl.

"Lyric, make me a promise," Bex asks as she reaches for the door. "Once you do your thing with the water bottle, turn off the magic mitten."

"Why?" I say. I can hear the defensiveness in my voice.

"You scared the guy at the last store."

I laugh.

"When that Slushy machine blew up, I thought he was going to have a heart attack," I say.

"It wasn't funny." She's dead serious.

"Bex, he wasn't hurt, and besides, I need the practice for when we get to Tempest."

She scowls and shakes her head.

"Promise me you won't use it in here, or I'm not going in," she says, and I can tell she means it. She takes her hand off the door as if she might march right back to the car.

"Okay," I say. I hide the glove behind my back.

She nods a thank-you, then steps into the frosty, over-air-conditioned shop. The bell tied to the door jingles a hello. I watch her approach the counter, suddenly wearing a smile she used to wear for me. She says something, bats her eyelashes, reaches out, and touches the cashier's arm, throwing out the bait. A grin stretches across his face as wide as the Rio Grande. *Reel him in, Bex.*

It's time for me to get to work. I unscrew the cap on my

water bottle and pour the contents onto the sidewalk. Then I shove my hand up under my shirt and, with the slightest amount of concentration, turn on the "magic mitten." The metal glows blue but, hidden beneath the fabric, it's not so noticeable if someone happens to drive by right now. Above the crackling power, I hear voices fluttering in my ear.

What would you have us do?

"Make some mischief."

I send the puddle into action, watching it seep under the crack of the door and into the store. I nudge it along so that it crawls up the wall to the ceiling, leaving a wet zigzag trail behind, until it finds its target, one of the dozen surveillance cameras mounted on the walls. The liquid invades the lens, swirls around in its electrical guts, and shorts out the entire system. A moment later it's blind, and I direct my little wet sidekick to the next camera, then the next, then the next, until all twelve are busted. Proud of myself, I power down my glove and push open the door.

The bell on the door announces my arrival. This is the moment when everything can fall apart and it's best to abandon the plan and look for another store. The jingle distracts the cashier, and he tears his eyes away from Bex and sends them my way. It is now that he will decide whether I'm suspicious or merely disappointing to look at. This part of the plan is hard on my ego. I don't get to be the hot one when we shoplift. I have to be the Plain Jane, only this Plain Jane looks like she sleeps beneath an underpass—no makeup, ratty hair, and a pimple on the end of my chin that could take out Pompeii. I tell myself that I am unattractive on purpose. If I strutted into this store looking all kinds of yummy, the plan would not work. Secretly, I hope that he can see past the grime. It hurts when they don't, but it means we'll eat.

He gives me the once-over. Blinks. Sniffs. Then turns back to Bex. Sigh.

"I am so lost," she coos.

"Well, maybe I can help," he says.

The Piggly Wiggly has four aisles and refrigerator cases on three walls. There's a soda machine and a microwave and a hot dog carousel. In my experience, the necessities are in the farthest aisle and the stuff that gives you diabetes is front and center, stocked on low shelves so little kids can grab it before their parents can say no. I hurry to the far back corner, where I find the first thing on my list—soap. You don't know how important soap is until you don't have it. Two bars of Ivory go into my pack, then a tube of Crest, a small bottle of green mouthwash, and—oh!—I can't believe they have dental floss! That's been on the list since I started making a list. A couple rolls of toilet paper are making things crowded, but after weeks of using gas-station t.p. . . . well, that's TMI.

You're stealing again, Lyric? I taught you better.

Oh, hey, Dad! I was beginning to think you weren't going to show up to make me feel guilty. Yeah, I'm shoplifting again, but desperate times call for desperate measures, and these are the desperate-est of the desperate times. I'm living in a car. I'm dead broke. I'm on the FBI's most-wanted list.

The second aisle is where the term *food* is thrown about with loose abandon. Here I find peanuts coated in honey, peanuts coated in peanut butter, peanut-butter-flavored protein bars, yogurt-covered raisins, "diet" desserts. This is the stuff that's killing me, but it's easy to carry and never goes bad. I stuff as many as I can into the pack.

There's not much happening in the next aisle. This is the Death Valley of all convenience stores: cans of motor oil, NASCAR T-shirts, dusty country and western CDs, and tattooed-girlie magazines. One shelf has a stack of those little tree-shaped car fresheners that smell like pine or green apples. I grab a couple and put them in the pack. The Caravan is getting pretty rank.

One more aisle and I'm out of here. I turn the corner and nearly fall over in shock. Food! Real food: apples, bananas, oranges, whole-wheat bread, cans of soup! In the refrigerator case nearby is milk, string cheese, bologna, pre-made tuna fish sandwiches, and a package of bacon. I have no idea how I'm going to cook it, but it doesn't matter. I've got bacon! Getting it into the pack is a bigger problem. It's almost full. Screw the toilet paper! I'll suffer. Once the t.p. rolls are out, I surrender a bar of soap and the mouthwash. Sacrifices have to be made, but now I've got room for a half gallon of milk and a loaf of bread.

The pack is now officially overflowing. I fight the zipper, then heft the whole thing onto my back.

It's time to go. As I pass down the aisle, I notice a newspaper rack. *USA Today* has a picture of my hometown on its front page. Coney Island is a battlefield. Soldiers charge toward the sea, firing rifles at dark-skinned Rusalka leaping out of a massive wave. There are two figures rising above the whitecaps who don't fit in with the monsters. I peer closer until I finally recognize them. The first is the prime, Fathom's insane father and king of the Alpha. He was bent on an invasion of the mainland even when his people were at their most vulnerable, and now he's got it. The second is his wife, Minerva, a cackling partner to his madness. More shocking to me is that it appears as if the prime is leading the Rusalka. How did the bitterest of enemies join forces?

Other papers and magazines give me more glimpses into the world I left behind. One reports on states rising up against one another, sending in their own militias to defend their borders. There are stories of lynchings and soldiers shooting people for trying to cross state lines. Food shortages are rampant, mobs, looting, and fires are a daily event. One paper speculates the tensions will lead to secession and to a second civil war.

But no matter what these papers are reporting, there is one thing they share: a hatred of Lyric Walker, teen terrorist-at-large. They use photos of me at my worst. Facebook shots when I was a little buzzed or a sweaty mess in the humid

Coney Island heat. I look unhinged, a bad seed who's been on the wrong path since she was born. I guess they can't exactly use the picture of me in my tenth grade homecoming dress. I wore a vintage lace shift with rose appliqués that night. I rocked that dress. Nope, I'm public-enemy number one, and I have to look the part.

I tell myself that it doesn't matter. I did what I could to stop everything that happened. They turned on me! *They* kidnapped my family and now *I'm* the villain? It's more of the same old racism now that they know I'm only half human. I guess it makes me all monster in their eyes. Well, let the world burn. It looks to me like it's getting exactly what it deserves.

Furious, I tear myself away from the papers only to find the cashier in my path.

"So, this little scam the two of you pull would probably work if not for one thing," he says.

Bex is just over his shoulder. She frowns and throws her hands up in surrender.

"I'm not a total idiot," he continues. "I've already pressed the silent alarm, so the police are on their way. Let's stay calm and let them handle this."

"How about if I put it all back?" I offer.

He hesitates, considering the notion, but it's too late. Two squad cars pull into the parking lot outside and stop. Four cops squeeze out of them, seemingly quadruplets, or at least clones — goatees, shaved heads, aviator sunglasses. Two of them circle around the back. I assume they want to make sure Bex and I don't sneak out a rear exit. The other two swagger through the front door and look around.

"Ladies, I'm Officer Perry and this is Officer Casto. Let me tell you what's going to happen here," he says as he takes off his sunglasses. Behind them are two oval-shaped patches of white skin in a sea of sunburn. "We're placing the two of you under arrest for shoplifting. It's best if you cooperate. It will go better for you when you go to court."

"Court," I whisper to Bex.

We can't go to court. We can't get arrested, either. The moment I'm put into the system, the military will march into this town and drag me away, probably to Tempest. No, when I show up there, it's not going to be in chains. Getting arrested is not an option today.

"Take off the backpack, please," Perry continues.

I do as he says, mainly because it will slow me down when we make a run for it.

"We promise we won't do anything like this again," Bex begs, still hoping this will end well.

"Sounds like we have a couple of Coasters, partner." Perry says to Casto.

Casto looks us up and down, then shakes his head like we're an infestation of vermin.

Coasters. That word pops up everywhere we go, like a hateful jack-in-the-box. It hangs in storefronts and gas stations. I've seen it on T-shirts and the front page of newspapers. We come from the East, places that people used to move to so they could be near the ocean. Boston, Savannah, New Haven, Providence, Norfolk, Miami, Fort Lauderdale, New York City, they're all devastated, destroyed by floods and tidal waves and monsters from the deep. People watch the tides. They leave everything they own when the Rusalka arrive. They run for their lives, but before they can get very far, cops and road-blocks try to stop them. The governors of places like Texas and Alabama tell us we are not welcome. They claim Coast-ers pose a threat to public health. They say it with a smirk. You don't have to read a history book to know that half of this country has been waiting a few hundred years for a chance to screw the other half. Now they've got their chance.

"That could have been a possibility if you weren't in viola-tion of the governor's executive order," Casto says in answer to Bex's offer. "No one from outside the state is permitted within Texas borders without the proper identification. I'm going to go out on a limb and guess you don't have it."

He pauses for Perry's laugh. It's a joke only he and his part-ner find funny.

"I'm going to search you now," Perry says. "Do you have anything dangerous in your pockets? Needles? Anything sharp I should know about before I put my hands inside? Drug para-phernalia? If I reach into that pocket and something sticks me, things are gonna get unpleasant."

"Really, you don't have to do this," Bex begs, but she's not looking at the cops. She's looking at me.

Perry pats me down and mutters something about "Coaster filth" and how I smell. He's "had it up to here" with "illegals" sneaking into his state, causing problems, "sleepin' in the parks." He's not having it in his town, "no, sirree, Bob." He's "drawin' a line in the sand" before the place he grew up in turns into another "stinkin' refugee camp."

"What is this?" he barks as he snatches my gloved hand and lifts it up to my face as if I have no idea it's wrapped around my wrist.

"It's jewelry," Bex lies. "She made it."

"Take it off," Perry orders.

"I can't. It's locked on tight."

It's the truth. This thing won't come off. I've tried vegetable oil, butter, soap, prying it open with a knife, smashing it with a hammer, everything short of amputating my hand.

"What are these markings?" he asks, twisting my hand roughly as he peers closer. "What is this? A wave or something?"

He looks into my face, maybe for the first time, and there's a burst of recognition. Yep, it's me. He's befuddled and turns pale as chalk, then falls backwards like I slugged him. On his way down, he knocks over a rack of candy bars, then a container filled with bottles of soft drinks in ice.

"Perry?" his partner cries. "What the heck? Get up."

"Casto, she's that girl from New York," he croaks while fumbling for his gun. When he finds it, he points the muzzle right into my face. "The terrorist!"

"Holy crap! The mermaid?" Casto cries. He aims his gun at me too.

Perry snatches for his radio with his free hand and drags it to his mouth. He pushes the buttons over and over again, like it's the first time he's used it, then screams for backup like there are thousands of me, all with bazookas and machetes.

A door at the back of the store opens, and the other two officers enter. Neither of them is expecting to find this scene, but in a flash, they've got their revolvers out as well.

"I thought this was a snatch-and-run," one of them cries.

"These are those girls from New York!" Perry explains. "The ones everybody's looking for."

I turn to Bex and give her a little "I'm sorry" frown. I have to break my promise. She flashes me an angry look, but what choice do I have? We can't go to jail. There are too many people counting on us. I will my weapon to life, admiring how it crackles, and quietly giggle when I hear four grown men gasp. Yes, I am awesome, thank you very much.

The whispers call out from every corner of the store, in the plumbing, behind the refrigerator doors, dripping out of the soda machine. There is so much water here, and all of it is as eager as a child waving her hand in class and hoping the teacher will call her name. All I have to do is ask for its help. So I do.

It starts with a banging in the refrigerator case behind the four cops, causing everyone to jump with surprise. A fizzy bottle of orange soda slams against the glass door, dancing a hyperactive jig.

"Lyric, no," Bex whimpers.

"Don't worry. I got this," I say to her as more bottles join the fun.

"Are you doing that?" Casto shouts at me. "Turn that thing off or I'll shoot!"

"You should have let us go," I remind him.

All the bottles shake violently, a deafening crescendo that cracks the air. There is an explosion of broken glass. Syrupy drinks splatter the walls, the floor, and the ceiling. Before the cops can react, they are soaked in water, beer, and sports drinks. Bottles rocket across the room like missiles, zinging past my head. A jug of coconut water tags Casto in the head and knocks him completely off his feet. He lands with a painful thud. His gun skips across the slippery floor just as a bottle of cola clobbers one of his colleagues in the jaw. A jug of iced tea streaks through the air and hits the cashier in the chest. A dozen cans of energy drink track the third officer like drones, hitting him in the temple, the back, and the gut. He slips and falls fast on the wet linoleum, face-planting the microwave counter on the way down and knocking himself unconscious.

Perry finally scrambles to his feet. The gun that he holds in his hands shakes like a leaf in a strong breeze.

"What are you?" he asks. It's a good question.

"I'm a Coaster, don't you remember?" I say, then urge a

two-liter bottle of mineral water to barrel into the back of his skull. He falls forward and his pistol fires. I hear the bullet whiz past me. It tugs the tail of my shirt, and when I look down, I see a faint trail of smoke drift out of the hole it made. My hands reach underneath frantically searching for a wound and the tacky traces of blood, but I can't find anything. He missed me, but now I'm angry. I stalk over to him, lying on the floor, terror in his eyes, and suddenly knocking him down doesn't feel like it was enough. This one needs to learn a lesson, one he can tell the whole world when the reporters come to ask him about his meeting with the terrorist teen, the Alpha monster, the girl who killed Coney Island. I can make sure he tells them all what I want them to hear: *Don't be stupid enough to get in my way.*

My hand glows as bright as my rage.

Bex grabs the pack, then me, and pulls me through the door and out into the parking lot.

"No!" I cry, trying to free myself.

"C'mon!" she screams. "There will be more cops any minute."

I'm frustrated, but she's right. We need to go. We sprint across the road, where Arcade is still sitting on the hood.

"You were attacked?" Her glove blazes to life. "Why are you running?"

"We have to go now," Bex shouts.

"A Daughter of Triton does not run from challengers!" Arcade says, releasing her second weapon, two jagged blades she calls her 'Kala,' serrated on their edges, which live in her forearms. They slide out with a *shhhkkkttt!*

"They're not challengers. They're police officers, and Lyric attacked them."

Arcade gives me a pleased expression. It's not a smile. She doesn't do that, but it still makes me proud.

"More are on the way," Bex continues as she pushes me into the driver's-side seat, "and thanks to that stupid stunt, every cop in the world is going to join them. Get in the car!"

Bex opens Arcade's door for her. The two of them share an unspoken battle of wills, then Bex throws up her hands in surrender and rushes around to the other side. She hops into the passenger seat and slams her door shut. Then she stuffs the key into the ignition and turns the car over for me.

"Lyric! Drive!" Bex shouts at me.

"This is shameful," Arcade mutters, then begrudgingly gets into her seat. Once her door is closed, I throw the car into drive and stomp the gas pedal all the way to the floor. Tires scream on asphalt, and we shoot down the road, steering haphazardly as Bex calls out turn-for-turn directions. Arcade watches the windows, her gauntlet glowing and ready.

"Turn that off," I shout to her. "You can see the light halfway down the road."

Just as Bex predicted, the air fills with sirens. Police cars tear down every street. Some streets are so crowded with squad cars that we have to double back, and there's a moment when we almost have to drive past the Piggly Wiggly again.

"Pull in there," Bex cries, pointing to an IGA grocery store. I make an insane hairpin turn that nearly causes us to fishtail into another car, but I manage to right us before an accident happens. I burn up an aisle and into an empty parking space. Bex reaches over, throws the car into park, and turns off the engine, then forces me to duck down below the steering wheel.

Huddled on the floor, I look over to my friend. Her face has turned from a scowl to utter disbelief.

"The only reason we haven't been caught is no one knew where we were," she whispers to me. "You just ruined that. Everybody with a badge and a gun is going to head to Texas to find us, which would be fine if we actually knew where we were going, but we don't, which means it's just a matter of time before we get caught."

"They were going to arrest us," I say defensively.

Bex drops her head into her hands and shakes it sadly.

"That's their job. We were committing a crime. When people commit crimes, police officers arrest them. That's how society works, but you were treating them like bad guys. They're cops. Just like your dad."

"They are nothing like my dad. They called us Coasters! They humiliated us."

"Fine! They are dumb cops in a stupid town. It doesn't give you the right to put them in the hospital."

"Lyric Walker did what was necessary," Arcade says.

"She was showing off!" Bex shouts at her. "And she just made our lives a million times harder."

The truth stinks. It took us forever to get to Texas from Brooklyn, two weeks of starving and hitching rides with perverts and sleeping on picnic tables. I just jeopardized all that sacrifice. What came over me back there? Why did I want to hurt those men so much? It wasn't just because they called us Coasters. I was overcome with something that was beyond anger. I was looking for a fight.

"Let them come," Arcade sneers. "When their fat bodies lie bleeding in the streets, it will send a message to those at Tempest who imprison our people."

Bex pounds her fists onto the dashboard, then opens her door and gets out.

"Where are you going?" I cry.

"We have to find another car," she snaps bitterly.

I watch her stomp off across the parking lot. Each step she takes away from me makes me anxious, as if she might get so far away that I'll lose her completely.

"We should leave her here," Arcade says.

"What?"

"She is not like us, Lyric Walker. She will be no help to us at Tempest. This is not her fight. She is human."

"I'm human!" I cry.

She shakes her head. "No, you are not. You are Alpha, a new kind, but one of us nonetheless. She is a helpless human girl with no fighting skills. She is slowing us down with her tedious lectures, and when we arrive at the camp, she will die anyway. Here she will live."

"We're not abandoning my best friend!" I roar, then push the car door open and hit the ground running. I chase across the parking lot, grabbing Bex by the hand and spinning her around.

"What was I supposed to do?"

"You think this is about *what* you did? It's not, Lyric. It's about how you did it. How you always do it. You can't see your face when you use that thing, but I can."

"What are you talking about? What's wrong with my face?"

"You're too happy. When you are scaring someone, or hurting them, you're smiling and proud of yourself."

"That's not true." But as I say it, I know it's a lie.

"Maybe you think you have to become this new Lyric so you can fight the bad guys, but you know what? The new Lyric sucks."

She pulls away from me, leaving me to suck all alone.

CHAPTER THREE

BEX FOUND AN UNLOCKED CAR PARKED IN THE BACK OF the grocery store. It's an ancient Ford Taurus, lime-green and as big as a boat. The shocks are spongy and the brakes shriek as soon as I turn on the engine. The back windows won't roll down and there's no air conditioning, but the keys were under the visor and it has a full tank of gas, so it's our new ride. I have to assume its owner is some poor kid who never thought anyone would want the rusty eyesore. Whoever it belongs to is not making bank. I feel bad, but we have to get out of town fast.

While Bex and Arcade load our stuff, I leave the owner of the Caravan a heartfelt and anonymous apology for its current state, especially for the dents and dings that weren't there when we "borrowed" it. I've smashed a few of these loaners in the last two weeks. I'm doing the best I can, but I don't have a driver's license. City kids don't usually get them. We walk everywhere or hop on the bus or subway. I never took a driving class, and I confess as much to the owner. My apology includes a sincere hope that the damage will not affect his or her insurance premiums, and also a "my bad" for the stink we are leaving behind after sleeping in it for a couple days. I hang one of the pine-scented car fresheners I swiped at the store from the rearview mirror, but I know it's not going to make a big difference. We're disgusting.

I carefully steer our new ride out of the parking lot and head to the edge of town, driving within a hair's breadth of the speed limit. We all have our eyes glued to the road, looking for cops, or for helicopters sent to track us from above. As many officers as there are on the road, none stop us or even give us a second look. I guess the police don't think anyone would steal this car either.

We're half an hour out of town when Bex discovers something in the glove compartment we have desperately needed for a long, long time—a phone charger. It plugs into the cigarette lighter and will work on both our phones.

"This solves, like, a million problems!" I say, selling the positive in hopes of changing Bex's mood, but I didn't need to. She can't hide her excitement. We haven't had phones in two weeks, which in teenage-girl years equals about a zillion.

She plugs the cable into the socket and then fishes her dead phone out of her shorts. Once it's plugged in, I realize how much I want it to work. We've all made sacrifices to find Tempest, but Bex has made the most. She left Coney Island not knowing if her mother survived the attack. We haven't heard from Tammy since. Is she alive? Is she looking for Bex? Plus, there are other people we both care about. Did they get out of the Zone before the disaster? It's been hard being in limbo, waiting for word, when the only conduit to the truth has been dead for weeks. This charger might give her answers, and it couldn't have come at a better time.

The screen lights up, and so does her face.

"C'mon," I cry, scorning the phone's snail-like pace. Where's the *shroom*, and the apple, and the buzz?

"I know!" she groans.

But none of those things happen. Instead, the screen gets weird. A purple smear appears under the glass, then some ugly brown colors and lines, and then what looks like something important melting and spreading. Everything shuts down. Bex pushes the power button again—and again—but nothing happens. She tries to force a reboot, but the phone won't respond. She unplugs the cord and tries it all over again, but there's no response.

"It needs to charge," I promise, ratcheting up the optimism until I sound like a cast member from *Annie*, but her face tells me the sun is not coming out tomorrow.

"It was in the water too long," she whispers, reminding me that I found her half-dead in the water before I dragged her to safety. That phone was submerged for heaven only knows how long. So was mine. "Try yours."

Dread hatches in my belly. My phone was soaked for even longer than Bex's as I swam around trying to rescue people. It was still working when we got out of Brooklyn, but then

I ran down the battery and couldn't charge it. What if mine is busted too? I will lose every email my mom and dad ever sent me, every text message, and every single picture I have of the two of them. There are no photo albums back home. There is no "back home" anymore. Everything about our lives was washed away. All that's left is on this little metal-and-glass machine.

I will lose the only picture I have of Fathom.

I plug the phone in with trembling hands like I'm cradling a baby sparrow I intend to nurse back to health. When I insert the plug, the screen is quiet and still. No *shroom*. No apple. No buzz. I don't even get the light. I close my eyes and negotiate the terms of penance with God for my less-than-moral life as of late. *I'll do anything,* I promise. All I want in exchange is one little electronic miracle.

Shroom.

Apple.

Buzz! Two weeks of messages and voicemails break through the levy and flood my inbox. Seven hundred and fifty-eight text messages appear before my eyes. The phone shakes like it's having a seizure.

"Maybe Tammy sent a message to me," I say hopefully.

Bex watches eagerly as I scroll through everything. I'd so love to give her some good news right now, but almost all of these messages are from people wishing me dead. They hope I get hit by trucks and bleed out in the street. They promise to do terrible things to my corpse. Some of them are from people I knew in the neighborhood, people I might have once considered friends.

"Anything?" Bex asks.

There's nothing. I check twice.

"I don't think she knew my number, Bex. She never called me," I remind her, which is true, but not at all helpful. "It doesn't mean anything. She probably sent you hundreds of them, and all we have to do is find a way to get them. They have to be in the Cloud. They store everything in the Cloud, right?"

She shrugs and turns toward the window.

"We'll get them," I promise, but I have no idea what I'm talking about. I don't know how to access "the Cloud." I don't even really know what it is. "Bex, c'mon. I'll help."

"Just let it go," she whispers.

Another text buzzes and I quietly ask God for just one more favor. Let it be Tammy. I pull it up only to find something a million times more surprising.

CHIHUAHUAN DESERT. MR. COFFEE.

I gasp and drop the phone.

"He's still helping me," I cry, reaching into the glove compartment for a map of Texas I spotted earlier. I pull it out and open it wide.

"Why do you speak in riddles?" Arcade says, suddenly interested in what is happening in the front seat.

"It's Doyle! He just told me where to find Tempest," I say, scanning the map for the Chihuahuan Desert. It's in the far southwestern-most edge of the state, hundreds of miles from where we are right now. It'll take days to get there, but at least we know where to go. "We're going to find them!"

Arcade nods, then snarls. "Move this machine, Lyric Walker."

"Well, let's get going already," Bex adds, without bothering to look at me.

"Bex?"

"Drive."

CHAPTER FOUR

TEXAS IS MASSIVE AND CROSSED BY INTERTWINING highways that lead you to endless tiny copies of the town you just drove through. Still, every dot on its map has a quirky claim to fame. Duncanville, Texas, once housed four nuclear warheads designed to protect Fort Worth and Dallas from the Russians. Hutchins, Texas, has the state's largest men's penitentiary. Terrell, Texas, is the birthplace of Jamie Foxx. Lindale, Texas, is the blackberry capital of the world. Chandler, Texas, boasts the state's biggest horseshoe-throwing competition. Corsicana, Texas, has an annual cotton-harvest festival. Canton, Texas, is the former home of notorious bank robbers Bonnie Parker and Clyde Barrow. I speed past each one, wondering at the lives of the people who call them home. I wonder if they're bored. I envy them. When this is all said and done, I'm going to move to one of these little towns and bask in the boredom.

Bex and Arcade have no interest in the scenery. They nap while the road ticks off the miles. To keep me company, I flip on the radio but keep it low so I don't wake up the happy twins. I've never seen anything as ancient as the Ford's stereo. It's a collection of clunky buttons with two knobs and a little window. I push one of the buttons, and a red line slides across the glass and lands on the number 1430. Static turns into polka music—lively horns and accordions. I push another button and land on a station playing a marathon of someone named Conway Twitty. I listen to a few songs. He's not bad—kind of a country-pop thing—but then he sings that he wants a lover with a slow hand, which completely grosses me out. I push the next button, and the music is replaced by a fiery tirade.

"So, America, more news from the frontlines, and the casualty list continues to grow. The Alphas continue their onslaught."

"Not the Alphas, dummy. The Rusalka," I grumble at him.

"As reported, the city of Norfolk, Virginia, the site of the world's largest military base, is lost. After several tidal waves and relentless flooding, the president has declared the base and surrounding neighborhoods a disaster area. FEMA and the Red Cross are on the scene, but there doesn't appear to be anything to do. Folks, there's no way to sugarcoat this. Norfolk was a terrible blow not only to our country but to our military. We just lost trillions of dollars in weapons, ships, tanks, and supplies, and it's the first American city to fall in this war.

"More coastal towns have been attacked, and as I have predicted many times on this program, the war between *them* and *us* is moving to small-town America. According to reports, the creatures came ashore in Jamestown, Rhode Island;

Portsmouth, Virginia; and Rowayton, Connecticut, to wreak havoc.

"We lost a lot of good people yesterday. A hundred of these monsters marched into Panama City, killing one thousand. Yes, you heard that right, one thousand servicemen and -women. There are reports that some of the bodies were stacked in mounds that spelled out the word *surrender*. Disgusting. Unfortunately, yesterday's losses bring this week's death toll to a whopping three thousand one hundred and eighty-eight people, more than twenty-five hundred of them military personnel. Like we do every day, we ask listeners to join us in a moment of silence to honor these fallen American heroes."

There's a long, quiet void where only the radio's hiss and the sound of tires on the road can be heard. The number of dead flops around like a fish in the bottom of a boat. Three thousand one hundred and eighty-eight people were killed in one week.

I flip off the radio. I can't think about those people. They're on their own.

I spot a sign for a rest stop, and since I haven't seen a cop in hours, I decide to pull off and take a break. The sun is setting out on the horizon, the end of a long, hot day, and the reward is a canvas of reds and purples and oranges.

Bex wakes and gives me a sleepy and confused look.

"I need a break," I whisper, leaning over her to get my phone.

"We all do," she grunts, and immediately drops back off to sleep.

I step out into the cool night and zip up my hoodie. I stretch, then walk over to the bathroom, where I wash my face and hands. I long to brush my teeth, but I'd have to wake the others up again to get into the pack. Instead, I wander over to a picnic table and lie down on my back. I take out my phone. I've got a decent signal, so I type the words CHIHUAHUAN DESERT into the browser, and a map appears. The area is huge, and it spreads into Mexico, New Mexico, and Arizona. It looks like a whole lot of nothing. There are county roads snaking through it and a handful of tiny towns. A big swath of it is a national park. I try to find the ideal place to put a camp. It would have to be in a remote spot, I assume, so that no one would find it. It's not going to be on a major road or near one of the towns. The problem is the entire region is barren. It could take us days to search it all. I hope Doyle sends me another message with more details.

I flip through my pictures to remind me of why I'm going to Tempest in the first place. One is of my mother, Summer Walker, in her ever-present flips-flops and cutoff shorts. She's on the beach doing yoga, strong in the warrior pose with the Atlantic Ocean behind her. She's so beautiful and strong, her black hair fluttering in the breeze. I hope they haven't hurt her. She is a Sirena, and I've heard what they do to Alphas at Tempest.

My father is in the next picture, the man Bex calls the

Big Guy. He's giving me a tired expression as he eats a bowl of cereal in his cop uniform. He loved to ham up his exasperated looks whenever I took his picture, but he's probably the most patient man I know. He's solid and honest and brave, but the last time I saw him, he was seriously hurt. I worry about the broken ribs he probably got when we wrecked the car. He begged us to go on without him. I will always regret that we did.

I flip through more pictures, feeling tears leaking down my face. Here they are, the two of them trying to decipher the instructions for it; the Big Guy's annoyed expression after he broke the IKEA coffee table; my mother standing off to the side, stifling a laugh. Here they are walking hand in hand along the sand, not knowing their daughter was capturing the moment on her phone. Here's Mom glowing in the sunshine. Here's Dad burning breakfast.

"I'm coming. Just hold on," I whisper, hoping the words drift out into the night and find their way to my parents' ears.

I skip forward to a photo of Bex and me, lying on my bed with our heads pressed close together so we can take a picture together. Our eyes are smiling and our mouths are puckered into duck lips. I don't remember when it was taken. It could have happened on a thousand different afternoons. We were inseparable then—so close, we didn't need other girlfriends. Here she is bumming cigarettes from the bouncer at Rudy's, and here is the time we tried to learn to skateboard, and here she is trying on a fur coat we found at the Salvation Army. I told her she looked like a polar bear. We laughed about it for weeks. I miss the girls in these pictures.

The camera roll ends with one of the last shots I snapped, and it steals my breath. Fathom and I are pressed close to each other in the bright Coney Island light. All six-foot-plus of him looks awkward and confused. I'm holding the camera and looking mischievous. I snapped it without warning, and when I showed him the result, his hard, suspicious features fell and a boyish version I never knew existed took their place. Was it magic? he wondered. Did I know how lucky I was to have a machine that recreated the faces of the people I love?

I do now.

What is it about you? Most of our days you were grouchy, or pensive, or just mean, but then you could be so kind. When you stepped close to me and locked your eyes with mine, I felt like I could melt onto the floor. Even now, this picture of you is enough to make me dizzy.

Could you really be gone? Arcade thinks so. She's packed you up and put you in storage like a stack of old sweaters she no longer needs. As cold as she is, maybe she's living in reality.

"I'm not ready to let you go," I whisper.

"We should train."

Arcade has materialized behind me, and I let out a little yelp of surprise.

"You scared the crap out of me," I cry. I fumble with the phone, not wanting her to see my photograph. I stuff it into my pocket and spring to my feet.

Arcade looks around at the deserted parking lot and the tree line behind the bathrooms. I take the opportunity to wipe the tearstains off my face.

"We do not have much time left," she says. "How long before we find the camp?"

"We've got about a half a tank of gas left, but it'll run out and we'll need another car. If we get lucky and all goes perfect, we could be at Tempest in three days."

She nods, then walks across the field toward the woods.

"Come," she calls to me over her shoulder.

"Can we cut the prayer down to fifteen minutes tonight?" I cry after her, but she says nothing.

I give the zipper on my hoodie another tug. It's going to be a long, cold night.

CHAPTER FIVE

ON MOST NIGHTS I AM EAGER TO GO TO SLEEP, EVEN if it is in the back seat of a stolen car. In my dreams, Fathom and I are together. He is healthy and alive. We are wildly in love. It is like the worst YA novel of all time, and it is absolutely delicious.

Tonight, we're lying on a beach, not the gross Coney Island beach littered with cigarette butts and hypodermic needles, but a tropical island. It's warm and bright, and the tide massages our toes. My cheek rides the rise and fall of his chest, and he clings to me like a drowning man holds a life preserver. Together we bake in the afterglow.

Or, at least what I think the afterglow must be like. I am still technically *beforeglow,* at least in the waking world. In my dreams, Fathom and I have been glowing almost every night —it's all hands and fingers and lips and arms and legs and then the fade to black. The nocturne gives me what the real world will not.

Fathom watches me with his hurricane eyes. His fingers

rake through my hair, and I lean into his hand, craving the tickles it conjures. He says something, but it's gibberish, as if this dream has spent all its creative energy and is slowly unraveling. I feel a pang of anxiety. I'm happy. I don't want to go. I like it here.

"Listen," he says, his voice suddenly clear.

"Listen to what?"

He sits up abruptly and scans the milky tide with narrowing eyes.

"I don't hear anything," I say, holding his arm like he might suddenly be pulled away into another dream.

"They're coming, Lyric Walker."

"Who?"

Fathom leaps to his feet, takes my hands, and pulls me to my own.

"The monsters!" he shouts at me, his voice barely audible over a rising shriek that is all at once everywhere and growing with intensity. I turn to the ocean, only to see it rise, higher and higher like a black titan, a looming giant of wrath standing hundreds of feet over my head. It's boiling and indignant, but I stand my ground, staring it down, daring it to come any farther. I plant my feet in the sand. My fists clench until they are red. My chin juts forward defiantly. In the water, I see forms emerge: arms, legs, claws, teeth.

I raise my fist, and it burns like a star, turning me into a lighthouse and illuminating the wave, which is suddenly no longer made of water. Now it is a living mass of Rusalka bodies stampeding toward the shore.

"Run!" Fathom shouts, but when I turn to him, he morphs into Bex. She grabs my free hand and tries to pull me away.

"We can't escape this," I say to her, but again she's changing, morphing into Arcade.

"Kill them! They're not worthy of your mercy!"

When I look back at the wave, it has changed too. It's no longer made of Rusalka. It's made of men and women in lab coats. They hold horrible saws and hooks and cattle prods in their hands, and at their center are my parents, thrashing for freedom.

"Let them go!" I scream.

A scientist leaps out of the murky soup and lands right in front of me. He's followed by another, and another, until I am completely surrounded on all sides. The scientists are no longer just people. They are hybrids of Rusalka and men, walking death with bloody gums; black, soulless eyes; and golden, glowing lights that dangle like bait in front of their terrible, ripping fangs.

"Make an example out of us," they taunt, and one last time they change. The monsters are gone, and in their place are hundreds and hundreds of identical copies of myself.

I wake with a jerk, all floppy limbs and foggy brain, and then *WHAM!* The crown of my head crunches against something hard and unmovable. My skull is a cracked egg with searing yolk dribbling down my neck, shoulders, and spine. Fireflies swoop in and out of my vision and the coppery taste of blood fills my mouth. I've bitten my tongue so hard, I'm worried I might have lost some of it.

"Calm down! You're okay. You're safe," a voice says from above me. Its owner is sitting on my chest.

I push off the dream, telling myself I am not a monster. This is not Coney Island. I'm in a lime-green Ford somewhere in the middle of Texas with a one-hundred-and-twenty-eight-pound girl sitting on my chest.

"Bex," I gasp.

Bex gives me a long, suspicious look as if she's weighing whether or not I've gone crazy.

"I can't breathe," I squeak.

She rolls off me and into her seat. She's sweaty, and it looks like someone poured a glass of water down the back of her T-shirt.

"You've been having a lot of crazy dreams lately," she says, pointing to my hand. The glove is awake and pulsating. It's never powered itself on before without my asking.

"It was so real," I explain as I turn it off. "I can still hear them."

Bex points to my driver's-side window. I crane my neck in that direction and spot a gang of burly guys sitting on motorcycles in the parking space beside our car. They laugh and shout at one another, gunning their motors so that a loud thrum rattles our windows, my teeth, the air, and probably God in heaven. One of them spots me and howls with laughter. He's amused that he scared the crap out of me. I give him the finger and he laughs even harder.

"Where's Arcade?"

"She's praying," she says, the words riding on a wave of irritation. "Were you two out training last night?"

I nod. There's a big purple bruise on my shoulder and on the right side of my rib cage. Bex gives them a quick once-over and shakes her head.

"Do the two of you have a plan when we get there?"

"Sort of," I say, but suddenly realize we don't at all, unless you consider "Attack the camp, free everyone, make people regret doing evil crap" a plan.

"Sort of?" she says. "And do you have a plan for me?"

"You're going to drive the getaway car."

"No, for when you die."

It's not like I haven't considered the possibility, but I also know I have actively avoided giving it a lot of thought. I don't know what is going to happen or how it's going to end. I also haven't thought about what Bex will do if I'm killed. Who the heck plans that kind of thing? This is a unique situation. I don't have a plan B, and she knows it.

"What do you want me to say? There isn't an instruction book for what we're going to do. I'm doing the best I can here."

"For just one second, can you stop fighting me and hear what I'm saying to you?" she says. "What should I do if you die?"

I fumble with words I don't have. I've been so caught up in preparing for this fight that I have forgotten about the consequences if it fails.

"Find somewhere to be happy," I whisper.

I watch a tear tumble out of her left eye and down her cheek; then she nods as if I just answered a question for her.

"Typical," she says.

Arcade opens the car door and crawls into the back seat.

"You have had enough rest," Arcade says. "Make this machine go."

I give Bex my best reassuring smile, but it misses by a mile. She turns her head away to the window again.

I start the car and pull out onto the freeway.

I've seen movies set in the desert, so I thought I knew what to expect: endless miles of golden sand, vultures, and some poor fool raving from thirst and hallucinations. The West Texas desert is nothing like the movies. Amazing colors are baked into everything: reds and rusts, mustards, browns and grays, and deep maroons, speckled by shocking blues and purples. It's a glorious painting, and the artist used every hue. It's also overflowing with life. Unfortunately, said life is freaking me out. I grew up in a place where the wildest beasts were the seven cats owned by the crazy lady on the tenth floor of my apartment building. Here, there are lizards as big as those cats. They sit in trees and lurk in the scraggly brush, spitting their lavender tongues at everything. Snakes whip their bodies into the road in defiance of my two-ton machine. Furry creatures with long tails skitter in the tall grasses that line the highway. I feel like I'm driving through a zoo.

When we hit a town called Goldthwaite, we lose the sixteen-lane superhighways that run through Texas, along with the eighty-five-mile-an-hour speed limit. This is where the poor carve out their lives. Gone are the monstrous SUVs and pickup-truck mutations designed to speed up climate change. These roads belong to the beekeepers and the day workers and the fruit pickers, to the Mexicans who work the oil wells, and to the people who live on "the res." The folks I pass have faces baked by hard work and years in the sun. They send me friendly waves when we pass one another. At least, I think they're waving at me. It might be the Ford they're waving at. It fits in nicely in this part of the country.

Unfortunately it's running on fumes, and when the engine finally ceases, we barely have enough to make it off the freeway and into a dusty gas station in the middle of nowhere. When we come to a stop, the motor pings and pops, then wheezes its final, dying breath.

The three of us are stuck. There is nothing out here for miles. Even this gas station is abandoned. By the look of the pumps, it filled its last car long before I was born.

"What now?" Bex asks.

"We walk," Arcade says.

"It's hundreds of miles!" I cry.

Arcade doesn't respond. She opens the car door and steps

out. I watch her walk along the road's edge. Bex snatches her hoodie and does the same.

"Guys, this is insane," I plead, but they are almost out of earshot. Exasperated, I grab the pack and step out of the car into the broiling heat. A hateful blister of a sun hangs in a jaundiced sky, melting everything into a Shrinky Dink. Thirsty trees lean forward, the crumbling sidewalk glows with angry sunburns, and everything is flat. We're definitely going to die out here.

As they walk on without me, I write a quick apology to the owner of the Ford, but it comes out more like a fan letter. I rave about how it handles, how the engine feels like something that belongs in a rocket. I apologize for stealing the phone charger but promise that it couldn't be helped.

I run a caressing hand on the Ford's hood when I'm finished.

"I'm going to miss you, beast," I whisper, because it's true. If I live through this, I'm going to buy a car just like this one. It's going to be ginormous. I might even mount a tusk where the hood ornament should be.

I do my best to catch up with Bex and Arcade. The heat and the running wind me, so I can hardly talk when I close the gap. I'm sure they don't mind. I'm not feeling particularly welcome. Bex's disappointment in me is palpable, and Arcade isn't exactly chatty. I hang back and walk at my own pace on the pebbly ground. After a few hours in the heat, I am really feeling the pack. It's bulky and awkward, and every step seems to add another pound. I'm regretting the bacon and the half gallon of milk and all the other stuff that is too impractical to carry on my back. Without asking the others, I slip it off and toss things onto the side of the road, where they are quickly attacked by a murder of crows. I probably should have talked to Bex and Arcade, but neither of them offered to help me with it. Unfortunately, when I hoist it onto my back, I can't feel much of a difference in the weight. I debate sitting down in the dust for a big cry, but I need to keep going. My parents don't care if the pack is heavy or if the sun is mean. I'm their only hope.

The sky is orange and purple, signaling the end of another day, when we come across a deserted ice cream shop. I kick through the overgrown grass and litter to a rusty metal picnic table and toss the pack on top. At some point the table was painted bright red with a big smiling clown logo in its center. Now the clown looks as if he's been sleeping beneath an underpass. Maybe we're related.

Bex digs into the pack greedily, pulling out everything. Neither she nor Arcade mentions the stuff I tossed out for the birds. Either they don't care, or this game of "don't talk to Lyric" is more important.

I snatch two protein bars and an apple and make myself a bologna sandwich, vacuuming them so fast, it's startling. Bex and Arcade do much the same. It's a silent affair. I look across the table at my besty, my partner-in-crime, my sister from another mister, and feel as if the tabletop is a million miles wide. I can't take it anymore.

"I hate this," I say, to both of them.

They meet my eyes but then look away.

"What is 'this' you speak of?" Arcade says.

"The way neither of you are talking to me!"

"I never speak to you, Lyric Walker, because the things you say make me angry and tempt me to kill you," Arcade says as she stands. She walks off into the brush. "Do not disturb me. I am sharpening my Kala and praying."

"So let's talk," I say to Bex.

Bex turns to watch Arcade settle in the dust, her back to us.

"She prays to Fathom," she tells me.

"She thinks he's dead," I mutter.

"Everyone grieves in their own way," Bex scolds.

"We're all grieving," I say, but it sounds selfish, and I can tell she hears it that way too. Bex lost the love of her life, then her mother. My family might be in danger, but they are still alive as far as I know.

"I'm grieving for you," she says.

"Bex!"

"What? Isn't that your plan? Suicide?"

"I don't want to die!"

"Good to hear," she says. "Maybe you should act like it."

Tires screech, and we turn our attention to the road. A sheriff's car has come to a skidding halt, and its driver is staring at us. I can see she's talking on her radio. We've had this happen to us a few times: an officer gives us a look that lasts a little too long, but never like this. I can see the panic on her face.

Bex shouts for Arcade while I slowly gather our things and put them back into the pack.

"If she gets out of the car, run," Bex demands.

"Bex—"

"I said run!" she shouts. "Split up and we'll meet back here at dawn."

"If she gets out of her car, she will regret it," Arcade says as she marches in our direction.

"Just don't!" Bex begs. "She's not your enemy. She's a cop trying to keep people safe. You don't need to attack her."

"Nothing must stop us, Bex Conrad."

"Just calm down. Maybe she'll keep going if we don't look like we're freaking out over here," I say, but I'm worried Arcade's right. If the sheriff gets out of her car, she's going to arrest us. She might even fire at us if we run. In fact, she's probably calling for backup right now so other cops can fire at us too. Attacking her might be our only hope of escape.

The officer gets out of the car with her gun drawn. She's a short woman, slightly round, with a broad brown face. Her eyes are huge and panicked, and her hands tremble. "Put your hands on your head right now or I will shoot!"

Bex does as she's told, like a normal person would do, so I take my cues from her, if reluctantly. Arcade, however, refuses and in defiance steps toward the cop.

"Arcade —"

"You will not stop us, woman," Arcade growls. "Put your gun down and go, or there will be a confrontation."

"Please get in your car and drive away," Bex begs.

"I know who you girls are," the cop says. "I know what you are."

"You don't understand what's going on," I tell her. "You've been told a story about us, and it's not true."

"I don't need your life story. Just stay put. There will be more officers here in a moment," the cop promises, then pulls the hammer back on her sidearm.

"Please, let us walk away. We're not out here to hurt anyone," Bex cries.

"You put three cops in the hospital yesterday."

"They took my parents, and I want them back," I explain. "They're good people, and I have to rescue them. You would do the same, right?"

"You murdered thousands of people!" the cop shouts.

"You don't under —"

"Shut up! I'm not here to negotiate with you," the cop barks, her words bigger than her body. She fires her gun, and it spits up dirt at Arcade's feet. "The next shot will not be a warning."

Arcade's hand is swallowed in blue flames. Bex shouts at her to stop, but I can already hear the rumbling beneath my feet. The world slows down to a crawl, so that even the blink of my eye sounds like the slamming of a heavy door. Suddenly, a waterspout erupts beneath the sheriff's car, forcing it off the ground. The geyser holds it there effortlessly, spinning it a little, until it comes slamming down on its side. The world speeds back to normal in a symphony of broken glass and smashed metal.

The force knocks the cop off her feet, and she falls hard to the ground. Arcade stalks toward the woman, her Kala sliding out of her forearms and shining like the sharp edge of a guillotine.

Bex is looking at me. She says nothing, but her eyes shout clearly enough. This is my responsibility. If Arcade kills this woman, she will blame me forever.

"Calm down," I say, stepping between Arcade and the officer.

Arcade's eyes widen in surprise.

"Are you challenging me, half-breed?"

"I'm making sure you don't do something you'll regret," I say.

"I have few regrets," she brags. "Get out of my way."

"Then I'm going to fight you if I have to," I say, hoping it sounds more confident to her than it does to my own ears.

The sheriff retrieves her weapon and climbs to her feet. She's shaken, working on instinct, and I know that at any moment she might fire again. I turn to her, bracing for the bullet, but her eyes are confused. She looks dazed and set upon.

"Do you hear that?" she asks, and then my ears are pounded by the sound of a whipping wind, and from out of nowhere swoops a black helicopter directly overhead. It's not like the kind they use on the news for traffic and weather. This one is long and sleek, like a bird of prey, and mounted on its sides are what look like rockets. From below I can see a logo painted on its belly—a white tower.

There's a single shot. I hear it drill through the air toward us, and then I watch the sheriff's body buckle. Her head flies forward, and she falls face-down into the dirt. The back of her head is gone, and there is blood everywhere.

Bex screams. I'm sure I would too if I weren't in shock. The people in the helicopter just killed a cop. Wait! *The people in the helicopter just killed a cop!* That means they are definitely *not* with law enforcement. But then who?

"Tempest," I gasp.

Arcade is the only one of us who has her wits about her. She sends another funnel of water up into the sky, and it plows into the chopper, knocking it out of its hovering position just as a second bullet screams toward us. This one crashes into the dirt inches from where Bex is standing. She's next.

I scan our surroundings for an escape. There is nothing out here, nowhere to go and hide that isn't open ground, except for the ice cream parlor, but getting to it keeps us out in the open, and then how do we get out? No, we're going to have to make a run for it.

I activate my weapon and concentrate on the water beneath

the earth. It's there, deep—several feet down in fact, but I can hear it and it can hear me.

"Come!" I shout.

It blasts through the soil, eager to please, forming a powerful spray that smacks into the underside of the cop car. The big machine totters back onto all four wheels with a heavy crash.

"Get in!" I shout to Bex, and we dart to the car. The passenger-side door is crushed and won't open, so we hurry around to the driver's side. Bex scurries in and I follow, happy to find a set of keys still in the ignition. I have no idea if the engine will start, but I have to try. It gurgles and groans but won't turn over. I try again with the same results.

"Keep trying," Bex says, staring out through the remains of her broken window. When I look past her, I see Arcade is still attacking the chopper and narrowly avoiding its gunfire.

I give the key another turn, and this time, with some grinding and sputtering, the engine comes to life. I rev the motor loud, just to let the car know my intentions are to drive it hard and fast. It doesn't stall out, so I take that as permission just as Arcade lands as nimbly as a cat on the hood. She leaps off and opens the back door.

"Go!" she shouts.

The helicopter falls out of the sky behind us. The propellers smack into the ground, break apart, and fly in every direction. The helicopter's tail end spins around toward us, threatening to saw off the back of the car.

"Drive!" Bex shouts.

I stomp the gas pedal and steer us all over the place, fighting a bent alignment. I manage to get it on the road just in time to watch the chopper explode into a ball of fire and fuel in my rearview mirror.

CHAPTER SIX

Bex cries. Arcade stares out the window. I'm too shell-shocked to know how to feel. I just saw a woman die in front of me, and I know it was my fault. She died because of me, but why would they kill an innocent police officer and let me go? Why not just kill me instead?

"What was that?" Bex cries.

"I don't know, but they shot her on purpose," I say.

Arcade leans forward.

"Why?"

"I don't know. It makes no sense to me."

"I believe they were trying to kill Bex Conrad and me as well," Arcade says.

"They weren't police or military. I think they were from Tempest."

"They know we are coming," Arcade says.

"We have to get off the roads, I think," Bex suggests.

I nod, and the first dusty path I see, I turn onto it, following the tracks of what looks like a large farm vehicle until I can't see the road behind me any longer. I park and sit in the dark for a moment, suddenly feeling the emotions that have been in limbo since I saw the woman die. I kick the car, and punch and scream. Then it's my turn to cry. Bex leans over and wraps me in a hug, the first affection she's shown me in days. Arcade sits quietly. I suppose the greatest kindness she can give me is to hide her exasperation with my tears.

When I'm myself again, we search the sheriff's car for anything useful. It feels terrible to steal from it, but we're desperate. In the trunk we find riot-gear helmets and batons, extra speeding-ticket booklets, something called a meth kit, and rolls of crime-scene tape. There are a couple of thin wool blankets, a bottle of water, and a pair of leather gloves. There's also a pair of pants that won't fit any of us, but we take them anyway. It looks like we're going to be sleeping in the desert tonight, and it's going to get very cold.

"This might come in handy," Bex says, snatching a small yellow case with the words ROAD FLARES printed on the side.

Bex and Arcade march out into the brush with whatever they can carry in their arms while I take a moment to leave a note in the car, knowing that its owner will never read it, but hoping someone will find it someday and understand.

To whom it may concern: We didn't kill her, I write. A helicopter with a white tower painted on its belly fired on us. They're responsible. I'm sorry. We're not trying to hurt anyone. I just want my family back, and then I'll disappear forever. You'll never hear from me again. I promise.

A photograph rests on the dash. It's a picture of the dead cop. She's standing next to a tall man with a big, happy smile and a dark black mustache. Next to her is a little boy in a baseball jersey and hat, and next to them, an elderly woman sitting in a wheelchair. They are all overjoyed to be together. The cop looks so happy, she might cry.

She can't anymore, so I sit in the car and do it for her, sobbing until my throat is raw.

We walk for hours, sometimes in pitch-black. Arcade's night vision is incredible. Having spent her entire life underwater, her eyes have adapted to see even the faintest flickers. She guides us along, warning us of obstacles to avoid.

Eventually even she is tired, and we stop to make a camp. Arcade scans the horizon, then stomps off to find wood. When she comes back, we light the pile she's collected with the flares. Soon we have a warm fire to huddle around. It doesn't come a moment too soon. My clothes are thin, and my fingers are so cold, I can't feel their tips any longer.

"Right about now, Ghost and I would lure fish out of the ocean to feed our people," Arcade says of her time in the tent city back home. "It took some time to adjust to the taste of cooked meat, but I learned to tolerate it."

"Yes, the protein bars are getting old," I say, opening up one that is *packed with peanut buttery taste.*

"You would be wise to get some rest," she says to me. "There will be more fighting before we get to Tempest."

Arcade takes a blanket for herself, and a few things to eat from the pack, then lies down by the fire.

"I am not killing anyone," I announce. "Not after what we saw."

"Good," Bex whispers back to me.

Arcade sits up and looks at me. Her face is painted with red flames and surprise.

"If you do not kill them, they will kill you."

"I won't do it," I argue.

She shakes her head, then lies back down, turning her back to us.

"You don't even realize it, do you?" Arcade says.

"Realize what?"

"You're already dead."

Bex edges toward me, taking my hand and squeezing it tight. She huddles close in the cold, and I offer her the sheriff's pants, since she's in shorts. We wrap ourselves up in the blanket as best we can and lie there listening to the creatures scurrying in the wasteland around us.

"Are you back?" I ask her, basking in her closeness.

She whispers a yes to me. "Stop being a jerk."

"I'm trying," I say softly.

"She looked like Shadow's mom," Bex says.

I nod. I saw the resemblance myself. She had the same round face and complexion. She could have been Mrs. Ramirez's sister.

I take out my phone and turn it on, flip through the photo

file until I find what I want, and then hand it to Bex. The screen illuminates her cheeks in soft blue memories and changes her face, turning her mouth from a worried line to a careful smile. She turns the screen so I can see a picture of her and her boy, Shadow Ramirez, our Tito, our sidekick. In it the two of them stand back to back, showing off their matching Halloween costumes from last year. Both are tricked out in fat gold chains, Kangol hats, tracksuits, and bright white Adidas, *sans* the shoelaces. Run DMC never looked so good.

I can't help but smile, but only because I can see what's really going on behind the silliness. It was taken before they admitted the truth about how they felt to each other, but you can still see it in their faces.

"He loved you so much," I tell her.

Bex's smile vanishes. She bites her lower lip to hold back tears, then rolls her arm across her face to hide her grief.

"I miss him too," I say.

I wrap my arms around her, pulling her tight, trying to take on some of the anguish that bends her backwards. She sobs quietly, and I do too, thinking about the friend we lost and the future he took with him.

She cleans herself up, then hands me back my phone.

"I saw his picture," she whispers.

"Whose picture?"

"Fathom's. Maybe you should let her see it," she says, tilting her head toward Arcade. "It might help her mourn."

"She's not mourning," I say.

"You know better than that."

Bex curls up all embryo-like, and soon she's asleep, leaving me alone with the dying fire and my thoughts. Across from me, Arcade slumbers. I pass Bex's idea back and forth in my mind as I watch Arcade's chest rise and fall, until I just can't stand it any longer. I don't want her to see that picture. It's all I have of Fathom, all I will ever have. Arcade had a whole lifetime of memories with him. She knows his secrets and dreams and his favorite kind of ice cream, and I know that people who live underwater don't eat ice cream, but that's not the point. He was hers, and in the end he chose her, and all I got were a few kisses and longing looks and one lousy picture! I look terrible in it too—my hair is sticking to my forehead, and neither of us is smiling. But it's mine. She wouldn't appreciate it anyway. As far as I can tell, his loss doesn't mean that much to her. No, I want to keep it all to myself. I know how to treasure things.

I take out my phone and look at him until I'm too tired to keep my eyes open. Then I sleep, and I dream of him.

CHAPTER SEVEN

IT'S DAWN WHEN BEX SHAKES ME AWAKE.

"You were doing it again," she says, referring to my dreams.

"Sorry. Was I talking?"

"Among other things."

My face burns with embarrassment.

"Where's Arcade?" I ask, looking around for her nervously. I want Arcade knowing what happens when I'm asleep even less than broadcasting it into the desert.

"She's training. Give her some privacy," Bex says. "I pulled up some maps and found a town about five miles from here. We should head in that direction. It's called San Saba."

San Saba is the Pecan capital of the world. A person can walk around it in about an hour and a half. There's not much going on here except for the twenty or so businesses that sell pecans. The smell is everywhere. I could twirl it around my finger and plop it into my mouth.

There are a few two-story buildings lining the streets, a

diner that hasn't seen a customer in a long time, and a lot of empty storefronts and parking spaces. I don't see a single person during our first silent stroll around town, which is good because we're on the hunt for another loaner.

The cars don't come. We try every door handle we come across, and all of them are locked. I do find a hatchback with keys in the ignition, but it's a stick, and I'm barely managing automatic. We circle the town again, making friends with a stray mutt who follows close behind, clearly hoping for some food. He's so skinny, we can see his ribs. Bex eventually breaks down and tosses him some crackers. Suddenly I feel bad for tossing out the bacon.

We eat our breakfast under the awning of an abandoned Woolworth, then our lunch beneath the awning of an abandoned Blockbuster Video. By dusk we're still wandering aimlessly and the heat that pressed down on us all day lifts and makes room for its frosty cousin. Bex is shivering. I can't hear myself think over my chattering teeth. We've got to find somewhere to stay.

"That park we passed might have something," I say.

Bex and Arcade respond with grunts, too tired and cold to argue or agree. They follow me back down the street, into the shadows, where we hustle double-time, staying away from streetlights. The park is a lot bigger than it seemed each time we passed it. Inside, it is massive and fancy, considering the size of the town. It has a small lake, baseball diamonds, fountains, tennis and volleyball courts, and a nature trail. We run through it all on our way to a gazebo at the center. It's an open-air building with a roof supported by sandstone pillars to keep rain and sun off, but not cold air. There we spot a couple of kids hanging around. One is using a picnic table as a skate ramp. The other kid is lying on top of another picnic table, staring up at the sky and burning a cigarette between her two fingers. I can't really see what she looks like, but the skater is unforgettable. His arms are covered in tattoos. He's also got piercings in his eyebrows and a huge one in his right earlobe. He's got that urban wildness I used to see in the kids who lived on the boardwalk back home. It's a combination of grime, nervous energy, and sunburns. I'm guessing they are probably homeless. They've got dogs with them, which is always a giveaway. Homeless kids love dogs. Maybe it's the whole "unconditional love" a dog is happy to give. The kids back home paid for that love with loyalty. They would let themselves go hungry to buy kibble.

"Maybe they know a squat," Bex whispers as we watch them from the safety of the shrubs.

"Can they be trusted?" Arcade asks.

I peer closely, wondering the same thing. My father told me that most of the homeless kids he dealt with were runaways trying to put distance between themselves and something back home. Others were dumped from the foster care rolls when they got too old and had nowhere else to go. They were all pretty harmless, he said, but he warned me that some had serious drug problems and mental health issues. But honestly, I'm more worried about how they might react to us. Bex and I come off pretty normal, if smelly, but one look at Arcade is all you need to know she's not human. Her features are too perfect, too symmetrical, breathtaking and otherworldly. The scars on her forearms where her blades jut out aren't exactly inconspicuous either. Maybe this isn't a good idea.

"You need something?" a voice says from behind me. Startled, we spin around and find a tall, broad-shouldered Asian kid in baggy camouflage shorts, a Burger King T-shirt, and road rash on his forearm. His hoodie is strewn with patches from hardcore bands I've never heard of, and like the other kids, he's got a beat-up skateboard under his arm.

"We need a squat for the night," Bex says bravely.

He studies each one of us, as if we're wearing little signs that read TRUSTWORTHY or UNTRUSTWORTHY. Oddly enough, Arcade doesn't seem to intrigue him. He spends a lot of time on me.

"Are you Coasters?"

"Yeah."

"Did you get dumped too?"

"Um, no," I say, confused by his question.

"You got through the roadblocks?" he cries.

"Yes," I say, though he doesn't need to know we used our magical mittens to make it happen.

He nods approvingly.

"You got anything to eat in that pack?"

"Plenty."

"Yeah, I got a place," he says with a smile, then gestures for us to follow him as he joins his friends at the pavilion.

The dogs are the first to notice us, and their barks are shocking and loud, like thunderclaps on a clear day. All their hostility is aimed at Arcade. A golden retriever charges at her and bares its teeth, then circles around her slowly, sniffing and snapping. A German shepherd takes the opposite approach, lying on its belly, a sign of submission. Even the dogs know Arcade's an Alpha.

"Easy now, Phil," Tattoo Boy says as he hops off his board and hurries to the retriever's side. He's calm and loving, caressing the animal's great golden head and neck.

The girl sits up and turns to us. She's beautiful in a way that's hard to define, with long black dreads that hang like ropes, light skin, freckles, big green eyes, and full brown lips. Unfortunately, all those amazing features are twisted and annoyed.

"You're scaring our dogs," she complains.

"Which city?" Tattoo Boy says as he rolls up to join us. He kicks off his board and it pops up into his hands.

"What do you mean?" Bex asks.

"You're Coasters, right? What city are you from?"

Bex flashes me a look, and I shrug. What's the point of lying?

"Brooklyn."

"Whoa!" he cries. "Near Coney Island?" our host begs.

I nod. "Near."

"Criminals or refugees?" Tattoo Boy presses.

Bex and I share a look, which makes him laugh.

"My favorite combination. They call me Duck," he says, and then he gives me a hug. Bex is next, but when he tries it with Arcade, she growls. He tosses his hands into the air in surrender. "Not a hugger. That's cool."

"Duck?"

"Yep. Do you like it?" he says, then lets his face unfold into a grin. Oh, boy, he's flirting.

"I'm Bex. This is Lyric and . . . Jill."

"Jill?" Arcade growls.

The Asian boy offers his fist for a pound. "Lucas. That's Sloan with the sour expression. Jill doesn't talk?"

"Jill doesn't talk. Will you take us to this squat or not?" Arcade cries.

"What did you do?" Sloan asks suspiciously.

"What did we have to do? We're Coasters," Bex says.

It seems like a good enough answer for Sloan. She shrugs and turns to lead us away when the retriever launches into panicked barking. The shepherd joins him, and this time their attention is on the road. As if on cue, a cop car cruises slowly by, shining a bright spotlight into the park.

"Is he looking for you?" Lucas asks.

"Maybe," I confess.

"I think that's Ferguson," Sloan warns us.

Lucas points toward a playground to the left of the pavilion. There, among the slides and swings, is a kids' tree fort. It looks like something out of the frontier age, with little windows and a rope ladder. It could be a great hiding place, or the perfect cage if one of these kids decides to rat us out. Sloan looks eager to get rid of us. Lucas and Duck, however, seem sincere.

"C'mon," I say, and Bex and Arcade and I race across the grass. We scamper up the ladder, then duck out of sight inside the tiny tower. It was designed for little kids, and scrawny little kids at that, not a gang of tall teenage girls.

"More hiding," Arcade growls.

"Shush," I say.

"You see any other kids out here tonight?" a voice booms. It has to belong to the cop they call Ferguson. "You, speak up. Have you seen anyone?"

I poke up enough to see its owner. He's short, maybe no taller than five foot four, with a port-wine stain smeared across his left eye. He's got a shaved head. What is it about the shaved head with cops?

"No, sir," Duck says a little too enthusiastically. I suddenly know everything I need to know about that kid. He's the one who never knows when to shut up, especially around authority figures and people who can make his life hard. He just can't help himself.

"What about you, girl? Have you seen any strangers around today?"

Sloan turns toward the fort and locks eyes with me. I bite down hard on my lip, sure we've been betrayed, but then she turns back to Ferguson and shakes her head.

"You speak English?" the cop demands.

"Of course I speak English," she snaps. I guess Duck and Sloan were made in the same factory.

"We haven't seen anyone, but we could keep our eyes open. What do they look like?" Lucas says, stepping between the cop and his friends.

"There are three of them. They're about your age; pretty girls. Two of them are wearing metal gloves."

"Metal gloves? Like Shredder?" Duck laughs.

"What?"

"The bad guy from *Teenage Mutant Ninja Turtles*," he explains. "His name is Shredder. He wears gloves with razors on them so he can shred. What did they do? Are they dangerous?"

"Heck, yeah, they're dangerous. Do you think I'm out here looking for them because they're selling illegal Girl Scout cookies? One of them is one of those fish things."

"Fish things?" Lucas asks.

"Forget it," the cop barks, then turns to Duck. "Are you sure you haven't seen them? You wouldn't be lying to me, would you?"

"No, sir," Duck says.

"Are you a citizen, boy?"

"I'm a Yankee Doodle Dandy, pal," Duck says.

The punch comes from nowhere. Suddenly, Duck is on the ground and Ferguson has his foot on Duck's head.

"You a Coaster, smart-ass?" he shouts. "Do you have your

paperwork? Did you sneak over the border? I bet you're all ille-gal. What about you, girl? Where are you from?"

"Sir, let him up," Lucas begs.

"Shut up! You kids are out here loitering day and night, and I never hassle you. I could send Social Services over here, but I don't. I'm a nice guy up to a point, but if ya'll push my buttons, I get angry. Girl, you better get a hold of those dogs, or I'm gonna put them down."

Sloan quickly grabs the dogs by the collar. She tries to calm them, but their frenzy of barking continues.

"Sir, please let him up," Lucas cries, panicked but trying to play by the officer's twisted rules. Unfortunately his pleas are ignored.

I watch in horror from the safety of the fort. Those kids are suffering because of us, and I can't let it continue. I shift so I can get my gloved hand out in front of me, but Bex pulls me back.

"C'mon, Lyric. Using that thing shouldn't be the first option," she hisses.

"Then what do you want to do?" I cry, bewildered.

She peers through one of the tiny windows.

"There are a million things you can do with it. Pick one that doesn't put him in the hospital," she begs.

I tuck my hand under my hoodie to block the light from radiating out and revealing our hiding spot. Then I strain to hear the water's call. There are pipes running beneath

Ferguson's feet, eager to explode and knock him down. There's a sprinkler system I could use to drown him. There's even a garden hose lying in the grass nearby that I could turn into a whip. All of them are deliciously vengeful, but for Bex's sake I'll try to be creative.

"Use some restraint," I whisper to the voices.

A second later, a fire hydrant in the street blows up and its metal cap sails through the air, landing at Ferguson's feet. A jet of water shoots into the sky and comes down on his car with such force, the back windshield collapses. Water floods through the broken glass and quickly fills the car.

"What on earth?" Ferguson hollers, and all of a sudden tormenting children is not at the top of his list. Duck scampers to his feet, embarrassed, angry, and hurt, but he knows better than to fight back. Instead, he steps as far away as he can from the cop.

Ferguson calls to his dispatcher. She accuses him of throwing a temper tantrum, then promises to send a fire truck.

"Get out of the park," Ferguson spits. "If I see you Coasters again, I'm calling Immigration."

He stomps back toward his squad car and suffers through the ceaseless spray to get behind the wheel. It's so powerful, it knocks him down before he finally gets the door open and crawls inside. While he's busy, Bex, Arcade, and I climb down from the fort. The kids eye us with both wonder and fear.

"Did you do that?" Lucas asks.

I nod.

"I won't hurt you," I promise.

"You're that girl from Coney Island," Sloan says.

"We need a squat for the night. If it's not cool, that's fine, but say it now, please, so we can keep looking before it's too late," Bex says.

She reaches over and gives my hand a squeeze. I return the show of affection.

Lucas speaks to Duck and Sloan. Tattoo Boy wipes the blood out of his eye and listens, his face full of suspicion, but then he eventually nods.

"You can come," Lucas says. "But whatever food you've got, you have to share, and Malik gets first pick."

"Who is Malik?"

"The guy who decides whether you sleep outside or not," Sloan explains.

She grabs Lucas by the arm, whispering something to him while staring at me the entire time.

"C'mon, we'll take you." Duck picks up his board and walks into the dark. Lucas and Sloan do the same.

CHAPTER EIGHT

THEY WALK US ALONG A LONELY ROAD TO A BRIDGE. Once there, we crawl down the embankment and find a huge metal drainage pipe big enough for a grown man to walk into upright. It leaks murky brown water into a muddy creek basin. Without hesitation, Duck plunges us into the dark. Sloan and Duck follow, then Arcade.

Lucas happens to have a small flashlight in his pocket, and he takes the lead for Bex and me. Soon we're so far in that I can't see the light of the entrance any longer. Along the way, Duck tells us his life story. He and his father left Newport, Rhode Island, when it was ravaged by the Rusalka—who he calls the "frogs." They packed all their belongings in the car, only to get stopped in their tracks at the Texas border. They were separated by the mobs, though, he admits, his dad might have ditched him.

"I wasn't his favorite child. Unfortunately I was his only one."

He laughs at his own expense, but it's not loud enough to cover up the pain.

Sloan says she's from a little town in Delaware that was overrun by the monsters. She and her mother and father abandoned everything they had and took off in the family's SUV. When they got to the Texas border, they were stopped and searched. The soldiers threatened to arrest the whole family, but her father bribed one with the car. He would only let Sloan pass through, all alone. That was a week ago. They were supposed to meet here but she hasn't seen them since.

Lucas, on the other hand, doesn't offer much.

"Are you from the Coast?" I ask.

"Yeah."

That's his answer for everything. He's like a male version of Bex. Getting him to share is like pulling teeth.

Finally we reach a ladder. Duck climbs up while Lucas shines his flashlight at him. When he gets to the top, he pounds his hand on a metal grate that blocks his way, first three times, then once, then four more times.

"Secret codes." Duck chuckles down to us.

There is movement from above, and then the grate opens and the tunnel fills with light. Leaning down into the hole is the face of a dark-skinned boy with a shaved head and the beginnings of a sad, thin mustache.

"What happened to your face?" he asks. He seems genuinely concerned for Duck, as if they were family.

"Ferguson."

He frowns, then peers down at us.

"Who are they?"

"They need a place for the night," Lucas replies. "Let us in."

"We don't have room for three more," Malik argues.

"You know we do, Malik," Lucas argues. "Let us in. I'm standing in sewage."

"We will only be here until morning, and then we'll be gone," I promise.

"They got anything to contribute?"

I take off my pack and hand it up. Malik snatches it and unzips it, peering inside. He rifles through it like it's his own, pulling out the last of the protein bars and the cans of soup, then takes out the package of bologna and smells it.

"One night," he says sternly, then moves enough to let Duck finish his climb. We all follow until we find ourselves in what appears to be an ancient boiler room, not unlike the one we used to have in the basement of my apartment back in Brooklyn. Once we're all out of the tunnel, Lucas closes the grate and then fastens a padlock to keep it shut. He hangs the key on a nail pounded into the nearest wall.

"You're gone by eight," Malik commands like it's the law of the land. He snatches the bread for himself, then hurries up a flight of stairs and vanishes from view.

"Don't mind him," Lucas explains. "He's sort of the mayor of this place, and he's very protective."

"Paranoid is what he is," Duck says.

"He needs to be," Sloan chastises.

"What is this place, exactly?" Bex asks.

Duck grins from ear to ear. "You're going to love this."

He hurries us up the stairs until we're standing in a room with soaring ceilings and a hardwood floor. Before us is a monstrous curtain that must be forty feet tall. There's ancient electrical work on the walls and huge black panels filled with tiny bulbs. Ropes, pulleys, and catwalks hang from a ceiling that soars to dizzying heights. Duck pulls back one end of the heavy curtain and urges us to step through. Once there, I find myself on a stage in a huge sloping room with hundreds of velvet chairs.

"It's a theater," I gasp.

I don't know how old this building is, but it was built with a lot of care and craftsmanship. The balconies are carved with cherubs, and the walls are decorated in a glitzy art deco design. There is a pipe organ to the left that looks as if it sinks into the floor, and the ceiling—oh . . . it's breathtaking. It shoots high above us, and it's painted to look like an endless blue sky dotted by chubby clouds made of milk. Unfortunately it's marred by water damage, and there's a hole up there somewhere that's allowing birds to nest. A few pigeons circle the room, spiraling around and around as if they are wheeling in a real sky.

"Welcome to the Royale," Lucas says when he joins us.

"It's incredible," Bex says.

"Malik found it a while back. He's been on his own for a couple years, so he cleaned it up. When Duck and I wandered into town a couple weeks back, he took us in."

"He's really not such a bad guy, just cranky," Sloan says.

The boys give her a "look who's talking" look.

She punches each one in the arm.

Lucas waves toward the seats. I was so overcome by the architecture, I didn't notice that there are people sitting out there, maybe thirty of them, both men and women, some teens and small children.

"Who are they?" I ask, peering out at their faces.

"Coasters," he says.

"Malik has been taking them in," Duck says. I can hear the respect he has for the boy in every word.

We descend a small flight of stairs and walk up the sloped floor. All the way, faces stare out at me. There are people in this theater who are brown and white and red and yellow. There probably isn't a better example of what America professes to be than in this room. Now they are refugees, unwanted in their own country.

"They all paid some guys to hide them in a truck and drive them across the borders. They were told they would be taken somewhere nice and put in a motel, but instead they got robbed and dumped in the middle of the desert in the pitch-dark. Every week there's more. Malik and I go out and check from time to time, then bring them back here," Lucas explains.

"How do you get them back here?" Bex asks.

"I've got a truck," he says.

"You've got electricity, too," Bex cheers, pointing to some lights glowing in the balconies and the back of the theater.

"We've got hot water," Lucas says. "You could take a bath in one of the sinks."

"If that is some kind of crack about how I look, I don't even care," I say with a laugh.

"Nothing wrong with the way you look," he says.

I blush.

"Look who gets to be the hot one," Bex whispers to me.

"Where should we sleep?" I ask.

"Find a spot. Anywhere, really," Lucas says, then points to one of the balconies that overlooks the stage. "Except for there. That's Malik's. He keeps his prayer rug up there, so be cool and find somewhere else. The place is huge. There's a couple rules. You can't hang around outside, and when you go, you need to use the tunnels. This place is off the town's radar at the moment. It has been closed for years, but when they shut it down they left the power and water on, which tells me someone still owns it and has plans for it someday. I have to assume it's a big company that doesn't care that it keeps getting bills, but there's no point drawing attention if we don't have to."

"Got it. We'll be gone in the morning," I promise.

"I said the same thing when I walked through that tunnel at the back of the theater," he confesses. "Ignore what Malik said about leaving tomorrow. If you need to stay, you can. We're all here for as long as there's no place else to go."

At some point a bottle of vodka gets passed around. It's the cheapest brand you can buy and bottled in a big plastic jug, which is never a good sign. I pass on it, but Sloan and Lucas each have a pull. They pass it on to Bex and Duck. I gave her a worried look and she gave me the thumbs-up expression. She upends the bottle, taking a long, slow drink, then wipes her mouth on her shirtsleeve.

"Easy there, cowgirl," I say, trying to take it from her.

She takes another swig.

"Don't spoil the fun, Walker," she teases.

Duck takes a drink himself, then drags Bex out of her seat.

"C'mon, I'll show you where I sleep," Duck says. I expect her to pull back, and for a moment she does stand her ground.

"Duck, let's keep the down low on where they're from," Lucas says in a low tone. "Some people will freak."

He nods, then gives Bex another pull. This time she lets him, and they skip into the darkness. I'm about to follow them when Lucas stops me.

"He's harmless."

"She's just very vulnerable right now," I say.

"So is he. Are you harmless?"

"Most of the time," I say as I look down at my glove. "And you? Anything I need to worry about?"

"Best behavior," he says. Oh, boy, he's flirting again.

"We must talk about Bex Conrad," Arcade says. "There is no room in my plan for her. We will leave her here when we go on to Tempest."

"What? No!" I cry.

"I am speaking to him," Arcade says, gesturing to Lucas.

"What? I'm confused," he says.

"You take in those without a home. I ask you to take in another. Our companion, Bex Conrad, cannot go any farther with us," Arcade says.

"No, Arcade. I can't leave her," I say.

"She is thin and weak. She has no combat training. She has never drawn the blood of an enemy. She will only act as a distraction and get in our way," she argues with me.

"Keep it down," I warn her, turning in my seat to make sure we're not being overheard.

"What is happening tomorrow?" Lucas whispers.

"Death," Arcade says matter-of-factly.

"I am not killing anyone," I remind her. "I'm not made like you, Arcade. I can't just kill someone 'cause they're in my way. The people we're going to run into in Tempest aren't the evil ones doing all the terrible stuff. We're going to be fighting the guards, at least at first, and they're just doing their jobs."

"What is Tempest?" Sloan asks.

"It is a house of evil where my people are imprisoned," Arcade explains, then turns back to me. "You see these guards as people who are just doing their jobs? Lyric Walker, the men who guard the camp are no less evil than the ones who work within. They labor to protect the horrors the others commit. You spoke to Terrance Lir, correct? He told you what happens there. They cut him open and emptied him out, filled his blood with poisons, and took saws to his bones. What was the word he used to describe it?"

"Torture," I say, ashamed.

"The surface dweller excels at the vile arts. It is dishonorable. I will kill anyone in that camp who participated in it— even the fools who sweep the floors. There are no innocents at Tempest, and I will make an example out of every last one. They will sing songs to warn the future never to practice this torture again or else face being cut down."

"I think we can rescue everyone without killing people," I argue.

She shakes her head.

"You are not that naive."

"What the hell are you people involved in?" Sloan demands.

"Bex Conrad does not have to die," Arcade says. "If you value her life, then you must put her safety first. She will most certainly die if we take her to the camp. Leave her here where she will be safe."

"I'm the only person she has left in this world," I cry. "If I dump her here, she will never forgive me. She's been abandoned so many times, I just can't do it to her again. She's been by my side nearly every day since the fifth grade. How do I walk away now?"

"Look at yourself, Lyric Walker. Look at me. We are Alpha. She is not one of us. This is not her fight. The men who are following us already tried to kill her once. Do you think they will go easier on her when we break into their camp? If she dies, it will have been avoidable and it will be as if you killed her yourself."

Arcade is right. Leaving Bex here is cruel, like letting a puppy loose on the freeway because you can't take care of it anymore, but at least she'll live.

"We can take her, of course," Lucas says.

"When we are done, we come back for her," I insist.

"If that gives you a reason to fight, then so be it," Arcade says. "In the morning we depart on our own. I must go and speak to the Great Abyss."

"The great who?" Lucas says, but Arcade doesn't answer. She stands and vanishes into the shadows, leaving Sloan, Lucas, and me alone.

"So, you're being followed?" Sloan asks.

"I blew up the world. Didn't you hear about it?"

"I heard things," Sloan says.

"Not true things."

"Gimme some truth," she says.

"My mother is what is called a Sirena," I confess.

"Which one is that?"

"As close to a mermaid as it gets."

"So you're half mermaid? Do you grow a tail?" Lucas asks after he takes a swig.

"Nope. Sorry if that's what you're into," I reply, snatching the bottle for myself. I take a cringing gulp.

"It's horrible, isn't it? I thought it would get better after a few drinks." He laughs.

"Can the two of you focus?" Sloan complains, then peers around again to make sure we're still having a private conversation.

"She was part of a group of twenty who came to the surface to learn about humans, and before you ask, yes, she was a spy, but she didn't know it at the time. She's a good person."

"With a tail," Lucas says. He's a little drunk.

Now I laugh. "With a tail."

"They say you made that tidal wave," Sloan says.

"They say a lot of things about me. The truth is I tried to stop it, and in exchange, someone kidnapped my parents and put them in a torture camp, along with a bunch of Alpha and their children."

"And that's Tempest? Where you're going tomorrow?" Sloan asks.

I nod.

"Tough girl, huh?" She gets up from her seat and gives me a nod. "Good luck. I'm gonna go feed the dogs."

A moment later, she's gone. I turn to Lucas. He is all smiles. I know that look, full of nerves and anticipation. I know that he's working on his bravery, and Sloan left because she's trying to help him. Nice wingman.

"I'm not going to kiss you," I say, blurting it out a little too harshly.

He looks at me hard for a minute, then shrugs.

"That came out wrong," I backtrack. "You're cute enough. It's just, I've got a . . . I'm in love with somebody."

"Lucky guy."

"I hope so," I whisper.

CHAPTER NINE

*B*ex!
I wake with a start. I'm in an old army cot in a dusty room filled with broken theater seats and yellowing movie posters, and I'm all alone.

I left her with a boy I don't know, and now my mind is working overtime, conjuring up endless ugly scenarios of what he did to her. Rule number one of the girl code is not to leave your friends alone with boys and not to let yourself be alone with one for too long. I'm not saying all boys are bad, but some boys are very bad. If she's hurt, I will never forgive myself. I can't believe I ever considered leaving her here with these people. I have to find her—now!

I push through the door into a hallway I don't recognize. It feels like I'm underground, though—it's cool and slightly damp. I find a flight of steps and race up and find I'm backstage. I step around the curtain, hop off the stage, and run up the aisle past sleeping people. She's not in the auditorium.

I charge into the lobby and up an elegant staircase. It leads to the second-floor balcony and the projection room. I push open one door after another and peer inside, waking up entire families. They stare at me in bewilderment. I don't stop to apologize. I find a door with a sign that reads STAFF ONLY, and I force it open. There I find my friend sobbing.

"Bex?"

"Hey, what up?" Duck is sitting on the floor, no shirt, but wearing a sheepish grin.

There's not a lot of thought that goes into what happens next. My hand explodes with power, I hear a pipe calling out to me behind this dumb boy's head, and I cause it to crack open. The water breaks through the wall, grabs him around the neck, and slams him to the floor.

Bex is shouting something at me, but I don't really hear it with all the rage in my ears. I am sick of people hurting the ones I love. I'm not going to take it anymore, especially not from some street rat with a face full of piercings. I'm going to fight back from now on!

"What is wrong with you?" Bex says, stepping between me and my newfound punching bag. "Let him go!"

"He doesn't get to touch you!" I shout.

"He didn't do anything wrong!" Bex cries.

It takes me a second to process what she said, but when I do, I turn off the glove.

"Then why are you crying?"

She looks at me with such disdain that I feel myself take a step back.

"I know that you want to make everything stop hurting," I say. "But this isn't the way. *He* would be sad if he knew what you were doing."

"Shadow is not here, Lyric. He left me," she cries.

"He didn't leave you—"

"He left me. He's gone. Just like my father and Tammy."

"You don't know if Tammy's—"

"She's dead, Lyric. That's one of the only two options a person has when they get close to me. They either walk out or die —either way, 'See you later!'" she rages.

"C'mon, I'll get you cleaned up," I say.

"Dead people don't get to tell me what to do!"

"I'm not dead!" I shout.

"You will be."

"What is going on in here?" Malik cries as he barges into the room. People have gathered in the doorway to watch our fight. Many of them are staring at me in complete terror. They saw me turn my glove on Duck, and they know who and what I am.

"Bex, we need to go."

"Get away from me, Lyric!" she shouts, and something in her eyes tells me she means forever.

This is it. It's the perfect time to grab my stuff, find Arcade, and leave. She's angry at me, and I will always hate myself for ditching, but it's all laid out for me to go.

"Fine," I say, because I can't find any words that explain everything I'm feeling. I turn and push my way through the crowd.

"Are you okay?" Lucas asks, bounding up the steps to meet me.

I can't talk. I want to be outside. This building is too crowded with ugly feelings, and the crowd is following me. Malik is with them. He hurries behind me with my pack in his hands.

"You need to go," he says.

"We're leaving right now," I say.

He tosses me the pack, and it's empty. Every single thing I took from the Piggly Wiggly is gone. There's also something else missing.

"Where's my phone?"

"What phone?" Malik asks.

"My phone. Where is it?" I shout, digging deeper into nothing. The power cord is missing too.

"I didn't take your phone," he says as he backs away.

"Someone stole it!" I cry. "I need that phone."

"You gotta keep an eye on your stuff," Malik lectures.

"My life is on it," I cry as the pictures of my parents and Fathom fly by in my imagination. Every picture of Bex is on it too. "I'm not leaving without it."

"Go, or I will make you go," he threatens.

"You challenge her," Arcade snarls as she appears at the top of the steps. "Please, amuse me by showing me exactly how you plan to make us go anywhere."

"Arcade, it's fine," I beg, stepping in between them. "We don't have time for this."

Arcade shoves me aside.

"This is your house and it is full of thieves," she says, pressing her face close to his. "Bring her property to me, or you will pay for the crime yourself."

"I don't have her stupid phone!" he bellows.

"Everyone just calm down," Lucas says, leading me down the steps. Arcade reluctantly follows but only after I beg her. "Where did you see the phone last?"

"I thought I had it on me when I fell asleep. Would one of these people sneak in and take it?"

"These are desperate people, but they're good, too," he says. I doubt it. "You had a lot to drink. Let's go down to the auditorium and look under the seats."

"If you call it, I'll hear the ring," I explain when we reach the first floor.

"You don't have your phone turned on, do you?" he stammers.

"Yeah, of course."

"Lyric, phones can be tracked!"

"Only if I make a call," I argue.

"There's a GPS built into smartphones so police can find you if you're having an emergency, whether you call or not," he cries. "Didn't you say you were being followed? If that's true, they know exactly where you are right now."

Malik rushes down the stairs, his eyes crazed and aggressive.

"You're one of those mermaid freaks!" he shouts at me.

Before I can stop her, she ejects her blades. Screams fill the room, and people fall over themselves trying to put distance between us and them.

Arcade's arm slashes through the air, and suddenly a thin trail of blood drips down Malik's face. She only nicked him, but there's a lot of blood.

"No bottom-feeding human filth is going to call me that word again," Arcade says.

I grab Arcade by the arm and pull her into the auditorium. Everyone has gathered and is following our every step. Paranoia grows around their thoughts like a choking vine. Something bad will happen soon. It always does.

"You should go," Lucas says. "And you should probably take your friend with you."

Bex pushes through the crowd until she's in my face.

"Walk out or die. You're doing both."

I fumble for the right words, finally giving up when I realize there are none.

"I was going to come back for you."

Bex blanches.

"Is this your idea or hers?" she asks Arcade.

"Your usefulness has come to an end. We go on to Tempest without you," Arcade says coolly.

"Bex, I'm trying to keep you alive," I plead. "We're going to find the camp today, most likely, and then it's going to get ugly. People will get hurt, and I don't want you in the middle of it. We're only doing what's best for you!"

"Enough! It is settled," Arcade says. "We are leaving now! Forget the phone."

It kills me to leave it behind, but I have no choice. I follow the Triton girl down the sloping floor and up to the stage. People are throwing things at us, mostly plastic bottles, but I see a chair cushion whiz past my head and know how this all ends. The mob isn't going to let us leave. They think I took their homes from them. They believe Arcade and I brought the monsters that destroyed their lives.

Bex pushes through the crowd and grabs me by the wrist.

"I have your phone. I was trying to locate the camp for you so you could see how dangerous it is. I wanted you to be prepared. I wanted to make sure you would survive because, you see, that's what I do. I'm Bex, the best friend. But you don't need me now, do you? You've got your magic mitten and you can move a mud puddle, so who needs Bex?"

"That's not true!" I cry.

Arcade grabs my hand and yanks me away. "Come, she is human. She does not understand."

"I'm human!" I shout at her.

"No, you are not," Arcade snaps. "You are Alpha. Your mother is Sirena. You have never been human, Lyric Walker.

You have only pretended. Your real people need you, and it is time to embrace your blood."

Arcade storms off backstage. I hear her snap the lock off the grate and lift the lid that leads to the drainage pipe. Bex and I stare at each other the whole time. I know she wants me to tell Arcade she's full of crap, but I can't. Part of what she is saying about me is true. I am not human, entirely. There are Alpha and half-human children locked in Tempest, too. They are my responsibility. Arcade is right. Bex can't understand and she can't help.

Something in her eyes shuts down, replaced with what I used to call "the hand grenade," that moment when Bex Conrad stops playing nice. I've never had it hurled at me, but I've seen it explode in other people's faces. Now the pin has been pulled.

Out of her pocket comes my phone.

"I'm doing this for *your* own good," she says, aiming her eyes and words right at my face. "Tell Arcade why the phone is so important to you."

Tick. She's talking about the picture of Fathom.

"Bex, no," I whisper.

"Tell her what you've been hiding from her!" she shouts.

Tick. She's going to do it. She's going to bust me.

"Arcade, Lyric has a photograph of your dead fiancé!" she shouts.

Arcade comes around the curtain.

"A photograph?"

"A picture," Bex explains. "Her phone can capture images of other people and save them even when the person is gone."

Tick. She's flipping through the files.

"Bex, don't," I beg.

But she won't listen. She's hands the phone to Arcade, then crosses her arms in defiance.

"I can't believe you were going to abandon me," she whispers.

Tick. Arcade takes the phone and looks down into the screen. For a long time her face is stone, frozen by confusion, but then her features give way to real emotions: pain, grief, and despair. I see feelings slamming into one another, and the destruction is too great to hide behind her steely Triton demeanor.

She turns her attention to me, and everything gets hot, like she can start fires with her eyes. "He was my selfsame," she says.

"And the second he died, you moved on!" I shout, surprised by my own fury. "Why do you suddenly care about some picture? You had a whole lifetime with him, and you tossed him out with the trash. I only had him for two weeks. I loved him!"

"You did not *have* him then . . ."

In one effortless movement, she snaps my phone in half. The broken pieces fall to the ground. Her boot heel grinds them into the pavement. Glass and chemicals and hardware spread like the guts of some electronic insect.

"... and you do not have him now."

I look down at the mess on the floor. I'm no longer embarrassed by what I hid, or ashamed of how important it was to me. I don't feel sympathy for her or sadness. All I feel is anger. My glove glows blue, and I aim it right at her. She does the same to me.

"All right, stop it," Bex says, suddenly the peacemaker. I almost laugh.

Arcade lunges at me, and in my shock I fall backwards onto the hardwood floor, a happy accident as I watch her blades slice the air mere inches from my face. The mob shrieks, and suddenly they are racing back the way they came, trampling the slow ones in their paths.

"Leave her alone, Arcade!" Bex shouts.

I force a waterspout up through the antique floorboards, and it catches Arcade so hard, her body is flung toward the ceiling. She slams into it with a sickening smack, then falls back down, crashing through the stage and creating a massive hole. I hear pipes bursting, and more crashes come from below.

I barely have time to stand when Arcade leaps up through the hole and lands on the balls of her feet.

"You are a vile, selfish parasite, Lyric Walker. My life has become a whirlpool of indignities ever since I encountered you. You have been scheming behind my back, disrespecting my role as his future queen. You think of no one but yourself."

"I wasn't trying to hurt you, either of you," I say, looking back and forth from Arcade to Bex.

"We part ways here, filth," she says through heavy breaths. "I will not dishonor myself by fighting at your side. I will go to Tempest alone. Do not follow me, or I will kill you."

"We need each other," I argue.

"I will never need you," she says.

There's a whipping sound outside, followed by a loud crash coming toward the lobby. I hear a bang, and something gets tossed through the lobby doors. It bounces down the aisle and lands right in front of the stage. It's a metal canister leaking a thick, ghostly gas that makes my eyes and throat burn. A moment later there are two, three, four more canisters flying into the auditorium, followed by a squadron of men in black riot gear and gas masks. All of them have the same white tower logo sewn into their clothes that I saw on the belly of the helicopter that killed the police officer.

"Put your hands on your heads! If you fail to follow instructions, we are authorized to open fire."

"Run!" Malik shouts.

"No!" I shout, but it's too late. The Coasters scatter like mice. There are popping sounds, and more canisters crash onto the ground. People fall left and right, overcome by the fumes. Children sob as they run through the chaos. Duck charges into the room, playing the hero, only to succumb as well. He coughs and clutches his throat and then passes out.

My first thought is Bex, even if she hates me. I have to get her out of here. I stumble through the haze and find her standing dumbfounded against a wall.

"Bex!" I shout, only to watch a soldier rush forward and shoot her with a Taser. She lets out a howl and falls to the floor, her body seized by pain and violent spasms. I am going to hurt this man. It will only take a single thought, but before I can break him in half, Arcade leaps into his path. She knocks his weapon out of his arms, then slices him across the chest with her blades. He lets out a terrible shriek and falls to the floor.

There's a ZAP. Arcade cries out in agony, struggling to yank out a collection of wires impaled in her back. I'm helpless to free her. Ozone and smoke are in my nose and eyes. I can barely breathe or see, but I can hear her agonizing cries.

Someone clamps a hand on my arm. I turn, prepared to break a few important bones in his body, only to discover it is Lucas.

"Come with me!" he shouts.

"I can't!" I cry, as guards haul my friends out of the theater.

There's another *pop,* and another canister lands at my feet. This time the smoke has a smell and a taste. It makes me dizzy.

Lucas lifts his shirt up over his nose.

"You can't do anything for them right now," he cries, then pulls me backstage.

"No, that's not true!" I shout, but my voice sounds like someone has turned the speed down on my mom's record player. Even the voice of the water sounds odd and distant.

Unleash us, it begs in a warbled whisper.

The floor buckles, and water spirals skyward. It breaks into a dozen tendrils, a multiheaded hydra that snatches soldiers off the floor and tosses them against walls. There are so many targets that it's hard to keep all of them straight, or maybe that's the gas. Are there suddenly more soldiers? Are they running down the aisles toward me?

I feel something stab my thigh. I look down and see several pointy darts attached to wires sticking out of my leg. A soldier is nearby with another of those weird guns they used to shock Bex. There's no way to brace for the pain, even though I know it's coming. A *zap* pushes me into a bonfire. My arms and legs are no longer mine to control, and they flail around like saplings in a hurricane. My head snaps up, and a scream boils over in my voice box. I fall hard, my face crashing into floor.

"You have to get up," Lucas demands, dragging me to my feet. He reaches down and pulls the wires out of my leg, then pulls me farther backstage and lays me down by the grate. Malik is there, and the two boys argue while I beg them to go back for my friends. Whatever I've been shot with has made me weak and confused. Everything seems to swirl before my eyes.

Malik gets the gate open and is nearly down the steps when Lucas begs for his help. The boy reluctantly takes my arm, and together they lower me into the tunnel, where we plunge back into the darkness. Lucas closes the trapdoor, and then he and Malik drag me through the irrigation tunnel.

"Why are you helping her?" Malik cries. "She's one of them."

"She's not what you think she is," Lucas cries.

"I can't leave them," I say, but it comes out like nonsense.

"You can't help," Lucas argues, but then I realize he's talking to Malik.

"I have to try. I'm going back."

"I'll come back once she's safe," Lucas promises.

Malik shakes his head. "That's the dumbest idea ever. I'm sorry, man. This is over. Go live your life. Get to California like your mom wanted. Go find that aunt."

He runs back the way we came, leaving Lucas to help me along by himself. He ignores my cries and pleading, and soon we come out into the bright sun under the bridge we first entered. I'm blinded by the light, dizzy and off-kilter.

"My truck is right up this hill," he says, nodding toward the embankment. He fishes a set of keys out of his pocket and then looks at me again. "Can you pull yourself together?"

"I'm not going," I garble, finding it difficult to raise my head so he can see my determination. The world feels like it crested the highest hill on the Cyclone and now it's roaring toward the bottom. The next things that happen appear only as small snippets, like YouTube videos edited together into something that barely makes sense. My feet stumble on pebbles in the street, sirens, more helicopters, a red pickup truck with black tires, keys in a truck door, the squeak of it swinging open, Lucas shoving me into the seat, the click of a seat belt, my hot-dog fingers struggling to free me.

"No! We can't leave them. I need them."

There's a sound by Lucas's door. An arm covered in tattoos

reaches in and takes the keys. Lucas is dragged out, and several men lead him away. My door won't open. A man in sunglasses stands by my window.

"Doyle?"

"Hello, Lyric. We need to have a talk," he says. His shirt has a logo. It's a white tower on a black background.

My head spins, and then everything goes away.

CHAPTER TEN

I'M SITTING IN A BOOTH IN A LITTLE RESTAURANT THAT HAS gone way overboard on the pastels and florals. Doyle sits across from me, sipping from a mug of coffee. He smiles.

"Where am I?" I ask.

"Menard, Texas."

I'm still loopy, and the black swirl in his cup hypnotizes me. I feel disconnected from my thoughts, like someone has cut the cord that connects communication between the two sides of my brain. Still, there is a feeling that something is really, really wrong. A little voice calls out from the fog. It tells me to run.

"You have had a rough two weeks," he says, eyeballing my outfit.

"Where's Lucas?"

"Lucas is fine, Lyric. I'm sure you have a million questions, but first, I'm very glad to see you, very glad that you survived the tidal wave. Better yet, I'm thrilled you found your way here. You are an incredibly resourceful young woman. Of course, you had a little help from me—"

"You're with Tempest?"

He nods his head, and I feel bile rise up in my throat.

"I'm what you would call an independent contractor. My job title is Combat Trainer and Strategic Engineer. In layman's terms, I train soldiers and plan security details for high-risk clients. I'm also an expert in crowd control."

"You took Bex and Arcade!"

He nods. "It was important to separate the three of you so we could have this conversation. I didn't want the others to sway—"

"You killed that cop."

"No, I wasn't there," he says as he gives me the "just a minute" sign. "And that wasn't how the operation was planned. The three of you were supposed to run, and my team would catch you one by one. It was regrettable, a breakdown in the command structure. The company has offered to pay for her funeral expenses and set up a college fund for her son—"

Before he can finish, I lean forward and slap him so hard, it's a wonder his nose doesn't come off and land on the table. I don't know if the noise attracted the waitress, but one comes strolling out from the kitchen with a pen and pad in her hands. She's a stout woman with hair braided so thick and long that it touches her belt. It's also streaked with gray and brown.

"It's hot out there today," she says, easy with the small talk.

She sizes us up, and I can see we're not what she was expecting. A middle-aged guy in a black jumpsuit and a filthy teenager with murder in her eyes.

"Do you have any pie?" Doyle says as casually as he can. There's a growing red welt on his right cheek that she can't see, but it might as well be flashing a beacon into space, it's so bright.

"Absolutely. We've got apple and blueberry."

"You wouldn't happen to have any cherry, would you?"

"I can check."

Doyle smiles wide and winks. "I would love you for it."

The waitress smiles warily. On her way to the back, Doyle begs her to turn on the television mounted on the ceiling. She obliges, and all at once, the screen is full of Coney Island. Soldiers are fighting Rusalka, who keep leaping out of the water. They fire M-16s and rocket launchers at everything as a reporter on the scene hyperventilates while trying to tell us that most of the military's efforts are having little effect.

"Oh, I hate watching this," the waitress says, but before she can change the channel, Doyle stops her.

"It's fine," he says. "Leave it."

"Suit yourself," she says with a shrug, then wanders off in search of his dessert.

"I don't want any more people to die while I work to keep you safe and alive."

"Nothing you say makes any sense, Doyle," I growl. "You and your company kidnapped my parents. You've got Alpha in a torture camp. You're experimenting on them. Now you're here to tell me you're trying to protect me."

"You really don't get it, do you?" Doyle says. "Lyric, you're the most important person in the world."

"Me?"

"You can put an end to the fighting, Lyric," he says.

"It has nothing to do with me," I say.

"It has everything to do with you," he argues.

"No! You know what could have helped stop the fighting? Thirty thousand Alpha living in a tent city in Coney Island. Maybe if people like you hadn't harassed them, they might have been willing to fight those things for us."

"I completely agree, and when this is all said and done, a lot of people are going to lose their jobs and go to jail, but right now pointing fingers doesn't solve the crisis."

"And exactly why am I supposed to care?"

He takes a deep breath, fighting the urge to continue the pointless debate.

"I need you to come with me, Lyric. I will take you somewhere you can do some actual good with that weapon on your hand. You can help me save the world," he says. "Look, there's the Secretary of Defense. You should listen to this."

Reporters gather in a room decorated with an American flag, blue curtain, and a podium with the government's official seal. Front and center is a gray-haired man. He looks tired and grim.

"Secretary of Defense Harris Abramson admitted to

reporters today what political pundits have been saying for days, that the U.S. military is not trained to handle an amphibious threat like the Alpha," a reporter says.

"Navy SEALS have been working closely with National Guard and Marine command, but many of their efforts are stymied by the flooding and the tidal wave attacks on East Coast military bases."

"What seems to be the problem?" a reporter shouts over the din of other questions.

"The enemy operate in relatively shallow waters that a submarine cannot reach," Abramson says. "Or they move into depths no human being has ever attempted. The Alpha have lived their whole lives underwater, and their bodies are suited for high pressures, frigid temperatures, and strong currents. They're physically more powerful and faster than human beings, even more so when submerged. Some, like the creatures with the teeth you've seen and read about, are particularly savage."

"Are there fears that there might be other things in the water? Reports coming out of the United Kingdom talk about a gigantic creature surfacing near Scotland," a reporter asks.

The secretary looks down at his notes, then wipes his brow.

"At this time, we have no information that would lead us to that conclusion."

"He's lying, Lyric," Doyle says. "There are other things. He's afraid of causing a panic."

"Sir, you keep referring to these creatures as 'Alpha,' and I'm wondering if there is a distinction? Is there no difference between the community who lived on the beach in Coney Island and these monsters who don't appear to be as intelligent? Can you please clear that up for us?"

"At this time, the State Department is not making a distinction. If it's in the water, we're shooting at it."

"That's all I need to know about your war," I say. "I'm just another monster."

The waitress returns with a smile.

"I've got one slice of cherry left."

"I'll take it," he says, and then waves his cup in a circle. "And some more coffee. She's going to have the turkey burger with bacon, sweet potato fries, and a chocolate milkshake. I'm going to have the stir-fry with tofu, and is the broccoli soup made with cream?"

She nods.

"Salad, then, and two big glasses of water."

The waitress nods and jots it all down, her pencil bouncing around like a rabbit. She scoops up our plastic menus, and Doyle gives her a wink before she disappears again.

"I'm not hungry."

"You need to eat something," he says before I can argue further. "I need you strong and healthy."

"You have my parents, and I want them back. I want Bex and Arcade!"

He nods. "I can make that happen, but you have to come to the camp with me."

I place my gloved hand on the table, then will it to come to life. It radiates blue, turning the entire restaurant into a bright sky. I put it in his face, then command the coffee in his cup to swirl up and out and dance around his face. He retains his composure, but there's fear in his eyes.

"You must think I'm stupid."

"Lyric, I'm not going to say the people I work with are good people, but we do have a good mission—saving the United States from an invading force. I can't figure out how to make it a success without you."

Filthy words line up in the back of my throat, jostling with one another to be the first to fly out of my mouth. Instead, I get up from my seat and head for the door.

"I'm trying to avoid a confrontation, Lyric. I told them that I could bring you in peacefully, and—"

I spin around to face him.

"Go to hell!"

He leaps from his seat and grabs me by the arm. I try to pull away and nearly fall from the effort. He's too strong. I can't get free.

The waitress peers out from the kitchen, and she's not happy.

"What's going on over there?" she says.

"He's a murderer. He killed people. He kidnapped my friends and drugged me. Please, help me," I beg.

"Jake, call 911," she shouts to someone I can't see.

"I'm sorry, ma'am. There's no need to call the police," Doyle says, attempting to turn on his charm again. "My daughter was out all night with a bunch of boys, drinking and doing heaven knows what, and I thought I'd sober her up here before I took her home to her mother. I apologize for any trouble."

He tosses a twenty on the table.

"I think we'll let the sheriff figure this one out," the waitress says. "Hey!"

Doyle pulls me out the door and into the hot parking lot. It's completely empty except for one lone red pickup truck.

"What did you really do to Lucas? Did you kill him like the others?" I scream.

"Lyric, stop! You have to listen to me."

"No, I don't. Not as long as I have this," I say, waving the glove at him once more. "Go back to your death camp, and let them know I'm coming. When I get there, I'm going to knock it down!"

"If you don't give this a chance, I can't help you later," he begs.

"If I ever see you again, I will kill you," I promise.

"Then I'm sorry, Lyric. I didn't want it to go down like this, but you're too important," he says, waving his hands in the air. Before I know it, I'm surrounded by a dozen armed soldiers, all dressed in black and pointing rifles at my head. They look exactly like the soldiers that invaded the theater.

"Get out of my way!" I shout. Reaching down into the

bottom of all my pain, I call to the whispers, demanding they be fast and furious and merciless. What comes is the most violent upheaval I have ever created, a shock wave of mud and concrete that cracks pavement. Thirteen spouts erupt beneath the soldiers, and the men flip into the air like rag dolls. Doyle is among them, and as he recovers, I dig into his pockets and find a set of keys. I assume they once belonged to Lucas, and I head toward the truck.

Doyle calls out to me.

"Fathom is there," he chokes.

I spin around and stare at him. My body feels hot and nauseous. I shake like my blood sugar has bottomed out. "You lie," I whisper.

"He's alive, Lyric. He surrendered to the Navy three days ago, just a few miles away from Coney Island. They brought him to us. He's at Tempest."

"Fathom would never surrender," I cry.

Doyle will not manipulate me. His words mean nothing. Fathom may be alive and well, but there's no way he's at Tempest. He's too smart to get caught. Doyle knows I care about him, and he's playing a game.

I will the water to pool around him and his thugs, then watch as they are swept away like they've fallen into a raging river. When they're gone from my sight, I turn and see our waitress gaping at me through the window.

I hurry to Lucas's truck and peel out of the parking lot.

Once I hit the freeway, the truth slams into me head-on. The reason we were never caught, never arrested, was because Doyle cleared our path. He has always known where we were and has made it simple for us to get here—the road blocks, the border fence, maybe even the stolen cars. It was all part of getting me to this point.

I found a receipt for gas on the floor of Lucas's truck, so I know Doyle filled the tank in Menard. It will get me pretty far, maybe all the way. It's a long drive, but that's fine. It will give me time to become as brave as I sounded in that parking lot. Everything is falling apart, and I don't know how to stop it. Worse, I'm terrified that my bad luck has yet to run out.

I search the truck's glove compartment and find a spiral-bound road atlas of Texas highways that allows me to trace a path with my fingers to my very best guess of the camp's location. I assume it would be in the desert's remotest area, maybe even on the very border of the U.S. and Mexico. It's a shot in the dark, but it's the only one I've got. After that, it's anybody's guess. The uncertainty sends me into despair. I think about how afraid Bex must be and how little help Arcade will be to her. I think about my parents in that camp with Doyle watching them every single day. I can't shake my certainty that he's watching me now, that there are cameras in the truck and my escape was part of the plan.

And then I think about Fathom. Not knowing if Doyle was lying to me or not is excruciating. I whimper for hours as I drive through Eldorado, Iraan, and Fort Stockton, where I take Highway 67 south toward the Texas border.

It's here in this barren landscape, the rocky climb into copper-stained mountains, that I feel loneliness for the first time. I expect Bex to lean over and change the radio station. She and Arcade are like a couple of phantom limbs. Their absence feels wrong. It needs to be corrected. Arcade wanted me to have a reason to fight, maybe even to kill. Doyle just gave me one.

It's nighttime when Lucas's car runs out of gas, half a mile from the nearest town. I let it roll off the freeway and as far into the scrub as it will go. Hopefully no one will spot it.

I find a blanket in the truck bed and a bottle of water under the seat, then spend ten minutes debating whether or not to leave Lucas a note. I doubt he'll ever see this car again. There's a good chance that he's not even alive, but it seems right to say something.

> *I'm sorry that you got mixed up in my problems. I had no idea the bad guys would go so far. I hope you are alive. You're good all around, and the world needs more people like you, Lucas.*

I place the note on the dash, wrap the blanket around my shoulders, and walk through the chilly night. When I get back to the road, I realize there are no streetlights out here. My only guide is the moon, so I use the light it reflects off the paint on the pavement to steer my course.

• • •

Half an hour later I walk into Shafter, Texas. The sign says the population is twenty-seven. I think it's exaggerating. Shafter is so small, I don't think it should be allowed to call itself a town. There are a handful of tiny homes surrounding a large white stucco church. It's imposing in the night, a white behemoth surrounded by black mountains. It's also quiet and a good place to camp for the night. I circle the outside and find a silver camper in the back. I listen at the door for signs of life, but there's nothing. I try the door, but it's locked tight. I consider breaking a window, but I doubt I'd fit through it.

The church has two entrances, one in the front and one in the back, but both are locked as well. I consider going back to the truck to sleep, because breaking into God's house seems really wrong—maybe so bad that my father's nagging voice might give up on me entirely. Still, it's so cold and I need to lie down. So I make the sign of the cross as best as I can remember and whisper a pre-crime apology into the sky. I find a heavy rock, wrap it in my hoodie, and smash a window. It was loud. I bet all twenty-seven residents are rushing down here in their pajamas to investigate. I wait for a light to come on or a police siren. After ten minutes, I reach my hand through the sharp edges and unlock the window.

The room I've broken into is a dank, stuffy place filled with rows and rows of pews and folding chairs. There are racks on the back of each seat where Bibles, hymnals, and paper fans wait for worshippers. A plaque on the wall explains how much money the church collected last month and how much more they need to meet their goals. There's a life-size sculpture of Jesus on the cross standing behind the pulpit. It's not fancy, not like the church Dad used to take me to, with the towering ceiling and the stained-glass windows and the little cushioned benches you could fold down when you knelt to pray. This is church without the special effects.

There are a couple of doors behind the pulpit. There could be a cot in the back. Heck, there could be a California King back there, but exploring feels icky. Instead, I choose one of the hard wooden pews and stretch out as best I can. There's something lovely about being able to lie all the way down after two weeks in a car, even if my back is going to kill me in the morning. It's all the pampering I need.

Once I'm settled, I look up and realize the statue of Jesus is hanging directly over me. He stares down as if waiting for me to go to sleep.

"Hey."

Like I said, he's not much of a talker. Still, I can't help but think about what Arcade said to me, how I needed to talk to the person in charge of my universe. I guess it couldn't hurt.

"So, we haven't talked in a while," I continue.

Jesus's eyes shine like moonbeams. He looks uncomfortable, but that could be the whole crucifixion thing he's dealing with at the moment.

"Let me bring you up to date. You can probably tell by the state of my clothes and hair that things are kind of bad.

I'm not blaming you. I made these mistakes. I know a lot of people think you get involved in our lives—you know, help people win football games and Grammy Awards—but I've always believed you are as surprised as anyone when a person gets hit by a bus or wins the lottery. My dad believes that you have some kind of plan for everyone. I don't know. Maybe you do. So if that's true, and part of your plan involves me dying in some horrible way, I'd like to offer an alternative. I could be the hero. Hear me out, 'cause this could be really exciting. First, you get me to Tempest. Second, I charge in, blow the place up, free a bunch of people, and then make an amazing escape. Sounds cool, huh? I'd pay to see that movie."

I turn a little to work out a cramp in my leg.

"But, you know, if the script has already been written, then can I ask that my mom and dad get out and find a little place to be safe and happy, and Bex—let her grow really old and still be super hot and find someone who gets her to drop her guard? And Arcade. Get Arcade into some therapy and, well, if Fathom is really alive, then I guess they should be together, but only if she really loves him and appreciates him, because if she doesn't, then let him find someone who will, but let that person look a little like me, so I can feel like he will never get over me. Yeah, that's selfish. Sorry.

"I know it is probably against the rules to pray for a painful death for someone, but that Doyle guy? Can't he choke to death on a cup of coffee?"

I know it's just the changing angle of the moon, but Jesus looks slightly confused now.

"Yeah, I know. I sound crazy. I wonder if the Great Abyss hears Arcade's rambling and thinks she's lost her mind too. So, anything you can do would be awesome. I guess I should ask for world peace. You know, something selfless? World peace would be cool. Well, thanks for Lucas's truck and this church and the bench and all."

I can feel myself slipping into sleep.

"Please take care of everyone," I beg.

Jesus looks noncommittal. I'm hoping it's just the light.

I open my eyes to find another man hovering over me. Unlike the Jesus statue, he has deep brown eyes and skin, a shaved head, and a well-trimmed beard. He's wearing a short-sleeved white shirt and a thin black tie. He smells like cocoa butter.

"I'm going to go out on a limb and guess that you are having a rough couple of days," he says.

I sit up, feeling embarrassed and panicked.

"Don't worry," he continues. "I'm not going to call the police. We'd have to wait forty minutes for them to arrive from the next town. What do they call you?"

"Lyric," I say.

"That's lovely. Lyric, I've cooked some eggs. Will you have some breakfast with me?"

This is the second strange man to offer me a meal in as

many days, but he has kind eyes and a smile to match. He gestures for me to follow him, and he walks to one of the doors behind the pulpit. Together we move down a long hall to a small cafeteria. There's not much more than a big steel coffeepot, but there's a little kitchen off to the side and a few tables made of Formica with matching plastic chairs. On one table are two plates of eggs, toast, and bacon. There are tall glasses of milk and bananas, too. My mouth waters like that of a dog eyeing a pork chop.

He pulls out a chair for me, and I take a seat.

"My name is Henry Tubbs," he says. "I'm the preacher of this church. I come by a couple of times a week to check on it. We had some break-ins a few months back, mostly desperate people from the East Coast who crossed the borders in the night. The window repair budget is in the red this month."

"I'm sorry," I say, sincerely.

He waves it off, then sits across from me.

"I'd leave the place unlocked if I could. It's kind of what God wants, but the congregation is a little more practical. So, dig in."

I look down at the food, my stomach angrily reminding me of how much I've neglected it lately. My mind argues back that we don't know if we can trust Henry Tubbs. The two of them fight about it. My stomach wins. I snatch the fork, and the first bite tastes like heaven. If it's poisoned, it's going to be a great way to go.

"So, I can assume you are one of our neighbors to the east?" he says.

I nod.

"Just passing through?"

I nod, tearing into the toast like I harbor a grudge against it.

He chuckles and slides his breakfast toward me.

"I'll make more," he says when I try to push it back. "You can eat all you want, but there's a price. You have to tell me your story."

"I'm looking for something," I say, hoping it will satisfy his curiosity.

"Breaking into a church is a good first step," he says with a grin. "That's the kind of thing every preacher dreams of hearing."

I can't help but smile. "Sorry, I'm already a believer. I'm looking for a camp."

He gives me a hard stare, then looks into his plate, nodding gravely.

"I know of it. What makes a young woman like you want to visit a place like that?"

"My parents are locked inside it," I say, too tired to make up a lie.

Henry peels a banana and cuts it in half with his knife, then spears it and plops it onto my plate.

"Are you like the people they lock inside it?"

I look up at him, dreading that face I have seen whenever

anyone finds out what I am, but it's not there. He's just curious.

"I'm half Alpha," I offer.

"That can't be easy," he says. "People who are different often walk the most difficult paths. I'm actually a big fan of a man who was different. Everywhere he went, he faced hostility. People threw rocks at him. They drove him out of town."

"People suck," I say, then burn with embarrassment. "Sorry, I've got a potty mouth these days."

He shrugs. "Don't give up on people. Most of us have good hearts. Some are just afraid of things that they don't understand. I'm sure everyone got freaked out when they saw Jesus walk on water. Actually, it sounds like you two have something in common."

I laugh.

"And you're going to this camp to cause some trouble."

I nod as confidently as I can.

"That's a dangerous place," he warns. "Lots of guns up there."

I put my gloved hand on the table. "I've got this."

He takes a drink of his milk, then points to my plate. "I'll get you some more. You're going to need a full belly for that kind of work. After that, I'll drive you up there."

"You know where it is?"

He nods. "Very hard to hide a thing like that."

Two more helpings of everything make a big difference.

The final effects of the tear gas have worn off, and the decent sleep from the night before has left me feeling better than I have in weeks. Henry looks through the donation box and finds me a fresh shirt and a warm parka that will come in handy if I have to sleep outside again.

We get into his rusty Ford Escort and putter down the highway. The engine struggles with the rising elevation, but Henry never lets up. He pushes the car onward into the craggy red mountain range.

"How does your gizmo work?"

"I really don't know for sure. I turn it on just by thinking about it, and then I hear voices that ask me for directions."

"Voices, huh? You know, lots of folks in the Bible heard voices."

"So did a lot of folks living on the F train platform near my old house," I say.

Henry chuckles.

"What do the voices say?" he continues.

"They offer me help. They seem to come from water, like there's a voice for every drop in the ocean. I'm like their boss, and when I ask them to do something, they do it."

"That might be a problem for you. The place they built this camp on is in the middle of a rain-shadow desert."

"Which means?"

"These mountains here," he says, waving out in front of us, "they block all the moisture from getting through. It's probably the driest place in the whole country."

"Predictable." I sigh. "I don't know why my luck should change now."

"I'll pray for you," he says, and for the rest of the trip, he is quiet. Maybe he's silently contemplating what a terrible idea this is, or maybe he really is having a one-on-one with God. Or maybe there isn't anything left to say.

The drive takes almost an hour and a half, up and down peaks and into valleys, until Henry stops his car outside a huge chain-link fence that stands three stories tall, and we step out. A sign reads CAUTION! PRIVATE PROPERTY. TRESPASSERS WILL BE ARRESTED AND PROSECUTED.

"I guess this is it," I joke.

"Not at all subtle," he says. "You sure you want to do this?"

I nod. "I don't see any other option."

"I assumed as much. I wish you luck, Lyric," he says, cupping his hands together. I step into them, leaping onto the fence and climbing up effortlessly.

"You seem to have some experience climbing fences," he calls up to me.

"Brooklyn girl," I joke. "I've grown up surrounded by a few of them."

The dirt road to the camp mocks me. It turns and doubles back over and over again, and what should really be a five-mile walk becomes a twenty-five-mile hike. I could be out here all day and night and still not reach the camp by morning.

Where is it you think you're going? What happens when you get there? What is your plan?

I don't know, Dad. I am seventeen and sheltered and stupid, but it's a little late to fix any of that now. I can't turn around, can't fight the magnetic pull the camp has on me. It won't let me abandon my family and friends.

I hear the roar of an engine approaching, so I dart into the brush and huddle behind a couple of tall cacti. A murky green army jeep careens into the scenery. There are two men in it, both wearing white T-shirts and jeans and sneakers. There are rifles strapped to their chests. They remind me of Doyle with their serious faces. Luckily they don't spot me, and they continue onward.

I hop back onto the road, unsure of how long it will be before they come back around or if there are more jeeps on the way. I do know it's time to pick up the pace. My walk turns into a jog—good and steady. I'm not an athlete, so I have to take breaks, but once I'm fine, I keep going.

Not to say that I'm high on determination. This totally sucks. My legs and stomach are cramping. My back hurts, and I'm definitely wearing the wrong bra for this marathon. I've got a blister forming on the outer parts of both big toes, too. All these aches and pains have illuminated something about me. I am a ridiculous human being, spoiled, soft, and lazy —just like Arcade used to say. Why didn't I take up a sport in high school? Why didn't I go for a run on the beach every single day? My mother was a great athlete. People paid her to teach them yoga! My dad is in perfect condition. He can chase down a shoplifter half his age. Where is the Olympic decathlon gene they should have passed on to me? Why did I get the binge-watching-Netflix DNA?

You're a force of nature. You're a wild thing. My mother urges me onward.

"Oh, hi, Mom. Thanks for showing up. Where were you when Dad was lecturing me about my sins?"

"Lyric Walker!"

My name booms from the sky. I scamper off the road, startled and confused. Huddling behind a thin tree, I search for the source of the voice, but I can't find it.

"My name is Donovan Spangler. Welcome to Area Eleven, part of White Tower Securities Incorporated, a joint agreement with the Department of Justice, the Department of Defense, the Central Intelligence Agency, and the United States Marines. White Tower has been contracted to operate this facility.

"I know why you're here and what you plan to do, but I'm hoping we can have a conversation first. I think we can come to a mutually beneficial agreement free of violence and drama. How does that sound?"

From my vantage point I can see the top of a watchtower, and I realize I'm closer than I thought. I don't see anyone in it, but I suspect that's where the speaker is amplifying Spangler's voice.

"Come on out, Lyric," he says cheerfully. "Let's be friends."

I crawl through the scrub on hands and knees, fighting the urge to stand and run back the way I came. I feel exposed, like I'm a little white mouse and someone is peering into my hidey-hole. I find a large boulder and hunch down behind it, pressing my back to it while I catch my breath and contemplate my next move.

It's clear they can see me, so I might as well throw out the sneak-in-and-free-everyone plan. No, now all that's left to me is a face-to-face confrontation. I think about Deshane back at school. He barreled through the halls, terrorizing people. Every day was a demonstration of his aggression. I can see he did it to avoid fights. Only the bravest of the brave called him out, but most of them were terrified of what he might do. Fear kept people at bay. On the other hand, he could have been a psychopath. Still, it worked. I might as well give it a try. My thoughts turn on the glove, and I reach out with my mind, sensing a huge well of water buried in a tank not far from here. It must be the camp's primary water supply. There's enough to level this place if I get close enough to it, but for now I need a little to put on my show.

"Now, there's no reason to turn on your Oracle," Spangler says.

Oracle? What's that? I look down at the glove. Is that what this thing is called?

"No one is going to hurt you, so come on in," he continues. "It gets hot out here around lunchtime. We've got air conditioning and showers, and the chef can make you anything you want for dinner."

I round a corner and see another huge fence in front of me. Its gate is wide open, inviting me to pass through. I whip my head around in every direction, searching for soldiers to pop out of nowhere and gun me down, but I don't see a soul.

"That's it, Lyric. You're going in the right direction. You're getting closer."

After I step through the fence, I hear a mechanical hum and turn just in time to see the gate close on its own. Then I notice the sign.

WARNING! ELECTRIFIED FENCE! CONTACT MAY LEAD TO SERIOUS INJURY OR DEATH!

I reach out to the voices, and the water comes, popping a hole in the tank buried beneath the ground and asking it to rise up through the sand. I send it flying toward the fence, only to watch the whole thing short-circuit in an explosion of sparks and fire.

"Now, Lyric, that's not nice. Those fences are expensive," he says. "There's no need for weapons."

"I want my family and friends. I want you to let all the Alpha loose!"

"I hear you loud and clear. Keep coming, and we will discuss everything."

I walk farther along the road and reach a curve that blocks my view of what lies ahead. I stop. I'm certain that walking around the bend will make me a perfect target. I need to be prepared when I do it. If I see guns, I'm drowning everyone.

"All right, girl. Get ready," I say to the glove. The massive tank roars eagerly. There's so much chatter in the water.

I take a deep breath and turn the corner, bringing the camp into full view. I don't know what I was expecting. A collection of tents? Long stables filled with broken people? Some kind of space-age evil lair complete with a bald supervillain and his hairless cat? No, it's none of those things. It's more of an office building buried in the ground with a roof that sticks out of the soil. The shingles are covered in dirt and flowers and stones to look exactly like the wastelands that surround it, something a plane wouldn't spot if it flew overhead. It's actually very clever.

Standing out front is a large group of men and women, about forty in all. There are soldiers in desert camouflage holding M-16s, but most of them look like scientists, wearing long white lab coats and carrying tablets. Standing in front of them all is a tall, thin man probably in his early thirties wearing tortoiseshell glasses and a smart, wavy haircut. He's got on a pair of black skinny jeans, a suit jacket with a hoodie underneath, and, to complete the look, a pair of white Chuck Taylors. He looks like an aging hipster from Williamsburg.

"Welcome to Tempest, Lyric," he says to me.

"Let them go," I demand, but it comes out squeaky and childish. I wave my glove around a bit so they can see it's on and powered.

"Now, now, Lyric," he says. "No one has to get hurt."

"That's really up to you. Let everyone go, and I won't fight you. We'll leave, and you'll never see us again."

"Now, I know you're not that naive. I can't let anyone out of here. These people, if you can call them that, are dangerous. There's a creature inside that has poisonous spikes that pop out of his skin. I know this might be disappointing to hear, Lyric, but the simple fact is that everyone inside is here because they pose a danger to our country."

"You're torturing them," I argue.

"Torture? That's an ugly word. We prefer the term *enhanced interrogation technique*. Isn't that right, David?"

The crowd divides in two, revealing another tall figure. David Doyle flashes me a sad look, a final reminder that all of this could have been avoided.

"We certainly had to pay enough to get everyone to use that term," Spangler continues. "Besides, terrorists torture people, Lyric. We're a corporation, we offer a service."

Two soldiers charge through the front door of the building. One has Bex; the other, Arcade. They push the girls into the sand, revealing that each has a noose around her neck. The nooses are connected to long steel poles the guards hold tightly. Bex and Arcade look drugged. Neither of them puts up a fight.

Something explodes inside me. I can't say what it is — maybe the last part of me that thinks people are mostly good. I came here to save people, and I hoped that I wouldn't have to hurt anyone to do it. I am not a killer. I know that for sure. But that doesn't mean I can't really hurt them. My mind calls out to water beneath Spangler's feet.

What would you have us do?

"Get creative," I whisper back.

The ground rumbles and quakes as something huge pushes to the surface, but Spangler is not concerned. In fact, he smiles at me as he taps away on his tablet, and all at once it's as if the power I feel all around me has been switched to the off position. I can't hear the voice. The whispers have been silenced, and my control over the water is gone as well.

"What did you do?" I ask.

"All right, people. Let's get out of this heat," he says.

A soldier steps forward and hands him a Taser rifle.

"Spangler, we talked about this," Doyle shouts at him.

"We tried it your way, David," Spangler says. He fires the weapon and there's a *pop!* I feel a stabbing pain in my chest, and I fall to the ground. When I look down, I see wires sticking out of the wound leading all the way back to the rifle. I try to pull them out, knowing what is coming next, all while studying Doyle's face. He stares down at me, disappointed and frustrated. His eyes say, *I told you so.*

I hear a *zap,* and suddenly I am on fire.

CHAPTER ELEVEN

I COME BACK INTO THIS WORLD SWINGING. I AM GNASHING teeth and claws on throats. My body's lust for damage burns like a dangerous fever. It takes several long moments of flailing before I realize that I am completely alone. Spangler, Doyle, and all their people are gone. I'm not even outside anymore. They've put me in a circular room with towering walls that soar high over my head. A steel door is built into a wall, but there are no windows on it and no windows in the room, either. The effect is not unlike being at the bottom of a well. Panic seeps into my thoughts. I've never been afraid of small spaces—I'm not claustrophobic in the least—but right now I want to scream and scratch and beg for help. My breath grows shallow. I start to wheeze. Everything is about to crush me into paste.

"Calm down, Lyric, calm down, Lyric, calm down, Lyric," I say between short, staccato gasps. "You need to think clearly. It's the only way to get out of here."

Though I'm not sure there actually is a way out of here.

I'm lying on my back on a paper-thin mattress tossed onto a cold concrete floor. It's the only furniture in the room—no sink, no toilet, nothing. Only a hole in the floor. There's a single light bulb dangling high above me that is so bright, it's hostile. I suspect it can shine right through my body to the other side. It sings to me: *Tick—tick-tick—tick—tick-tick.*

Suddenly, there's a clang at the door.

"Inmate 114. Stand in the circle," a voice barks, but, as outside, I can't find the speaker.

"Where am I?"

"Stand in the circle," the voice repeats with growing impatience.

I try to sit up, but my whole body revolts. I feel broken, and my limbs are uncooperative. My head is a soft avocado. On top of that, one of my shoes is missing and there's blood on the big toe of my sock.

"I'm hurt," I say.

"Last warning, inmate! Stand in the circle."

"I don't know what you're talking about," I whimper, falling back to the mattress.

There's a loud clank, followed by an electronic buzz, and all at once my body becomes a herky-jerky marionette, thrashing in agony. My teeth grind together, holding back shrieks until the buzzing and the pain stop.

"Stand in the circle painted on the floor of your cell," the voice demands.

I hear him, but my brain and body are too busy rebooting to obey. My eyes, the only part of me that's not in full shutdown, find a circle on the floor painted in bright yellow. It's wide enough to stand inside, but getting into it feels like an impossible request.

"Stand in the circle, or I will shock you again!"

"Please, I'm trying," I beg, then weakly crawl in its direction. Every movement is a Herculean effort, but I somehow manage to get into the circle. It feels like hours before I can actually stand.

"Confirmed," the voice says, followed by a soft click, and then nothing.

"I need a doctor!" I shout.

There's no response.

"Let me out of here!" I shriek.

I cry. I can't help myself. The tears come out in violent convulsions, igniting a shaking fit that I can't stop. Everything inside me rattles, bones crash against bones, organs shake like jelly, and my knees buckle. I tumble face-first, hard. Unable to brace myself, I hit the floor with a hard smack.

Now I'm on my side, half on the mattress and half on the concrete, and I'm still alone. I sit up and feel a sticky pull on my face and arms. The mattress is damp and has a big red stain with a brown border. It's blood—my blood—and there's lots of it.

I search my body, looking under my shirt, wondering if I

really was shot, but there are only three tiny burns forming the corners of a pyramid. I gingerly remove my sock and see the nail on my big toe has been torn away. It wiggles when I touch it and delivers a shocking pain into my back. Still, there's not enough blood to have caused what I'm seeing. I reach up to my scalp and slowly probe my hair until I find a lump as big as a hard-boiled egg on the back of my head where my skull meets my spine. There's a lot of crusty stuff too, which I guess is dried blood. Running along the top of the lump is a wound. It's angry, and even a soft graze from my fingertip sends daggers into my skull. I cry out, and when I look at my fingers, there's fresh blood on the tips.

"I need a doctor!" I shout to silence. My stomach threatens an eviction of Henry's breakfast. *No. Calm down. Someone will come. Spangler will send a doctor. I'm important. Doyle said so. He won't let me die. They'll stitch up my head and clean me and bring me a new mattress and a pillow and a sheet. They will do these things because they are human beings.*

"Hello?" I shout.

The only answer comes from the light bulb hanging over my head.

Tick—tick-tick—tick—tick-tick.

There's a commotion at my door. I hear a rattle and the sound of keys. The slot at the bottom opens wide, and a silver bowl of food slides into the room.

I crawl toward the slot and peer out into the hall, but I don't see anyone.

I have never been so hungry in my life. There's bread and something that looks like mac and cheese, and two brown things in sticky syrup. When I look closely, I realize they are slices of rotting apple, but I am too ravenous to care. I tear at the bread and it crumbles in my hand, dry and stale. I nearly choke to death on it and have to slow down because they haven't given me anything to drink. I eye the mac and cheese next and reach for a spoon, only to realize they haven't given me that, either. I scoop it up with my fingers, feeling like an animal. It tastes gritty and definitely not like mac and cheese. I can't place the taste at all. It's a bit like Cream of Wheat, but there's a vinegary flavor. I'm too hungry to care. I shovel it into my mouth and lick my fingers until I see something squirming on the tip of my finger. I eye it closely. It's a maggot.

I wretch and everything comes up, burning through all that's left of my energy. I lie back down, pull my knees close to my chest, and rock back and forth. If my mother were here, she'd rub my back and tell me jokes until I laughed.

"Where's my mom?" I whimper. "I want my mom."

Is she in a cell like this one? Could she be across the hall? I know I am not alone in this prison. There are shouts and screams seeping in from beneath the crack in the door. Someone is slamming metal on metal. I hear footsteps and an argument that turns into a fight that turns into an agonized scream. The noises never stop. They bear down on me, grind at my skull. Every shout is a punch in the gut. Every cry for mercy is a stab in the heart. They're proof that I am not alone, but they are no comfort to me. I wonder if that person is Bex. What if it's Arcade? What if it's my father? What if it's Fathom?

I failed them all.

I hear a rattling, and the slot opens. There's a hum that terrorizes me. I brace for electrocution, but instead the bowl rattles around on the floor, then skids toward the door as if seized by an invisible hand. It slams against the door, bounces around a bit, then zips through the narrow space. The slot closes. Footsteps fade away.

I must have fallen asleep, because suddenly Spangler is in my cell. He taps on his tablet, but when he notices I'm awake, he puts it away.

"Lyric, do you know what an alpha is?" Spangler asks. "Not the people, of course. I'm talking about in the animal kingdom. Alphas are the leaders of the pack. Apes, lions, even birds, have them. Sled dogs are a great example of animals that have an alpha. They get their name because they are the most dominant animals in the group. The alpha isn't born into the position. Usually it has to fight for its power, and then it has to train the others to be submissive using sheer aggression and intimidation. Every once in a while, one of the dogs on the sled forgets its place in the pack and it challenges the alpha.

Do you know what usually happens? The alpha rips the other dog's throat out. Here at Tempest, I am the alpha dog. Do you understand what I'm telling you?"

I nod.

"Good. Your parents didn't get it at first. I'd hate for you to have to learn the way they did," he explains.

My heart beats hard enough to blow out of my chest.

"Are they alive?"

"You could be a great help to our little sled-dog pack. I'm confident that you can learn to cooperate, but my patience will go only so far."

"What do you want me to do?" I ask him.

"I want you to be a good dog."

Panic attacks rise up and batter my mind. The trembling strips me of my strength even more. I sob unexpectedly until my face is smeared in mucus. I don't have the energy to care. I curse myself for being here, for not having a plan, for not preparing myself for this kind of fight, for being afraid. I curse myself for assuming I would be killed if I didn't rescue my people. I never thought I'd be locked up inside with them.

When I'm too tired to cry, I hoist myself up so I'm sitting against the wall. My cell can't be wider than nine feet—just long enough for the mattress and a tiny bit of exposed floor space and that painted yellow circle, of course. I study every-thing closely, hoping for some way of escape. I can't crawl up the wall to whatever is above me. It's too smooth. There's no lock on the door and it's made of heavy steel. I peer into the drainage hole dug into the floor. I can't see too deeply into it, maybe six inches at most. The light above will permeate only so far. It's too narrow for my body to fit inside, but still, maybe there's something useful about it. I lean forward, listening closely, praying for the familiar gurgle of water. Something shines down there. I activate my glove, realizing I can still use it as a flashlight, but it isn't much help.

The things I could do if it still worked. Spangler shut it off, but how? I remember when the Rusalka attacked us on the beach, our gloves suddenly didn't work. I know there was a moment when it seemed we combined our efforts and shut down theirs, but maybe it was White Tower all along. Doyle was in Coney Island that day. Anything is possible. I just don't know what to do without it. When it's activated and talking to me, I feel like a giant. Now that I can't access its power, I'm like a kid with a broken toy. I am so screwed.

During the night, I feel something nudging my foot. I sit up to find a rat chewing at the heel of my sock. I shriek, but it's not afraid of me. A moment later I discover why. It is just one of a flood of rats that pour out of the hole in the floor, each with a long, hairless tail and hungry pink eyes. I kick at them the best I can, knocking a few against the wall, but they don't stop coming. Soon, there are so many, I can't see the floor anymore.

Overwhelmed, I scream as they bite at my shoes and leap

at my legs, and then, just like that, they all scurry back down the hole, crawling over each other as they go. When I finally find the bravery to sit back down, I look at my battered sock and realize the rat nearly chewed all the way into my heel. I drag my mattress so that it covers the hole, then huddle on the other side of the room to calm myself.

I wonder if there is a camera on me. I wonder if they are listening. I'm even afraid they might be able to hear my thoughts. If it's true, then they know I hate the light. They know how much I want to destroy it. I spend hours concocting plans for how to get at it and smash the little person inside it that keeps making music.

Last night I tried to be clever. I unbuttoned my shirt and slipped it off. It was filthy, with caked black blood on the back, and barf on the sleeve, but I knew it could block out the light. I draped it over my eyes and enjoyed the closest thing to darkness I've felt in . . . I no longer know how long I've been in here.

I heard a clang, and then the door opened and men stomped into my space. I was shy. I tried to hide myself, but they were on me before I could. One of the soldiers kicked me in the chest and the other snatched my shirt. A moment later they were gone. The pain spread in hot waves across my ribs, but the despair was more agonizing.

The light still shines, still watches, still ticks. I know it is part of Spangler's plan. The mattress, the hole, the sleep deprivation, and even the rats are to torment me. He's training me to be submissive. He's turning me into a dog.

The door rattles. Now I jump up and prepare to get into the circle. I've gotten very fast at following their orders. This time, however, the door opens all the way. On the other side are three armed soldiers, two of whom have M-16s pointed right at my head. A third one is carrying a long pole with a noose attached to the end. It's exactly like the ones they used on Bex and Arcade the last time I saw them. They've come to kill me. They've had it with my begging. They are pissed that I've been looking for their secret eyes. They know I want to murder the light bulb. I'm tempted to scurry back into the corner and push my mattress between them and me, but I put out my hands. I submit.

"Don't move," one of them barks. Suddenly the noose is around my throat, cutting off the air and my voice as they drag me to my feet. They lead me through the door and into the hallway, and I stumble along, panicked that I will trip and hang myself. The noose is unforgiving. It feels like it's shredding skin and muscle. My lungs tighten. Spots float in my eyes.

Suddenly we're through a door and in a room as wide and as high and long as an airplane hangar. The lights in here are so bright, I can barely see, but I can make out a maze of chain-link fences in every direction, forming tiny little cages barely big enough for a full-grown man to stand. I'm pushed along the path, passing each cage, and inside I see the contorted faces of people I used to know. They are all adults, men and women, all with broken spirits and sad eyes. I hear someone say my name, but the guards keep pushing me along, so I can't stop. They shove me deeper into the labyrinth, finally tossing me into an empty cage of my own. They force me to my knees, and the noose comes off. Finally I can take a ragged, desperate breath.

"Turn around and face me," one of the soldiers demands.

I do as I'm told, fully expecting to see his gun in my face, but instead I find him with his smartphone aimed right at me.

"Smile, freak," he says, and then I hear a click.

"Get one with me," the other soldier says, stepping into the shot. I can see he's grinning as he gives the camera the thumbs-up sign. Everyone gets a picture with me as I stand shaking and bewildered.

"What is this place?" I ask.

"We call it the kennel," one of the soldiers says.

"Looks good," the cameraman says as he stares down at the phone. Then they lock the door and leave me alone.

"Let me out of here!" I whimper.

The soldiers ignore my plea, then turn and walk away.

"Lyric?" a voice crackles from the next cage.

I turn to my left and find a rag doll of a girl with dark rings around her eyes. Her skin is ashen and her lips chapped. Her fingers poke through the fence, eager for human contact.

"Do I know you?" I ask.

I kneel down so our faces are close, then nearly fall back when I recognize her.

"Bex!" I cry, "Where are they keeping you?"

She shrugs. "It's a maze, and I can't keep track of it. I'm in a cell by myself."

"Me too."

"This is the first time I've seen you here. We get an hour a day in the cages. I think it's so they can clean our rooms," Bex says. "Lyric, we all thought you were dead."

"We?"

Bex gestures to the other cages. I peer into one and realize I'm looking at another familiar face. I don't know his name, but I know he is married to a Sirena. I used to see him on the boardwalk when I was a kid. He liked flying kites. Yeah, I know him! In the next cage is another familiar face—Rochelle Lir! I call out to her, but she doesn't respond. I ask her if she's seen Terrance or Samuel, but she's sleeping, I hope.

"Have you seen my mom and dad?"

"I've seen the Big Guy," Bex whispers, as if talking saps her strength.

"He's here?" I stand and study the cages for as far as I can see. I don't see him, but they go on forever.

"Dad!"

A few people stir, but no one responds.

"Leonard Walker?" I shout.

There's a long pause.

"Lyric?" the voice comes from the other side of the room and echoes off the ceiling. "Is that you, Lyric?"

"Dad?"

"Thank you, God!" he cheers.

"Mom?"

"They don't keep the Alphas in here, honey," he explains. "Are you okay?"

The man in the cage across from me hisses. "Keep it down—they'll come back."

I ignore him. "I'm banged up but all right. How are you?"

"I'm fine," he says. I know he's lying. The last time I saw him, we were dragging ourselves out of a car crash. He was hurt so bad, he couldn't even walk. I'm sure he's got a couple of broken ribs but he doesn't want me to worry. "Keep quiet. It's not safe to draw their attention."

"Dad, what are we going to do?"

His pause haunts me.

"Lyric, I love you."

"I love you!"

The next few moments hover with anticipation. One of us should shout that we have a plan and that the other shouldn't worry because we will all be safe and together soon. We should be sharing hope with one another right now, but all we have to offer is silence and uncertainty.

I sit back down next to Bex, pushing myself against the fencing so that I am as close to her as possible.

"Bex, I'm—"

"I'm sorry, Lyric," she says, then breaks into a coughing fit. "I'm sorry for what I did."

"Don't be stupid," I say. "I was being an ass."

"I was so afraid of losing you, I held you back. If I had kept my mouth shut, maybe we—"

"We never had a chance, Bex. Doyle orchestrated everything. We were always going to end up here. Now we need to concentrate on getting out. Have you seen Arcade?"

She shakes her head.

"They keep saying I'm important. They want something from me," I explain.

"What is it?"

"I don't know, but if it gets us out of here, they can have it."

"Don't trust them," she begs. "They're all liars."

I'm not always in a cage next to Bex. Sometimes I'm next to someone completely new, like Jacques, who hasn't seen his son, Pierre, or his Sirena wife, Anna, in a year and a half. Sadie is a pale-skinned lady who was probably very pretty before they captured her. She tells me she's thirty-two, but she looks closer to sixty. She hasn't seen her husband, Mark, or her daughter, Breanne, in almost three years. Bruce is forty, and he and his wife, Raina, were friends with my mother. He hasn't seen his wife or his three girls, Alexa,

Dallas, and Priscilla, in a long while. He's lost track of time since they locked him up. Robin was a schoolteacher who didn't even know his wife, Beth, was an Alpha. He's bitter about the deception and resentful that he doesn't have a picture of his daughters, Tess, Emma, and Jane.

And then there are the ones teetering on the edge of mental illness, who can't trust anyone or anything. They watch me, suspicious of my every move. They accuse me of being a spy.

"I don't want to talk to you about what I've seen," Kirsten whispers angrily. "You can't fool me, Lyric. I know you tell them every word."

"I'm not telling anyone anything. You have to trust me. We need to work together to get out of here," I say. "You might know something that can help."

I alienate more than a few of them with my persistence. A tall, graying man actually rats me out to a guard when they come to take us back to our cells.

"She's planning an escape!" he shouts, pointing a wild finger at me. "Tell Mr. Spangler that I told you. Tell him I'm not a troublemaker. Ask him for more rations, please."

"Good dog!" I shout at him, then feel remorse. We're all doing things that aren't in character these days. I should be more sympathetic.

A guard listens to the man, then eyes me closely, finally laughing as if he's heard the funniest joke ever.

"Good luck, kid," he sneers as he slips the noose around

my neck. "The only way you're getting out of this place is in a body bag, or maybe, in your case, we'll flush you down the toilet, fish girl."

One day I find Bex next to me again. She looks worse than the last time I saw her. She's getting thinner and has trouble keeping her head up.

"You're rocking the pixie cut," she whispers to me, her voice no louder than a breeze.

I have to get her out of here.

Getting to go to the cages feels like a treat. They take me in the same rough way as always, dragging me like a wild beast and tossing me in before I can fight back. One day, as they lock the gate, one of the soldiers swats me on the nose with a newspaper, then throws it into the cage.

"What's this?" I say.

"You're front-page news." He laughs.

I snatch up the paper and find a picture of a young girl. Her eyes are hollow, her cheeks thin and sucking. She's wearing ragged, filthy clothes and is desperately skinny. There's a feral look in her eyes. I'm confused. I don't understand what this is about. I stand and bang on the gate, demanding that he explain it to me, but he laughs and walks away.

I look at it again, hoping for some clue, and then I read the headline.

CONEY ISLAND TERRORIST APPREHENDED. 17-YEAR-OLD LYRIC WALKER ARRESTED IN TEXAS. PUBLIC CALLS FOR DEATH PENALTY.

The girl in the picture is me. It's the photo the guards took of me. I look like I've lost my mind.

A woman is standing over me wearing a long white lab coat. She's got red hair and a pinched face. At first I think she's a dream, but she yelps when my eyes focus on her. Dreams aren't startled by the dreamer. I try to bolt upright, but I'm strapped to a bed. I'm not in my cell. I'm in something similar to an emergency room, though it doesn't look very sterile. The walls and floor are concrete, and it's cold. My nurse is not happy.

"She needs more Pentothal." Her voice is tinged with panic.

A soldier is on me, holding down my arms while she injects something into my shoulder. I want to fight back, but I feel like I'm melting.

"The gas should have done the job," the solider barks at her. "You said it would work."

"Well, it didn't! She's like one of the kids," she snaps. "She's tougher than a normal person. Just relax. I've got it covered. Now help me. We've got to get her ready."

"Please help me," I beg, but I'm already sinking into sleep as the nurse and the soldier look down on me.

"She hurt her head," the soldier says.

The woman sighs.

There's a gurgling sound nearby that causes me to jerk. The rats must be coming up the hole again. I struggle, but the guard holds me still. The tinkling is coming from bubbles rising inside a bag of liquid that swings back and forth above my head.

"Where am I?" I say, but my voice sounds slow and flimsy.

"She's not supposed to be talking, is she?" another voice asks. "Give her another dose."

"And stop her heart?"

"If she wakes all the way up—"

"Calm down, Calvin," the nurse demands. "She doesn't have the strength of a pureblood."

"How do you know? Just because the others seem normal, that doesn't mean she is. She's got one of those gloves," the guard warns.

"They've turned it off, so relax. You make this job impossible sometimes."

"I didn't sign on for this," Calvin complains.

"Who did?" the woman snaps. "If you hate it so much, ask for a transfer. I hear there's an opening in the tank. You can feed those things. They'll give you your own bucket of chum."

The guard growls. "Don't even joke about that."

"Then stop whining and do your job," the nurse scolds.

I hear a buzzing sound, but I can't tell where it's coming from, only that it's near my ear.

"All right, let's get this over with," the nurse says. "The client wants to see the product, and she can't be a filthy mess."

There's a tickling sensation on the back of my skull that is curious, but I can't keep my eyes open any longer.

Now I'm nude, strapped down to a table, and terrified.

"Stop shivering. You have to be still," a voice broadcasts from a speaker I can't see.

"What are you doing to me?"

"We're taking x-rays," the voice explains.

I hear buzzing and I jump, sure that I'm about to be shocked like so many times before.

"I told you to hold still," the voice complains.

"I'm trying. I'm so cold."

After x-rays, Calvin and the nurse enter and wheel me to another table. They transfer me to it, then slide the table, with me on it, into a tiny hole like I'm entering a casket.

"The MRI takes an hour, so lie still," Calvin snaps.

"I have a lot of electricity in my brain," I say as I fade. "When I was little, the doctors said so."

I don't know how long I was out, but it was long enough for them to put me back in my cell. I feel groggy and soft. Chemically induced sleep must not be as good as the real thing.

They've given me a bath and put me into a black jumpsuit with the White Tower logo on it. There's something on my head, too — a bandage, and when I reach up to see if they've stitched the wound, I realize my head has been completely shaven. All that's left is stubble.

I sob. I know it's stupid. My hair is the least of my problems right now, but I can't help myself. It's not from vanity. It's the vulnerability, the helplessness, that crushes me. These people can take whatever they want from me. I have no control over anything, not even a single strand of hair.

CHAPTER TWELVE

I'M ON THE SHORELINE IN MY BARE FEET, AND THE COLD Atlantic water swallows my toes. Stretched out before me is a turbulent brew, spinning in the sky. A storm is coming, one that promises to wipe Coney Island off the map.

"Are you finally ready?" Fathom says, materializing by my side. He slips his hand in mine, and I hold on to it tightly.

"To do what?"

"To fight."

Suddenly, the black wave that destroyed my home is hanging over me. Ghost, Luna, Thrill, and Arcade appear, all of them whole and alive. Ghost takes my other hand in his long, white spindly claw and turns his bulbous eyes to mine. His mouth is grim.

"You are not allowed to give up, halfling," he hisses to me.

"I can't do this."

Black figures break through the wall of liquid, but they are not Rusalka. They are soldiers in White Tower Securities uniforms. Their claws shift back and forth from sharp talons to M-16s.

"Fight them, Lyric!" Luna begs. The scales on her neck are fiery red.

"You have to let loose whatever power is inside you," Thrill demands.

"But the glove doesn't work!" I try to explain.

"You don't need it," Arcade says. "You have other weapons."

I turn to find my mother. Her raven black hair cascades down her shoulders. She's in her jean shorts and her flip-flops and she is as beautiful as I have ever seen her. She steps into the warrior pose, a staple of her class, and something she taught me to help fight my migraines. Her arms extend from either side of her torso. She looks at me and smiles.

"Don't tell me you've forgotten."

The buzzer shocks me awake just in time for me to see a bowl slide in from under the door. I crawl over to it and stare down into the slop. Today is the worst yet. I wonder if Spangler is cooking these meals for me personally. I'm tempted to fling it at the wall, but I'm afraid of what the punishment would be, so I leave it where it sits and crawl back onto my mattress. I lie there, looking at my light bulb, and consider the dream.

Tick—tick-tick—tick—tick-tick.

Eventually the slot opens and I hear the hum of the magnet that steals the bowl away. I watch it skid across the floor, but this time it doesn't line up properly. It bangs against the lip of the door, then tilts upward, eager to heed the magnet's call but unable to get through. I'm tempted to help out the idiot on the other side and move it to where it should go, but then the hum fades away and he starts cursing. The bowl falls to the floor and is still.

The voice crackles on the speaker. "Inmate 114. Stand in the circle."

I do as I'm told, then hear another buzz, followed by the clank of a lock. The door slowly opens, and on the other side is a guard I've never seen before. He's carrying a keycard about the same size as a credit card. I realize this is how he locks and unlocks the door.

"Don't move," he says. His eyes are wide and his gun is out. He looks like he's twenty years old, too young to have a job like this.

"I promise."

He leans down without taking his eyes off me, snatches the bowl away, then slowly backs out of the room.

"Give my compliments to the chef," I manage before he slams the door again. I hear the clank of the lock and then his footsteps. I lie back down on my mattress, but face-down, because I don't want the cameras to see the gigantic smile on my face. I just discovered a crack in the system. I think I've found a way out of here.

CHAPTER THIRTEEN

MY MOTHER'S VOICE IS DRIFTING THROUGH MY thoughts when I wake up the next morning. *Fight like a wild thing.*

"I hear you, Mom. I hear you loud and clear."

I stand, lean my mattress against the wall, and then sit cross-legged on the floor. Closing my eyes, I focus on my breathing, blocking out the shrieks from beyond my door and the light that never dims. It's a lot to ignore and it takes longer than it should, but I find my place, the silent, still white place where my brain goes to meet with the *Om*. It's there, waiting for me. I'm ready.

I press my hands together in prayer, nod respectfully to the big unknown, then rise to my feet. Stepping forward with my left foot, I lunge back with my right, turning it ninety degrees toward the wall. I extend my arms until they are parallel to the floor; then I stretch into it, dipping my knee and letting my toes, ankles, and quadriceps wrap around themselves to do the hard work of balancing me. I can't stay in it for long. I'm rusty and weak, but tomorrow will be better.

For the next hour, I work through a routine my mother used to teach daily on the beach. I'm sloppy and unbalanced. I can't really stay in downward dog very long, and when I plank, I cheat with my knees. Holding some poses sends my muscles into tremors, and my feet and abs twist into cramps. There are a lot of cranky areas in this body, which is to be expected.

That's why they call it a practice instead of a workout.

My goal today is to get through it, reminding myself that I'm both exhausted and near starved. I am also an emotional wasteland, but I'm doing something proactive that will make me strong and ready when someone makes another mistake on the other side of my cell door.

When the routine is done, I sit myself next to the closest wall, prop my legs straight up against it, and lie back in a ninety-degree angle. I focus again on my breath, trying to ignore my pissed-off muscles, embracing their anger. It is so much better than the fear I've been manufacturing since they locked me in this room. I lie still for as close as I can estimate to thirty minutes, feeling my head clear, feeling more like myself than I have in a very long time.

"I am Lyric Walker, Daughter of Summer," I whisper when I open my eyes. She taught me these lessons, and I abandoned them. I've been a fool.

The days pass, and I get stronger with every one. The guards try to interrupt my practice by having me stand in the circle over and over again. At first the intrusions kill my concentration, but eventually I learn to slip right back into the workout once they are satisfied.

I wake eager to get started and end each day with another hour-and-a-half session before I go to sleep. I can feel my muscles tightening in my shoulders and arms, and soon the tremors and cramping are gone. I was never good at handstands, but my mother tried to teach them to me anyway, so I know the basics. I use the walls to brace myself, falling over many times, banging the back of my head once so badly, I'm sure I've ripped out the staples, but I get back up and do it again and again and again, until I can do a handstand pushup. At the end of the second week, I can do five of them. At the end of the third week, I can do thirty. My posture straightens, and I'm able to tune out the noises a lot better. The panic attacks still come around, but I'm able to fight them off with some focused breathing.

The hardest part is the food. It's always the same, always rancid, and there's never anything to drink, but I eat every bite. It's the only way I'm going to get stronger. I wish I could just gorge and swallow it fast, but I know it will make me sick to eat too quickly, so I close my eyes tight and try to think of my mother's spaghetti and meatballs, or meatloaf, or anything. Even the charred black stuff my dad made while destroying the kitchen every morning is better than this. His burned eggs and toast and scorched oatmeal sound delicious.

I think about pizza from Famous Ray's, and chili dogs from Nathan's, and cotton-candy afternoons. I think about fried oysters and clam strips at Rudy's Bar. I think about everything but barfing, and aside from some gagging, it works. I lick every crumb in the bowl and tell myself it will turn into muscle. I'm still working on the rotten apples when the slot opens. I snatch what I can as the bowl is pulled out of my hands, skitters across the floor, and disappears.

I crawl to the door and laugh.

"I ate it all!" I shout. "You couldn't get it before I was done!"

And I pray. Not like Arcade, but certainly inspired by her. My father is a nonpracticing Catholic, and Mom has her Alpha beliefs, so we never really went to church on a regular basis. I know the basics, but I'm not really talking to God or Jesus or the Great Abyss. I'm talking to whoever is out there and is listening. Sometimes I imagine that it's Henry from the little church in Shafter. He tells me to pray out loud, unapologetic and vulnerable.

And the rest of the days, I lie on the mattress, silent and mindful. They must think I'm sleeping, but that's not at all what I'm doing. I'm listening to the noises, the ones that used to drive me insane. I'm counting their rhythms and taking mental notes on their patterns, quickly discovering my meal delivery is a fairly reasonable time-keeping method. I can't know for certain the exact time of day it is, but I know I get three meals and then there is a long run until the next one arrives. I assume that span is nighttime, when everyone is supposed to be asleep, including me. So the first meal is the beginning of a new day. In between those meals, I'm counting how often someone checks the lock on my door—nine times. I'm noticing that someone demands I step into the circle eight times. There are three times each day when there are lots of people in the halls—shift change. All of it soon forms a predictable schedule, in which I know what's happening outside my door without ever seeing it. Their routines are telling me plenty about how this place works.

The only thing that breaks up my training is when they steal me away to run tests. I never expect it, and it occurs in the nighttime when I'm asleep. I assume they pump some kind of knockout gas into the room, but I never hear the hiss. During the tests, they poke and prod. The nurse takes blood and tissue samples. She studies my eyes. They drop me into a tank and film me as the scales appear on my arms and neck. They examine the gills on the undersides of my jawline and the webbing between my feet and toes. They want urine and skin samples, and they scan and x-ray me to the point where I'm concerned about getting cancer, but I don't fight them. My strength is reserved for other things.

"This one needs a bath," Calvin complains.

"Well, ask Spangler if you can give her one," the nurse snaps.

"Damn, Amy. You're a real pill."

Amy. That's the nurse's name. She's the one who shaved my head. She stitched me up and inserted the IV needles. Amy. Such a nice name, a name that seems kind and pleasant, like it's associated with springtime and flowers, and yet there's such ugliness inside her.

"I've got a brother in the Guard, and he's stationed in Brooklyn," she snaps at him. "Those things nearly killed him this week, so excuse me for not being Little Ms. Sunshine."

She reaches into her pocket and takes out a tube of lip gloss and spreads it across her ugly mouth. Then she selects a needle off the tray and injects it into my bag.

I would kill for lip gloss, I think, feeling their sedatives crawl through me.

"Oh, sorry. Is he okay?"

"He can't tell me anything," Amy says calmly. "My mother is in hysterics. She's got two kids working around sea monsters. She keeps blaming herself, like she did something wrong."

"You told her?" Calvin says. "I thought all this is classified."

She shakes her head. Calvin is intolerable to her. I can't help but laugh at her misery.

"It seems like every couple months something uglier crawls out of the ocean," he adds. "Did you see what they brought in here the other day?"

Amy grunts. "Disgusting."

"Did you read that story about the captain who spotted the giant squid?"

Amy scowls. "I had an uncle who was on a fishing boat. He was always drunk too."

"Unless it's true," he argues.

"Jeez, you were right, Calvin. She does need a bath."

"Can't we hose her off or something?" he asks. "She's not going to hurt anybody. She can't even keep her eyes focused."

Amy shrugs, grabs me by the jaw roughly, and flashes a penlight into my pupils.

"Yeah, get the hose."

The nurse pulls the IV needle out of my arm, swabs my skin with alcohol, and puts a bandage on the wound.

Moments later, they're blasting me with a stream of water so intense, I slam into the wall behind me and pass out cold.

"Inmate 114. Stand in the circle," the voice says.

I rise, step into the circle, and hear the buzz.

"What, no sarcastic remark?" the voice asks.

"I'm a good dog," I say, *with a very mean bite.*

Once I hear the click, I start my practice, beginning and ending with the warrior pose, then lie down to calm my mind and focus on my breathing. It isn't long before I hear the slot open. I don't even look as the bowl scrapes across the concrete floor. I just stand and retrieve it—the same as every day, and I eat, slowly and methodically, like it's my favorite meal in the world—a grandma slice from Neptune pie. This is the last meal I'm going to eat at Tempest.

I've timed it so well, I know when the slot will open and the bowl will go, so I'm finished when it happens. I hear the buzz, but this time I give the bowl a swift kick. It flips up into the air and lands flat against the door, then scurries back and forth, unable to fit through the hole. I watch it move to the left and then to the right as the guard outside does his best to alter the angle of the magnet to no avail. It falls with a clang when his machine powers down.

"Inmate 114. Stand in the circle," the voice demands.

I nod and do as I'm told. There's a buzz, then a clanking sound as the door is unlocked, and it slowly swings open.

Fight! Fathom shouts in my ear. He's joined by my father, and my mother, Bex, Shadow, Arcade, Lucas, Ghost, Luna, Rochelle, and Terrance—by everyone I have ever met, living or dead, all shouting for me to beat this guy's ass. I leap forward and kick the door with everything I've got. It's a gamble. I have never been able to figure out if the door will automatically lock when it closes, but it's a chance I have to take. From the other side I hear an "oof," and a cry of pain. The guard's gun rattles to the ground as loud as a fireworks display and then settles, silent and waiting. The door slowly creeps open, and I step out into the hall.

His nose has exploded. There is blood all over it and a gash on his forehead leaking down his face. It's Calvin, the soldier who is helping Amy experiment on me. His eyes meet mine as if he's wondering whether I've got the guts to go for his pistol, and then they widen because he knows I do. We leap at the same time, scrambling for possession, but he's faster, stronger—he's not living in a box and eating gruel—so I slam my elbow into his nose with every ounce of aggression I can. He screeches. It's enough for him to loosen his grip on the gun, and I snatch it away.

"Kid, you're going to wind up shooting yourself with that," the soldier warns, his hands up in front of his face.

I click off the safety, cock the hammer, and shake my head.

"My dad's a cop in the Sixtieth Precinct. He taught me how to use this when I was fourteen. Get in the cell."

"No."

"Look at me, Calvin. I look pretty desperate, right?"

"You'll never get out of here," he warns as he surrenders to my demands.

"Just give me your keys."

He unfastens his key ring from a chain around his waist. Among them is a keycard with a White Tower logo printed on its face.

"Aren't you going to wish me luck?" I ask.

He laughs despite himself, and I slam the door shut. I wave the card over a sensor panel mounted on the wall and hear the buzz and clank of the lock. That was easier than I was expecting, and it takes me a second to wrap my head around the fact that I'm actually standing in the hall without a guard. I scan both directions. There are doors on either side of the hall, and each one has a sensor pad.

"Anybody in there?" I say as I swipe the card over the nearest door. I hear a whimper when it swings open and find a woman about my father's age with chocolate-brown hair huddled on the floor.

"We're leaving," I say, then dart to the next door and repeat the routine. Soon, every door is open and a scrawny, half-starved person is taking his or her first tentative steps toward freedom. A forty-something man with a full beard creeps out of his cell. His eyes are wild, and he's rocking back and forth with nervous energy. I can't tell how long he's been here, but one look at him tells me there's a good chance he's lost his mind. It dawns on me that none of these people might be capable of escaping. A few of them are too afraid to leave their cells. I give them all a second look to make sure Bex and my mom aren't among them, then run to the end of the hall, find a door marked STAIRS, and push through it. Up a flight of steps I go with a gun in one hand and a keycard in the other. I careen through a second stairwell door and right into Amy on the other side. A tray of hypodermic needles she was holding flies into the air and comes crashing down around us.

"Hello." I level the pistol at her face.

"I'm sorry," she blubbers. Fat tears rolls down her cheeks so quickly, I wonder if they've been waiting for this moment since I arrived. "Don't kill me."

"Where are you keeping the others?"

"Lyric, you can't—"

"I have friends and family in this camp, innocent people, Amy, and we're going home."

"Your father is right there," she says, pointing to a door across the hall.

I push her against the wall and swipe the card on the sensor.

The door opens with a heavy clank. Amy wasn't lying. My father is on the floor. He's lost some weight, but he's not as bad as some of the people in this camp. He looks up at me, confused, like he's not sure whether what he's seeing is real or a delusion.

"Lyric?"

"Dad, can you walk?"

He tries but gives up with a groan.

I pull Amy into the room.

"Help me get him on his feet. You're going to be his crutch!" I shout.

She does as she's told.

"Lyric, this is crazy," my father says.

"Crazy is all we've got," I say, helping him into the hall.

"Now, where's Bex?" I demand.

"Who?"

"Rebecca Conrad!" I shout.

"She's upstairs."

"With the Alpha?" I demand.

"No, they're on the floor above that. They're in the tank," she explains.

"The tank? What the hell is that?" I ask.

Amy whimpers. "It's on the top floor. I have nothing to do with it. I don't work in that section."

She points down the hall to another exit sign. I suddenly realize how hard it's going to be to get everyone out. There must be at least sixty adults, maybe even more, all as sick and weak as my father. Who knows what kind of state the Alpha are in, and then there's their children. I don't even know where they're keeping them. We'll never find them on our own.

"You're going to have to come with us," I say to Amy. Her eyes drop down to the hypodermic needles on the floor. She's considering going for one, jamming it into me, maybe knocking me out.

"Lady, I don't know if I can kill you, but I know I can shoot you. If you don't help us, I'll put a bullet into something you need. Now go!"

She nods and, OMG—I've got a hostage.

I unlock all the cells while my father leans on Amy. I don't even bother to look inside the rooms. I don't have time. I tell myself the best I can do for them is to let them out.

"Are there soldiers on the other side of those doors?" I ask, pointing to the end of the hall.

She nods, but before we can make a plan, the door behind us flies open and one of the prisoners I released appears. He's the bearded one with the wild eyes, and like all the others, he's filthy beyond belief. White foam forms in the corners of his mouth like a rabid dog.

"I need a weapon," he says to me.

"I think those needles have something bad in them," I say, pointing to the floor. "Stick Amy here with one if she tries to get away."

He scoops up a handful and nods.

"I can do that," he offers.

We hurry down the hall, pounding on cell doors and telling everyone they are free. Along the way, my new sidekick tells me his name is Charles and he's married to a Sirena named Melissa. They've got a daughter named Georgie, and he hasn't seen either of them in two years.

When all the doors are unlocked, we shove Amy through the double doors, and as she said, a soldier is on the other side. He's sitting in front of a bank of video screens eating a bologna sandwich. He couldn't be more unprepared for us. He fumbles for his rifle leaning against a file cabinet, but I've got my pistol in his face.

"My friend needs to borrow your gun," I say.

The guard frowns.

Charles pricks the side of Amy's neck, and she sobs.

"Darren, just give it to him!" she shrieks.

Darren reaches over and timidly picks up his weapon, then hands it to Charles. Wild Eyes tosses his hypodermic needles into the corner, then swings the rifle around and aims it at Darren. I'm sure he's going to shoot him, but instead he snatches the bologna sandwich and swallows the whole thing in three bites.

"Darren, we're not going to kill you," my father explains, eyeballing Charles as he talks. "We're not going to kill anyone. We need to open all the doors. You'll be able to go home afterward, you'll be able to get another sandwich. But if you don't help us, I'm going to give my daughter permission to shoot you and we'll just figure it out on our own. I've seen this kind of security before. I know there's a master lock that releases everything. Where is it?"

Darren gets up from his chair and crosses the room. There's a metal box mounted on the wall. He opens it, inserts a key, then turns it with a click. Suddenly the air is alive with a piercing wail. Darren has sounded the alarm.

Charles slams the butt of the rifle against Darren's head and knocks him out. Amy lets out a little yelp and then starts to whimper.

"Unlock the doors!" I shout at her.

"I don't know how! I swear. I'm just a nurse!"

I have no idea if she's being honest or not, but the alarm is freaking me out. We need to get away from here.

"All right, take me to my friend and then my mother!"

"I want my wife and daughter now!" Charles screams.

I lean down and snatch Darren's keycard off his chain, then hand it to Charles.

"Find your kid," I tell him. "Get her and all the children out of here. We'll find your wife and meet you outside."

He nods eagerly, then runs to the elevator, swiping the key-card to activate it. When the doors slide open, he lets out a disappointed groan. I turn just in time to hear a gunshot and see him fall backwards.

"Run!" I scream, and the three of us bolt through the door-way, only to find another flight of stairs. We climb them one by one, my father struggling but doing his personal best. Amy is really what's slowing us down, with all her whimpering and shrieks.

"Prisoners have escaped their rooms on Level Three. This is not a drill. I repeat, this is not a drill," a voice booms through speakers on the walls. "All unarmed associates are to fall back to their secure locations. Security associates, please load your sidearms and turn your radios to channel eight for further instructions."

We're almost up the steps when I hear a gunshot. The bullet ricochets off a wall, sending dust into my eyes. I howl, sure that the next one will hit me. There's another shot, then another.

We duck through a door onto a floor that looks much like the one below, more cells lining both sides of the hall. I hear men shouting in the stairwell and have to make a terrible choice. I can't open them all in time.

"Which one has my friend?" I demand, shoving the key-card into Amy's trembling hands. She looks at it for a moment, then helps me take my father from her. She walks down the hall, and we follow closely until she stops at a door. She swipes the sensor, and the door opens. Standing in her own little yellow circle is my friend. When she sees me, her eyes fill with tears.

"You are so kick-ass, Lyric Walker," she says.

"We have to hurry," I beg. She lets my father wrap his arm

around her shoulders, and together they do their best as they stagger down the hall. At the end is a door with an emergency alarm bar. Its alarm adds to the already piercing sirens. Still, we push through and slam the door behind us.

"Lock it, Amy," my father demands.

Amy frowns but reaches into her pocket. She takes out her own set of keys, inserts one into the lock, and gives it a turn just as I hear banging on the other side.

"They're going to try to shoot their way in here," my father says, and no sooner does he warn us than we hear a loud bang. "This door is steel, so it will buy us a little time. We can't waste it. We have to find your mother. You should leave me here."

"We tried that once," I say, and drag him down another hallway. There's a turn, then another. It's a maze.

"Where?" I demand, putting the gun to Amy's head. I know she could help without me asking. I suppose it's dumb of me to be irritated that she won't take the initiative.

She points forward, and we run through another set of doors and find an elevator.

"Aren't there stairs?" I ask.

Amy shakes her head. "The elevators are the only way into the tank."

I'm dreading this, but I have no choice but to use it. I swipe the card on the sensor plate and wait until the elevator opens on our floor. I shove Amy in front of the elevator door in case a soldier with a happy trigger finger decides to shoot before looking. When it opens wide, Amy blubbers. We push her inside and step in ourselves. I search the buttons and find a p for penthouse. The doors close, and we slowly rise while a Muzak version of "Smells Like Teen Spirit" plays. Yes, this place is truly that evil.

"The Alphas are in there," Amy cries when the doors swing open. "Just let me go. You don't need me."

I can't think of a reason to keep her, so I let her go, giving her a shove so that she falls to the floor of the elevator.

"You suck," I say, because I'm all out of quips, then watch her disappear when the doors close.

When we turn, I find out why this place is called the tank. There are rows and rows of big water-filled tubes. Some are large enough to house many people. Inside them are Alpha, all in their undersea forms: gills and fins and tails and odd append-ages. Scientists scurry about, taking readings and recording data. They don't even realize we are here.

I clear my throat.

Suddenly, all the buzzing and work comes to a stop. The scientists see my gun and cry out in fear, alerting the whole room.

"Get out. Every one of you," I threaten. They scurry like rats fleeing the exposing light.

"What is this place?" Bex asks.

"This is the torture chamber," I explain. I peer into each tank. There are Rusalka and Sirena and Nix. I see a Selkie and

Tritons and Feige and even some creatures I've never seen before.

"We need to find your mother," my father says. "If she's not hurt, she can help get us out of here. She's a lot stronger than a normal person."

"Find Arcade, too," Bex says.

I leave her with my dad. Racing down the aisles, I realize the whole place is like a zoo. There are fourteen Ceto in a single tank, ranging from elderly to small children, bobbing up and down like transparent blobs. They're very close to jellyfish, except for the pinkish heart that beats steadily and pumps black blood through millions of veins. One tank has three Sirena, two females and a male, covered in gorgeous scales that range from blue-green to red-pink. Their legs are gone and their long, muscular tails swing back and forth, but my mother isn't among them.

There are seven Nix crammed in one filthy tank. Their spindly arms and legs have transformed into gray fins lined with terrible spikes. I realize they look a bit like eels, with their yellow eyes. There are more Selkies, bloated and brown, with whisker-covered snouts. Their back legs are gone, replaced with tails, but their arms are still huge with rocky muscles.

In one tank at the back of the room are five small creatures that at first appear to be octopuses, but on closer look, they have dozens and dozens of tentacles, and that's pretty much it —no head, no eyes, no body—just tendrils lined with suckers, all whipping around in a frenzy and smacking against the glass. It's the creepiest, most unnatural thing I have ever seen. They're what nightmares are made of.

I shake off the chill they've given me and turn down another aisle, searching tank after tank. I stop before a huge creature with charcoal-colored skin and a round, puffy body. It has quills sticking out of it and a foul expression on its big face.

"Nathan." I met him in the Alpha camp back home.

The tank next to him contains three Feige with murky green skin. The one after that hosts something that looks an awful lot like the Creature from the Black Lagoon. There are others, some with skinny legs, others with claws like lobsters, and some that have huge shells on their backs. There are so many different kinds, it's hard to process them all. Arcade told me there were other people in the ocean. Now I believe her.

"My God." I gasp when I come across the next tank. It's filled with body parts: limbs, heads, hands, like some kind of nightmarish junk drawer where these bastards keep the stuff for which they don't have a place.

Some tanks have Alpha who look like they have been experimented on. They're missing limbs, and their chests are split open from neck to naval, so their internal organs are exposed. There are some so wounded that it seems a miracle they are still alive. This is the horror show Terrance Lir warned me about, the one he swore he would die before going back to, but Tempest has Rochelle. I'm sure he's here somewhere.

"Lyric, you have to hurry!" Bex shouts to me.

I turn a corner and finally find my mother. She looks intact, healthy and serene, like she's taking a long bubble bath. Her mermaid tail swishes back and forth in the water. She's more beautiful than I have ever seen her.

"If they've hurt you—"

"She's never been touched, Lyric."

Donovan Spangler appears behind me with two armed guards. I turn and point the gun at him.

"Let her out."

"There are a few specimens we have decided to keep as is, you know, in case we needed them as bargaining chips. Like her, for instance," he says, gesturing behind me. "And, of course, this one."

I follow his gesture to another tank. Inside it floats a boy with golden hair and skin, his arms marred by scars, and a face that has visited my dreams almost every night since the last time I saw him.

Fathom.

I peer through the thick glass, suddenly wondering if I'm dreaming or, worse, hallucinating, and that Spangler actually broke me and this is all a delusion. I slam my hand against the tank until my knuckles split open and spill blood onto the floor.

"Is he alive?" I ask.

"Oh, yes," Spangler says, smacking the tank himself. "In fact, he seems to prefer being in there."

Guards escort my father and Bex. They hobble toward us with guns pointed into their backs.

Fathom opens his eyes, and he smiles at me. He says something, but I can't make it out.

"Miss Walker, I'd like to make you an offer. Just hear me out, and if you do, I'll let your mother and your boyfriend out of these tanks. How does that sound? Just five minutes of your time?"

CHAPTER FOURTEEN

SPANGLER HAS AMY BRING MY FATHER A WHEELCHAIR. She's jumpy and angry at the same time. I suspect she was hoping for a little sympathy after what she just went through. I'm too shocked and confused to enjoy her disappointment.

Doyle meets us at the elevator. He gives me a pleading look, a *Please, will you behave?* expression I used to see on my parents' faces when I was little. He won't look at my father or Bex at all. He keeps his head down and escorts us out into a hallway until we enter an employee cafeteria. There are round tables and plastic chairs, a salad bar, and a soda machine. Everything is painted bright white. A rich and savory aroma wafts into my nose, and my stomach rumbles. I can see it's having the same effect on Dad and Bex.

Doyle leads us to a big table in the center.

"What does he want?" my father asks Doyle.

"He wants what we all want," Doyle says as he points to me. "Her help. And if you're smart, you'll tell her to give it to him."

"Is that some kind of threat?" my father says. He tries to stand, but his face turns white. His ribs must be killing him, but he doesn't cry out. He's tough, and I'm sure he wants Doyle to see it.

"It's not a threat. It's a plea for common sense. I know you have done a great job with her, Leonard. She's strong and smart and stubborn as hell. Right now she needs to make a good decision," Doyle says as he takes a seat at the table next to us. "He's not going to take no for an answer."

Spangler enters with his tablet in one hand and his smartphone in the other. He's got a pair of fancy headphones some hip-hop guy invented strapped to his ears, and he's talking about delivery dates and shipments. Whoever he's talking to needs a lot of assurance, and Spangler seems to be a pro at appeasing fears. He makes promises and promises, then says that when the person he's talking to arrives, he wants to take everyone out to dinner. When he's done, he unplugs his headphones and pulls them down so they wrap around his neck.

"Sorry about that. I've got a very nervous client on my hands," he says, rolling his eyes as if we can sympathize.

"You're not with the military?" my father asks.

Spangler chuckles like he's listening to children.

"Do you think the government could put together something like this? I mean, it's nothing fancy, but the budget for half of this place would get lost in committee until the end of time. Congress would dither over which state got the tax breaks. I'm sure a small handful of them would raise a stink about the Constitution, and human rights issues—due process—you know how they can get. Anyway, all that haggling might be good for getting a bridge built, but it's not very practical when the end of the world is on your doorstep. No, when they need something done and done quickly, they go with private enterprise."

"Or when it's against the law," my father adds.

"Yes, the ugly stuff is usually done by corporations. We're difficult to prosecute for war crimes, at least in America. Here you can send a soldier to jail for atrocities, but who do you point the finger at when a business does it? Truth is, I find some of it a bit distasteful myself, but are we going to let the world go to hell in a handbasket waiting for bipartisan support? That's why they need us. We're in the business of results."

"We don't care about your business plan. We want out of here," my father growls.

"But, Mr. Walker, Lyric is my business plan. Who's hungry? I'm hungry."

As if on cue, two women dressed in pencil skirts, white shirts, black ties, and aprons enter with trays. Another woman places a napkin in each of our laps, then sets the table with plastic utensils and a real plate. We're served roast beef and gravy, mashed potatoes with pesto, and string beans and almonds.

Spangler looks down at his and smiles.

"Look good? Go ahead, eat."

I stare down at my food. I'm not going to lie. I'm tempted to bury my face in it. An old shoe would be more delicious than what they've been feeding me. Bex and Dad look even hungrier. Still, they both push their plates away. It's an act of strength and defiance like I've never seen, and I have never loved either of them as much as I do right now. I look back down at my plate, and as casually as I can, I fling it at Spangler. The china crashes to the table in front of him, and the food splatters his face. I catch my father's grin as Donovan cleans himself.

The waitress returns with another plate of food and sets it in front of me like nothing has happened. Before she can take a single step, I chuck it at our host.

"Dammit, Lyric," Doyle says. He's got his face buried in his hands.

A soldier steps in from the hallway with his gun ready, but Doyle commands him to leave. I suddenly don't feel so brave, but I have no regrets.

"Lyric, the temper tantrum is wasteful, and really, that kind of behavior is an obstacle to getting what you want," Spangler says. "Someone bring her another plate."

"Maybe you should put it in a doggie dish," I say.

He takes a deep breath.

"Yes, I had my doubts about that approach. It was the client's idea, a bit dramatic, but you know that old saying, "The customer is always right"? I tried to explain that you wouldn't be broken. I knew it the second you started your yoga practice. That's defiance. I quietly cheered you."

My waitress is back with a new plate. When I reach for it, the waitress does the same. She's much stronger, so I throw my hands up in surrender. She gives me a little look of triumph, but when she turns her back on me, I toss the plate and hit her right in the shoulder.

Bex laughs.

"Maybe Ms. Walker will have something to eat after our chat," Spangler says, dismissing the irate waitress.

"What do you want?" I say.

I feel my father's hand on my leg, his way of saying to tread carefully.

Spangler flashes me a strained smile.

"I've watched all the footage of that day in Coney Island. I not only saw what you can do, I saw what you tried to do. You're not the terrorist they have painted you as. You're a hero, and I'm offering you a second chance at it," he says. "Before you can do that, I realize we have to start over. No more solitary confinement. No more whatever it is they are feeding you. I'll free your mother. I'll let the prince and the Triton girl out of their tanks. In return, you have to accept my job offer."

"Job offer?" I cry.

"Saving the world, Lyric. You've seen the news. This country is on the verge of collapse. The attacks by the prime and his army have all but crippled our defenses. It's maddening to everyone involved that a few thousand barely intelligent creatures have managed to decimate the greatest military power the world has ever seen. In the time you have been here, things have gotten much worse. Just yesterday, the air force dropped a small nuclear device into the water outside Norfolk, Virginia, in hopes of reclaiming a base. They used a low-grade weapon, a 'bunker buster' is what they call it. They're meant to take out a village or a cave system, not to fight an amphibious army, but that's how desperate things have gotten. Want to guess how it turned out? The prime smacked it back like a tennis ball. It leveled eight city blocks and destroyed the base entirely. Casualties were low, but no one will live in Norfolk for fifty years. That place is poison."

My father's face turns pale.

"The East Coast is rubble, and now we're seeing new threats. Did you happen to notice the things with all the tentacles during your daring escape? There's a spike under all those limbs. It leaps onto your head, jams it into your nervous system, and then drinks you like a milkshake. How do you think that's affecting morale on the frontlines? Lyric, the prime is kicking our butts, and it's not just a handful of cities with six feet of water, it's farms and crops, industries, mining, oil production, and finance. Wall Street is in a no man's land. Do you understand what that means? The financial center for the entire world is closed for business. There are food shortages, gasoline shortages, mobs, looting, and clashes between citizens and soldiers. This morning, West Virginia officially seceded from the rest of the country. They say Texas will be next. It's my job to make sure it stops. You're going to help me."

"I am, am I?"

"Yes, because I am desperate." Spangler's eyes drill into my cranium. He's not trying to charm me now. He's done trying to manipulate me. He's done torturing me. He's a businessman, and none of this is good for business. "So if you're not going to have lunch, perhaps you would like to go ahead and get started. David, why don't you show Ms. Walker your park?"

"Where are you taking me?"

"It's easier to show you than to tell you," Doyle says.

Doyle has some of his soldiers take my father and Bex to the infirmary. They are both suffering from malnutrition, and my dad's ribs are killing him. I could tell by the sweat on his face all during the meeting with Spangler. Doyle gives Amy a lecture on treating them well. She seems intimidated by him, but maybe it's all an act. I can't tell, and there's nothing I can do about it anyway.

"This could have been so much easier," he says as he leads me down a hall.

"No, it couldn't," I say defiantly. Soon we approach another elevator that requires his keycard. Once it's activated, he pushes a button that says sb for subbasement.

The elevator stops, and we're let out into a hallway with a concrete floor and cinder blocks for walls. Once again, I realize how practical things are here at Tempest. It's not the evil fortress in a comic book. Everything except the device that jams my glove seems ordinary and familiar. Even the tanks look like something they bought at a hardware store.

"In the comic books, the bad guy's secret lair is usually tricked out," I say.

"You would be better off if you stopped thinking about all this as a war between the good guys and the bad guys," Doyle says. "I've found that most people are a mixture of both."

"That's what the bad guy in comic books always says to the hero too. I'll try to remember that the next time I walk by a tank full of human hands," I hiss.

"Sometimes you have to break a few eggs to make an omelet," he says when we get to the end of the hall.

"And that's your problem. You think your job is making omelets. Sorry, Doyle. Your job is making sure this madhouse works. If it weren't for people like you, none of this evil could happen."

He swipes his keycard again, and the door opens into something my mind is not prepared to understand. As we step out onto a catwalk, I see a massive green space as big as a soccer field. The grass is bright and lush. The trees have fat pears hanging from the limbs. There are rows and rows of blooming flowers—marigolds, lilacs, tulips—in whites and blues and yellows and oranges. Everything is manicured and tidy, with a stone pathway beckoning to a swing set and a carousel. I see basketball and tennis courts, a baseball diamond, and a running track. There's a trampoline and archery targets and places to picnic.

"What is this?" I ask.

"It's many things. A military facility, a training center, a place for the children to feel special," he says.

"Children? You mean the Alpha kids?"

A loud buzz blasts the air.

"C'mon, I want to keep you out of sight for now," he says. He walks me into a shadowy section, far from the lights, and he sits down on the edge of the catwalk, letting his boots hang over the side. He invites me to join him, but I refuse.

Below, two double doors open at the far end of the space. Dozens of kids run through it, grinning like it's the last day of school, singing and dancing in their black jumpsuits with the White Tower logo on the back. They range in age, some as old as myself but others hovering around seven or eight. A couple could be as young as five. The little ones take to the monkey bars, swinging on swings, zipping down slides, riding teeter-totters, and laughing among themselves. The older kids ride skateboards on a professional fiberglass halfpipe. Others fall to the grass and braid one another's hair. I peer down as best I can, recognizing a few faces. Angela Benningford's eleven-year-old son, Cole, is shooting hoops on the basketball court.

"This is what I've been doing here, Lyric. White Tower was originally built to imprison these children and their Alpha parents. I believed the kids were special. When the first one morphed in the water, I realized they could be useful. I've battled a lot of CEOs—they come and go pretty fast around here—but I got my way. I built this park, and I've been training them ever since."

"Training them for what?" I ask, eyeing him suspiciously.

"Remember in the diner when we watched the press conference? The Secretary of State said that we aren't prepared to fight an amphibious threat? He's right. We aren't. Not with guns and boats and bombs, until now," he says as he gestures to the children. "They're our amphibious weapons, soldiers who can breathe underwater, who have been trained in combat. They're our best chance at fighting the prime and his army. They can help put a stop to the devastation."

"They're babies."

"They're hybrids, half human, but, more important, half Alpha."

"You're going to toss those kids into the war?" I seethe. "You're going to get them killed."

"Not if we give them their own gloves."

Suddenly I understand what he's planning. It's so revolting, I have to take a step away from him.

"Lyric, all of them have migraines just like you did. They have the right genetics to activate the weapons. With a little training—"

"You want me to train them?"

"We recently got enough gloves for each of them. You will

teach them how they work. I've done the rest. They're near experts in hand-to-hand combat, survival techniques, and marksmanship—"

"Marksmanship? That kid down there is five!"

"I've prepared them for anything," he says. "But I can't help them with the gloves. That's why we need you."

"You're insane. It will never work."

"Lyric, it has to. Listen, this isn't a movie. There isn't a secret government organization filled with supertechnology that's going to save the world. There aren't any superheroes. There's no plan B. You and those kids are all we have. I wish the brains in the tank could have figured out how to crack those gloves. I'd love to put them on some real soldiers. I'd love to have thousands of them, but what I want and what I have are two different things. You and those kids are the best chance we have."

"Arcade would be better at this than me."

"I think we both know she's not going to cooperate."

I stare down at the alien weapon wrapped around my wrist. Suddenly it doesn't seem as powerful and scary as before. Now it feels tiny and impotent.

"I'm not good with this thing, and even if I was, you couldn't convince me to help. Those are children down there, not soldiers. How many are there, thirty?"

"Thirty-two," he says. "With you, it's thirty-three."

"Thirty-three babies against thousands of flesh-eating monsters, some of whom wear the same gloves. Plus, from what I hear, there are squid monsters that drink your insides now. And let's not mention the prime, who is insane, and his wife, who makes him look healthy. You remember they threw a battleship at us, right?"

Doyle stares down at the children while their songs of laughter drift up to us.

"Desperate times," he says. "Do you think anyone wants this to be our last, best hope? You heard Spangler. We're desperate."

"I won't do it."

"Then I can't protect you and your family any longer."

"If my time in here is what you call protecting me—"

"It is, Lyric." he says. "You have no idea how hard it has been to keep you all alive. Your mom and dad and Bex? They're just a drain on resources to him, a few more useless mouths to feed that seep profits and raise overhead. If you don't cooperate . . . there are worse things than solitary confinement, Lyric."

"You disgust me, Doyle. You'd let him kill us?"

"He won't kill you, Lyric, but he'll kill everyone you love, then he'll send those kids to fight anyway. He's made a deal with the Marines. He's delivering thirty-three hybrid kids to the beach whether you are ready to fight or not. You have a chance at keeping them alive. You may not care about the soldiers who are fighting, or the people who have lost everything, but you have to care about your own kind, right? If you turn your back on them, they're as good as dead."

I look down at the children. A group of kids who should be in the second grade are running through a sprinkler. Their giggles float up to us like party balloons.

"But they're just kids," I say.

"No, Lyric, those are weapons. Once you've taught them all you can, you will lead them back to Coney Island to reclaim the beach, then move up and down the coastline until it is safe again."

Doyle doesn't take me back to my cell. Instead, he escorts me to a suite at the end of a long hallway. Inside, much to my surprise, is what looks like a spa—one as fancy as any I've seen in Manhattan. There's a single chair with a drop-down hair dryer and a shampoo sink, a steam room and a sauna, a table for skin scrubs, and a Japanese soaking tub that must be three feet deep. Steamy water is pouring out of a tap while two Latino women with round faces smile at me.

"What's this?"

"The beginning of something new, Lyric," Doyle says. "By the way, these women are illegal immigrants and don't speak a word of English. They're only here because White Tower has promised green cards to them and their families in exchange for their silence about what they see and hear. They are not part of this place. Enjoy your bath."

"Screw you!" I shout—well, I actually say a lot worse than that, but most of it he doesn't hear once he's left the room.

The ladies are somewhat dumbfounded by my anger and seem concerned. I realize what I must look like to them. I'm filthy, I'm covered in bruises and bandages, and I've got a shaved head. Plus, I was hand delivered by an armed soldier.

"Sorry," I say, even though I suspect they don't understand. I mime myself drawing a smile on my face and hope that helps.

The ladies try to help me out of my uniform, but I resist. It's not some weird shame about my body; it's that I'm tired of being vulnerable. Eventually, though, I surrender and take off the jumpsuit. The call of the tub and bubbles is too great. I step into the steamy water, which should be heavenly, but I'm covered in fresh wounds. Burn marks on my chest are bright red, and my knees are raw. All my damages sing with agony. Crimson welts and scars rise up where there were none.

Eventually, the pain dulls and I allow myself to melt like a slab of butter buried inside a stack of pancakes. The women wash me like I'm a helpless baby. They scrub my arms and back, my feet, my face and neck. It's odd to be bathed, but I'm so tired, I let it happen. The women are gentle and kind, even when they gingerly remove the bandages from the back of my head.

They both gasp.

"Is it bad?" I ask in a panic, but I know they don't understand.

One of them rushes to the door and pounds on it. A soldier opens up, but I can't see what's happening because my other helper has spread a gigantic towel in front of me to block his sight line. My other "stylist" shouts at him in rapid-fire Spanish, but he's just as clueless as me. He calls for Doyle, who briefly speaks to her, then closes the door.

When she returns, she looks at me with a sad, sympathetic face and points to the back of her own head. I don't need an interpreter to understand my wound is infected. The other lady holds my hand tight while the first pours hot water over it. It feels like lava, and I shriek and cry.

I hear an argument in the hall, and then the door opens. Nurse Amy steps in with a small medical kit. She approaches the tub like it's full of venomous snakes. My ladies scream at her, shouting hostilities in her face, pointing to my head, telling her off in the universal language of "you suck."

After she examines my wound, Amy tries to open a tube of ointment, but the women snatch it from her. Like before, one takes my hand and the other pours the water. It's just as painful, but when they're done, they let Amy apply the cream, supervising her every move until she wraps it in a fresh dressing. Then they take the ointment from her and point to the door. Amy stalks off, and I ease back into the bath and smile up at my saviors.

"I love you, ladies," I say.

When I'm done, they help me out of the bath and rub moisturizer all over me — my back, my scalp, my feet and face. They apply more ointment to wounds and scratches Amy ignored, then help me into a robe and slippers. They lead me to the sink, where a tube of toothpaste and a brush await me. As they remove the toothbrush from the packaging, I stare into the mirror at someone I don't recognize. I'm gaunt, tired, and pale, like a ghost who refuses to believe she is no longer alive. It's a wonder that Fathom knew who I was when I saw him. I'm ashamed, which is stupid, but it kills me to know he saw me this weak and broken. I'm almost glad my mother didn't wake up and see me too.

I squeeze some toothpaste onto the brush and go to work. The mint has a shocking bite. Dental floss feels like lasers shredding my mouth apart. Still, I force myself to do my best, spitting out one red mouthful after another. I turn the knob for water to wash it down the drain and watch it swirl around in the bottom of the sink. Odd that I've missed hearing its whisper in my ears. I suppose Spangler will have to turn off whatever it is that jams my glove if he wants me to train those kids. Wait! I'll have an opportunity to get us all out of here this time, and not as some mad unplanned dash through a maze of hallways. I will have my power back.

I nearly sprint out of the bathroom, and I make my way to the door. I want the guard outside to know I'll train the kids. I want him to tell Doyle right away, but before I can get there, I see my ladies smiling at me from ear to ear.

"What?" I ask.

They point to a chair in the corner. Fathom is here. He's in shorts and a T-shirt, all with the same stupid logo, but who cares? He's here. He's alive and in my room, and I have suddenly forgotten how to breathe.

Neither of us waits for the women to leave. He's out of the seat and wrapping me inside his arms before I can really process him. I don't even hear the click of the closing door. All my attention is on his face, his eyes, his mouth.

"I thought you were—"

He stops me with a kiss. It's firm but gentle, romantic but passionate, everything I have ever dreamed a kiss could be and a few ways I never dared all at once. I wrap my arms around his neck, and he pulls me in with his. Our mouths never part. I'm not sure they can.

I don't know how long it lasts—minutes? Days? We might live out the rest of our lives connected by this kiss. Fine with me. Eventually he pulls back, rests his hands on my shoulders, and looks me up and down.

"Did they harm you, Lyric Walker?"

"Yes, but I'll be okay. I'm just a little beat up," I admit.

He blushes a little.

"What?"

"I'd like to see," he says.

I'm stunned and taken aback. It's my turn to blush, not because he's flirting, but because I want to show him, but there are too many faults and scars and wounds and I'm too thin and my head is shaved and my lips are chapped and I would do almost anything for a tube of lip gloss.

But then I take a deep breath and I drop the robe.

I feel like I'm going to cry. I wonder if I will ever be able to be vulnerable with another person again. I lean down to grab my robe, but he takes my hand, steps close, and wraps himself around me.

"You have a long way to go if you are trying to collect as many trophies as me," he whispers.

He kisses me gently and runs his hands along my shoulders.

"I need to tell you something right now, while I still have the courage to do it," I say.

"I love you, too," he says.

I can't help but smile, because that was actually the coolest thing any boy has ever said to me, and this guy, he's not so good at being a boy or being cool. I realize then that all along, as intense as this feeling has been for him, it was always infatuation and lust, but now it actually is love.

Then, well . . . then we fade to black, and I learn about the afterglow.

CHAPTER FIFTEEN

I WAKE UP ON A BED DRAPED IN MY ROBE, ALONE IN A SPARSE white room. I sit up and call for Fathom, but there's no answer. At first I'm hurt that he's not here; then I panic that they took him in the night. I tell myself that dragging him out of here would have caused a lot of racket, so I know he left under his own power. I don't know how to feel about it. When I imagined the night I just had, I really only pictured the beginning, with all the kissing followed by the waking-up-and-smiling-at-each-other part. I was looking forward to the waking and smiling. I feel cheated.

I pad out of the room into the spa area and find a mirror over a sink. I know it's silly, but I want to see if I look different, like if someone could tell what has happened just by looking at me. Sadly, I'm just as rough as I was yesterday, though maybe cleaner, and my hair is coming in a little. I guess the difference is inside me, which is actually the best place for such a thing. No one can get at it there. Spangler, Doyle, Amy, the guards, the client—they can't take last night from me. It's not on a phone they can snap in half.

Arcade.

I didn't think about Arcade. I didn't consider her for a second. Last night the only people in the world were Fathom and me. Even now, the only shame I feel is that I don't feel ashamed. Last night he came to me. He made his choice. She can't blame me.

And besides, their relationship was forced on them. It's not real. What he and I are is real.

There's a knock at the door and I cringe, wondering if it's her, then realize that Arcade would just charge into the room without knocking. I hurry to open it, hoping that it's Fathom on the other side. We need to talk about what we're going to say to her. She's strong and has swords in her arms she can stick into my soft parts. *Aargh.* We shouldn't have done what we did before we talked to her. I broke the girl code on that one, but she's got to understand. We're in love.

I throw the door open, but it's not him. It's my mother and father, as well as Bex.

"You look better," Bex says.

My mother wraps me up in the greatest hug of my life. My father joins her, while Bex hovers on the borders. I am thrilled to see them, of course, but I'm having trouble shifting gears.

"My baby girl," my mom weeps, giving me big, hard, wet kisses all over my face.

"It's okay, Mom," I promise. "We're all together now."

Behind them is Doyle.

"I hate to have to break up this reunion, but Lyric needs

to get dressed. We have to get started as soon as possible, but I will bring her back as soon as I can," he promises.

Bex slams the door in his face, and he's smart enough to leave it closed.

I tell my mother and father everything that has happened to us so far, filling in holes that Bex left out, and editing out a few things that will break their hearts. I explain what Spangler wants me to do. My mother doesn't like it.

"I don't have a choice," I explain. "But I think it might give me a chance to get us out of here. If he wants me to train them to control the water, Spangler's going to have to let me use it myself."

"Will Fathom help you?" she asks.

"I haven't asked, but I'm sure he will," I say, then blush, thinking about him. I can't help it, and it isn't lost on Bex. She flashes me a curious look but says nothing.

There's another knock at the door, and my spa ladies enter. Doyle tentatively follows.

"They're here to take care of the rest of your family," he says to me.

"You're going to love this," I tell them, then look at my mom. "Actually, you might want to supervise Dad."

"Lyric, please," Doyle says. "The team is waiting."

"Let me get dressed," I say. I walk to the closet, where a dozen fresh black White Tower jumpsuits are hanging. Putting one on physically repulses me, but there's nothing else to wear. I snatch one off the hanger.

"Bex, feel free to steal anything you want from my closet."

I head to the bathroom to put it on, with Bex in tow.

"Something's different."

Again, I blush.

"Fathom was here last night."

"NO WAY!" she shouts. It's so loud, I have to clamp my hand on her big mouth while she jumps up and down. "Oh, Lyric, you are like a trouble magnet."

"What's that mean?"

"You thought Arcade was pissed at you for having that picture. Wait until she finds what else you've had," she says.

"Gawd, do you have to say it like that?" I groan, then eye her sheepishly. "Am I horrible?"

"You love him, right? This isn't a Stevie Brinks thing?"

"That was the third grade!"

"You knew Heather Stamp liked him, but you kissed him by the bumper cars anyway. It was scandalous. Arcade is not Heather Stamp. She can break you in half."

"I know." I cringe. "But I do love him."

"You have got to tell her, Lyric. Maybe not right now, when we're locked up like this, but soon. They've been together since they were little. I'm not trying to make you feel guilty, but you need to be prepared for some of her hostility."

"I am . . . I will be."

"Still, you're such a hussy," she says with a giggle. "Shadow called it. The first time he saw the two of you together, he knew you'd be a couple."

"Bex, back at the theater. Duck . . . did you—"

She shakes her head. "That was a hard day, and I really just wanted to crawl out of it, but no. I let him kiss me. I thought he might be a nice distraction, but it just made me sad. I miss my boy. He broke me for everyone else, Walker. He's in my head, in my dreams. He's hanging on more than he did back in the fifth grade."

There's a tap on the door.

"Ms. Walker, please!" Doyle calls from the other side.

I get dressed and say my goodbyes, making Dad promise to be nice to the spa ladies. I follow Doyle out into the hallway that leads to his park. Once we get there, we step onto the catwalk and descend a flight of metal stairs that lets out onto the lawn. The ground beneath me is as real as it looked from above, slightly spongy and cool, like the great lawn in Kaiser Park, back in Brooklyn. It takes me back to times when Shadow, Bex, and I would lie beneath a tree and smoke cigarettes she squirreled out of her mother's purse. I reach down and let the tips of grass tickle my palms. I wonder if it will affect my allergies.

"Pretty cool, huh?"

"Shut up, Doyle," I say, irritated at how proud he is of his battlegrounds.

"Put this on," he says, undeterred by my tone. He hands me a black skullcap. "I think the bandages will scare the little ones."

"These kids need to get used to being scared," I say.

"This place is supposed to be pleasant, or at least as happy as it can be. They'll see plenty of ugly things later. Here, they're safe."

I slip the cap over my head and tuck it down over my bandages just as I hear a buzzer sound. Taking a deep breath, I close my eyes and tell myself to stay focused and wait for my opportunity. *If you do everything right, you can destroy this place, and these kids will never know what they were being trained to do.*

The double doors on the far wall open, and the children rush into the space. Familiar faces are among the crowd, and a few even smile and wave to me. Most hover around a nine-year-old with bushy black hair and sad blue eyes. I guess this is Georgia, Charles's daughter. His last moments replay in my memory, the way he looked so eager before he pushed the elevator button, and how his head snapped back when the shot was fired. He was being brave. I wish I could tell Georgia, but Doyle asked me not to speak about it with her.

Angela Benningford's children, with their bright red hair, gather around me. Angela was the last Sirena to be captured by the government, at least until they got my mom. The oldest of her kids is McKenna, who is my age, pretty with a pale complexion and freckles. She reminds me a bit of Luna, the Sirena girl who died when the Rusalka arrived. I realize that all Angela's kids are beautiful; in fact, every kid in this park is gorgeous. It's the Sirena part of them.

Emma Sands and her two sisters, Tess and Jane, are brown-skinned supermodels. Danny Cho and his sister, Sienna, are adorable. Finn and Harrison Cassidy, the twins, are transitioning from cute little boys into handsome adolescents, but there's something else about all the children I'm starting to notice. They all look tired. Many of them have dark rings around their eyes, a telltale sign I know all too well. They are all struggling with migraines. Samuel Lir and I had the same problem for most of our lives. They kept me awake, forced me to hide away in dark places until the pounding and the lights stopped. It all ended when I put on the glove.

Spangler follows them out, then wades through their midst, leading them all to me. His smile reaffirms our agreement, and he expects me to reciprocate. I nod and grin. He doesn't need to know that my smile is motivated by revenge and the many ways I intend to destroy everything around me and bring the roof down on his head.

"Children, if you don't know our new family member already, let me introduce you to Lyric Walker," he says.

"She's joining us here in the park every day as your new instructor, helping David with your training. Can everyone say hello?"

The children say hi in unison like an elementary school class. They give me gentle, shy smiles, all except one. A boy in the very back grins wide. He's tall and lean, around my age, maybe even a year or two older. He's fresh-faced and olive-skinned, clean and happy, with thick eyebrows and a head full of brown hair. I recognize him from the neighborhood too. His name is Riley, I think. I feel like I've been at a party with him, but I can't be sure. Bex would know. She remembers all the cute ones. I'm not sure about his name, but I remember that smile. I think he went to private school and his mother is a graphic designer, and they had a lot of money for Coney Island standards. He's looking at me like he remembers me, too.

I break his gaze and turn back to the kids, counting them one by one. Including me, there are thirty-three, as Doyle promised. Only, he told me I would be training *all* the hybrid kids, and there is one who is not here.

"Where's Samuel?" I ask.

"Who?" Tess asks.

Spangler frowns. "Samuel isn't able to join us."

"Does he have a migraine too?" Emma asks.

"No, he has a few disabilities that keep him from doing things, but he's one of us and I think he should be here, don't you?"

The children nod.

"Perhaps we can bring him tomorrow," Spangler says, stiffly.

"That's great," I say. "He's very special and you will all love him."

Spangler asks each one of the children to take turns introducing themselves to me, and all at once they're squabbling over who gets to go first. I meet Lilly, and Danny and Geno, and Alexa, and Dallas, and the boy in the back turns out to be Riley after all. I try to remember each name, but I can't. It doesn't matter. I'm not going to be here much longer.

"Did your mom and dad get sick too?" Georgia asks me.

"Sick?" I ask.

Spangler clears his throat.

"Yes, children, Lyric's father got sick like your human parents. He is helping us develop a cure."

I turn to Spangler, ready to demand an explanation for this ridiculous lie, when a little girl with a strawberry blond pixie cut and bright green eyes pushes through the group. She can't be more than six and holds a stuffed rabbit in her hands with the White Tower logo sewn onto the bottom of its foot. Her name is Chloe, and her bunny is Mr. Fluffer. She's Sam and Jill Norris's daughter. They managed a furniture store in Park Slope, and she's the mirror image of her mother.

"Have you seen them?" Chloe asks me, her face drawn and full of worry.

"Lyric hasn't been here very long, and as you know, kids, all the infected people have to be kept away from the healthy people. That's why we can't let you see your families right now. You could get sick too," Spangler explains. "They need their rest, but I can take them messages from you, like I always do."

The children deflate with disappointment, but none of them argue. Even the teenagers seem satisfied by his story. He's got them trained very well.

I don't know what to say to them. Everything in this place is a lie. All of this deception against children is gross. Now

Spangler and Doyle want to include me in their ugly fairy tale. I didn't sign on for it. They need to know this is all an illusion.

"I'm going to tell these kids the truth," I hiss.

"Ms. Walker—"

Something in his voice is threatening. I stare at him for a long moment, and I can see it in his expression. He will hurt everyone I love if I pop his balloon. I let him sweat a few more seconds and then turn back to the kids.

"A few months ago, a man known as the prime attacked Coney Island."

"The evil king," Cole says.

"Yes, he is evil. He came out of the sea with a group of people called the Alpha, who, as you know, are related to you. The prime wants to kill everyone who lives on the surface and take it for himself, even though his people disagreed. He used a bunch of scary monsters called the Rusalka to help him. My friends and I tried to fight them, but they were too strong, and our hometown was destroyed."

"Coney Island is gone?" Breanne asks. She tugs on her braid nervously.

I nod.

"The Rusalka used a machine that controls the ocean, and they sent a huge wave to destroy everything in its path. Your homes are gone. I wish I could make up a story that wasn't as sad as the truth, but I don't want to lie to you."

"Uncle David showed us videos. We saw you fighting them," Dallas says.

Uncle David?

"Unfortunately, I didn't fight them hard enough, and now they are attacking other cities, so we need your help."

"The children have been preparing for this for a long time, Lyric," Doyle explains. "Some of them for as long as they have been here. They know all about the mission and how important it is. They've worked very hard. All they need is for you to show them how to use their secret power."

"Secret power?" I say. He's so awful. Now who's living in a comic book?

Spangler taps a few buttons on his tablet, and I feel a rumbling of motors beneath my feet. Suddenly the ground jerks. The kids hoot and holler, leaping away as the floor slides aside. Chloe takes my hand and pulls me along.

"C'mon, silly, before you fall in." She giggles, leading me to safety as a massive swimming pool is uncovered. It's probably twice as big as the one at the YMCA, tiled in blue, with diving boards and depth markers along the perimeter. The salty smell of seawater tickles my nose when it's finally exposed.

"Kids, do you see the glove on Lyric's hand? We call that an Oracle. Remember how I talked about the Oracles? Well, Lyric knows how to make one work. Lyric, why don't you give us a little presentation?" Spangler asks.

"I think the battery is dead," I say.

He taps his tablet and then smiles smugly. "Give it a try."

A tiny bolt of electricity zips through my bloodstream, around my mind, along my shoulders, and down my arm into my hand. The metal explodes with crackling light, bathing everything in blue. The children ooh and ahh like we're at a circus, and I realize that's what this place is—Tempest is a circus, and Spangler is the ringmaster, and we're a bunch of poodles leaping through rings and walking on balls. I stare at him. I hate this man. I hate how he has all the answers, how he's planned every detail. I hate how confident he looks that this is all going to work out for him and his company and his clients.

I'm going to love showing him how wrong he's been.

What would you have us do?

"End him," I whisper.

A huge greedy hand reaches out of the pool. It grabs Spangler tight, and with lightning speed it drags him in and pulls him to the bottom.

Guns are drawn and soldiers rush at me, aiming their weapons at my head. I hear them click off their safeties. I'm surprised by how much I don't care. They can shoot me if they want. In fact, they probably should, because once Spangler has taken his last breath, they're all next.

"Lyric, you should let him up," Doyle says.

"I'm just showing the kids what their *Oracles* can do, *Uncle David*," I taunt. "No need to worry."

The children murmur with concern. Spangler has won all of their hearts with his big smiles and promises. It makes me wish the pool were deeper. I could drag him down and let his skull crack open from the pressure.

"You're hurting him," Geno says.

"No, no! He's going for a swim," I say. "He's enjoying himself."

"Lyric, that's enough!" Doyle demands.

"Let him up. He's human. He can't breathe down there," Priscilla begs.

"It's going to be okay, kids," I promise. "I'm going to make this all okay."

Four guards storm my way, but with a single thought, funnels of water slam into them and send them flailing.

"I'm counting to three," another soldier says as he levels his rifle at my face.

"I'll only need two," I whisper to him.

"Lyric Walker, release him!" a voice booms from the other side of the room. I turn in shock, because I recognize it. Fathom is here, racing toward me like a blur until he's got his hand clasped around my wrist. "That is enough."

"What are you doing?" I cry.

"Spangler is necessary," Fathom says to me. "I cannot let him be harmed."

I yank my hand away from him, horrified by his betrayal.

I turn off the glove, not because he asked, but because I am shocked that he asked. Of all the people in this world, I thought Fathom would want Spangler dead.

Our captive swims to the surface and takes a strangling gasp of air before Fathom helps him out of the pool. Spangler hunches on hands and knees, coughing up water. At the bottom of the pool, I can see his tablet.

"Kids, it's fine! Lyric and I planned this all along," Spangler cries. "We wanted to show what you can do to an enemy. Sorry, we weren't trying to scare you. We . . . we were showing off. The Oracles are pretty cool, huh?"

The children's faces move from shock to eagerness; then they break into applause.

"When do we get our Oracles?" Riley asks.

"Soon, and you can thank our new friend Fathom. He brought them to us all the way from the ocean," Spangler says, climbing to his feet to shake Fathom's hand. I'm horrified to see Fathom return it. "Lyric will show you how they work. Then we're all going to go back to Coney Island to save the world."

The children cheer and clap. Their eyes are full of wonder and excitement. Chloe hugs her bunny and grins at me.

I am sure I'm going to scream.

CHAPTER SIXTEEN

TWO GUARDS WALK ME BACK TO MY ROOM, EACH WITH a loaded pistol aimed at my head.

"That was a pretty stupid stunt," one of them says to me.

"It was only stupid because it didn't work," I mumble.

Once inside my room, I find chaos. Furniture lies broken and strewn about. There's a hole in one wall shaped roughly like a person. It opens into the bathroom. There are a few more like it on other walls. Glass shards litter the carpet. Bex and my mother hover over my father, who is slumped against a wall. Two more soldiers tower over him. Each have busted knuckles and batons.

I try to activate the glove, but Spangler has turned it off again, so I rush to the guard holding my mother down and swing. He blocks my punch and pushes me down to the floor.

"Be smart, freak!" he bellows.

The door opens, and Spangler enters the room with a dozen guards behind him.

"You did this to him?" I ask as I get to my feet.

He nods, then taps something on a new tablet. When he's finished, he gives me a cold stare.

"You need to understand a few things. When you don't fall in line, I will hurt the people you love. I took the liberty of preparing your family's cells this morning. They are ready for their return. The science team is prepped and ready for experiments. Gentlemen, let's empty this room."

The guards step forward, revealing that each is carrying a long, black stick. They press a button on their handles, and they hum with electricity.

"No! Leave them alone!" I shout.

"You challenged the alpha dog, Lyric!" Spangler shouts. "Throats must be ripped out."

One of the soldiers pulls my father to his feet, causing him to groan in agony. Another drags Bex toward the door, but I step in his way. He shoves me hard, and I fall. This time I grab his leg and wrap around it like a snake.

I hear my mother scream when they hit her with one of the batons.

"I'll do what you want!" I shriek. "Don't take them. I'll do whatever you want. I promise."

Spangler waves his hand, and the guards release my family. They exit the room, leaving Spangler standing amid the destruction.

"Am I a fool?" he asks me.

"I don't know what you mean."

"I'm trying to be a nice guy here. Am I being a fool?"

I shake my head.

He measures me for a long time, then kneels down to my level. He removes my hat and then rubs the top of my head like I'm a dog, even going so far as to scratch behind my ears. His touch makes me cringe, but it's the humiliation that sets me on edge.

"Can you promise to behave?"

I hesitate and he clamps his hand on my jaw and gives my head a jerk.

"Can you behave?"

I nod.

"Good dog," he says, as a smile creeps across his face. He stands and looks around at the chaos of the room. "What a mess. I'll send someone down to help clean this up."

A moment later he's gone, taking his soldiers with him.

My mother gets to her feet and helps my father sit in the only chair that survived the beating. I wrap Bex in my arms and do my best to calm her trembling.

"This is my fault," I say.

"No, it's not," my father says between painful winces. "Besides, your mother did most of this. She's mean when you make her angry."

"Don't joke," she lectures. "This is serious."

"Then I blame Fathom," I say. His name is bitter in my mouth.

"Fathom?" Bex asks.

"I had a chance to end this, and Fathom stopped me. He's working with Spangler. He brought all the kids their own gloves."

"Did he . . . was last night . . . ?"

"What happened last night?" my father asks.

"Nothing," I lie.

There's a knock at the door, and we all go quiet as mice. My mother stands and moves toward it.

"Stay behind me," she urges, her muscles tense and ready. When she opens the door, Fathom is waiting.

"I wish to speak with Lyric Walker," he says.

A million ugly words fight to be the first to come out of my mouth, but I never get the chance. Bex steps forward and points her finger in his face.

"You don't get to talk to her anymore. Do you understand me?" she shouts.

He looks over her shoulder to me, clearly hoping I will intervene. All I can think to do is give him the finger.

"I've tolerated your brooding crap because she loves you," Bex continues. "But we're done! Your stupidity and arrogance bore me, and now you're a traitor, too? There's something wrong with you, man. Your head isn't right, and we've got all the crazy we can handle right now, so turn around and go. In fact, why don't you go back to your fiancée and try to explain to her what you've been up to? I doubt she's going to be happy about it. I might not be able to kick your ass, but I know she can."

"Lyric Walker?" he pleads. "Just a few words."

For so many days and nights, Fathom has given me the strength to keep going. He's been the escape from a terrible reality. Last night was more than I ever hoped it could be—gentle, passionate, loving, and when we fell asleep against each other, I was sure I would never trust anyone as much as I trusted him. Now he's made me regret the best moments of my entire life, and I hate him for it.

"I'm such a stupid little girl," I say out loud, but it's not meant for anyone else but me.

"Please," he begs.

"Leave me alone," I say, and I turn my back on him. "I don't ever want to see you again."

I hear Bex slam the door. The sound rattles my heart. She takes my hand and leads me past my bewildered parents and into the bathroom.

"Can someone explain what is happening?" my father shouts when Bex closes the door.

"Let it go, Leonard," my mother says.

Bex sits me down on the side of the tub and puts my head on her shoulder and lets me cry and cry and cry. We have been in this same exact situation before, maybe not locked in a camp, but on the edge of a tub sobbing about some dumb boy. It's oddly comforting that in this nightmare life of mine there are still some things that are familiar and dependable. Bex will always be here to let me cry.

"He's not good enough for you," she whispers. "You're Lyric Walker, the second-hottest babe in Coney Island, behind me. He was totally dating up."

I laugh through the crying.

"Plus, the whole love triangle thing played out in 2005. Why would you put yourself through that tired cliché? You're better than having to try to convince someone to pick you. In fact, I know you are sad, but I have to be honest and tell you I'm really very ashamed of you. What the hell happened to your self-esteem?"

"I couldn't help myself," I cry defensively.

"At the center of every love triangle is always a complete ass." She sighs. "He gets to be Captain Wishy-Washy while the dummies who love him fight for his attention. It's manipulative and pathetic. They should call them loser triangles."

"You're still trying to make me feel better, right?"

Bex laughs and squeezes me tight.

"Well, I was saving this for your birthday, but I think you need it now," she says, reaching into her jumpsuit and pulling out a tube of cherry lip gloss from the pocket. She places it in my hand. I pop off the top and smell it. The scent is fruity and biting.

"Where did you get this?"

"From Luisa and Carmen," she says.

"Who?"

"The spa ladies! We're tight. You know, you really should learn some Spanish. It's kind of embarrassing."

I apply a coat and taste the phony cherry flavor on my tongue, then hand it to Bex, who does the same.

"This is the worst hotel I have ever stayed in," she says.

I laugh and laugh, and then I cry some more.

"When we check out of this place, we're stealing the towels," she says.

Doyle comes for me in the morning. He doesn't say anything, but he watches my father and mother as if he's concerned for them. He's smart enough to know we don't want him around, so he retreats to the hall while I get dressed.

"Honey, if you get your chance today, take it," my mother whispers to me. She looks around the room as if she suspects we're being listened to. I hate to admit it wasn't even something I'd considered, but now I can't stop imagining microphones hidden in the beds and pillows.

"If I fail, they will hurt you," I whisper back.

My mother nods that she understands, then my dad, then Bex.

"Take the shot," my father says.

Moments later I'm on the catwalk above the park, looking down as the children race through the trees. They're playing a game of hide-and-seek, giggling as they scamper for their favorite spots. I marvel at their joy. Doyle said he wanted this place to be a safe harbor for the children and it's working. They really don't know what's happening here. They think their parents are sick, bravely fighting some imaginary illness, rather than starving in solitary confinement just a few floors above. They don't realize that their Alpha parents are guinea pigs in a mad scientist lab that's only an elevator trip away. How can they not know that something is wrong? How can they not suspect that everything around them is a lie?

As I watch, I can't help but think about what my family wants me to do and how it will turn their lives upside down. *Take the shot.* And then what?

If I go after Spangler, I will have to attack Fathom and Doyle and the guards and quite possibly the children. Chloe is hiding in a shrub near the carousel, her face as clear as if she were sitting right next to me. I wonder if she would try to stop me if I had a chance to get us out of here. Would Harrison? Georgia? Finn? Priscilla? Would Riley stand in my way too? Is Spangler's hold on them so powerful that they can't see the difference between right and wrong? It sounds far-fetched, but I'm not so sure it's impossible. Fathom betrayed me to protect him, and he is the most strong-willed—no, *stubborn* person I've ever met. Even I felt it a bit when I was locked in that cell. I remember hearing the buzzer and leaping up to get into the circle. I was so eager to please. It hurts to admit it, but I wanted Spangler to be proud of me. I wanted to be a good dog.

I don't know how to stop him without ripping the throats out of all his pack. First, I need to figure out how he's blocking my glove. If I can find the switch, I can do some serious damage. I could find Arcade, and we could finish what we set out to do. She must be in the tank with the other Alpha, but—

"You'll never make it work," Doyle says. He's been standing beside me the whole time.

"Make what work?"

"I can see what you're thinking. You might as well put it on a billboard. You're working on scenarios."

"I don't know what you're talking about," I say, then turn my back on him so he can't see the lie.

"I'm not going to tell you to stop. It's how you're made. I'd do the same thing if I were you. We're the same kind of animal. I'm just saying it's not going to work. I helped design this place and—"

"You and I are nothing alike," I hiss.

"Let's work it out together. How do you get all the Alphas upstairs out of their tanks? How do you get all the parents out of solitary? How do you free these kids? How do you avoid the guards and Spangler and me and get your injured father out of his room and still turn off the EMP device all at the same time?"

"EMP?"

He chuckles. "I like you, Lyric. You'd make a good soldier. EMP stands for electo-magnetic pulse. It's what's turning off your power. It's used in military-grade weapons to knock out electronics. Thing is, your weapon doesn't run on electricity. We really don't know what makes it work, but the EMP has the same effect. Any idea what makes that thing on your hand tick?"

"Always the soldier, Doyle. If I knew, I wouldn't tell you. Unless you want to tell me where to find the EMP?"

He laughs. "So you're going to try again?"

I don't respond.

"You'll fail, Lyric," he continues. "You might kill Spangler, but they'll replace him with someone worse."

"I don't plan to stick around to find out."

"And what about the kids?"

"If you want to send a daycare center into a war zone, that's really on you," I say. "Because as much as you've trained them and prepared them, that's a playdate down there and nothing more. Chloe won't let go of her stuffed bunny. Geno can't tie his own shoelaces. They're not killers."

"You underestimate them," he argues.

I can't stand to be near him any longer.

"Let's get started," I snap, then descend the steps to the park.

Spangler spots me and calls the children in from their games. The little army rushes to meet me and gathers around with their eager faces.

"Today is a big day, kids," Spangler says. "We're being joined by some new faces."

The door opens, and Terrance Lir enters. He looks like he's aged forty years. His eyes are watery, and his hair has turned white. He pushes a wheelchair with his son, Samuel, in it. I haven't seen Sammy in so long. I run to his side and kneel down, hoping to catch his eyes.

"Sammy. It's so good to see you."

He struggles to look at me as his whole body shakes. When the gangs back home found out that he was half Alpha, they beat him and left him for dead. He was once a promising basketball star; now he can't feed himself. He can't talk, but he gives me a little smile to let me know he remembers me.

"They told me that we owe you our freedom," Terrance says.

"I'm working on getting us all out of here," I whisper.

He sighs, as if hope has let him down so many times, he can't stand when it's in the room.

"Take care of my son," he says, then walks back through the doors.

"C'mon," I say. I push Samuel until we are standing in front of the group. "Children, this is Samuel Lir. He is one of us. His father is Sirena, and his mother is human. Sammy here is going to keep us company while we train."

"That's not all," Spangler interrupts. "That's not the end of the surprises. I have presents."

The doors open, and a parade of scientists in lab coats stream through, carrying large silver cases and video equipment. They put everything down at Spangler's feet, then go to work setting up cameras and tripods. As they finish, Spangler unlocks the cases, revealing a collection of gloves identical to mine. He removes one and holds it out for all the children to see.

"Fathom brought one for each of you," he promises.

Fathom enters and the children thank him, then they crowd around Spangler, reaching for the glove like it's a bag of free candy.

"Now, now, let's line up and—"

Fathom tries to catch my eye but I refuse to look at him. His presence makes me angry. I can't tell whether giving the children gloves or the person who brought them is more disgusting.

"Wait!" I shout.

Spangler gives me a wary look, and I'm chilled.

"What is it, Ms. Walker?"

"If you put one on, you need to know that it doesn't come off."

One of the teen girls steps forward. I think her name is Abigail. She looks confused. "Ever?" she asks.

"I don't know about ever, but I think so. When you go out into the real world, people will see it, and everyone will know you are different. People may react with fear and anger because you have it on. Lots of people don't understand what we are, and it scares them—"

"Because of the sickness," Spangler interrupts. "But soon they'll understand that you aren't contagious. When that happens, you'll all be seen as the heroes you are. Now, there's something that I didn't mention. The Oracles will take away your migraines."

Chloe takes my hand. The rings around her eyes are deep and purple. She must have been up all night with headaches.

"Is that true?" she asks. There is so much hope in her eyes, and why shouldn't there be? If I had known that I could be free from my pain if I wore a cool metal glove that gave me superpowers for the rest of my life, I would have leaped at the chance.

I nod, defeated.

"I want mine!" Riley cheers, pushing to the front of the line.

Spangler hands him one, and the boy turns it over and over again in his hands, studying the metal and the carvings. He fumbles with it, trying to put it on the wrong hand, until Doyle flips it over and closes it with a snap. It locks itself in place, and Riley's eyes glow like someone turned a strobe light on inside his skull. A second later, his hand joins the laser light show.

"Whoa!" he says. "That's crazy."

Scientists buzz around him, taking pictures and videos. One waves a machine that looks like a Geiger counter over the boy. Its needle bounces around wildly.

"How do you feel, Riley?" Spangler asks.

"It's hard to explain."

"Please try," Spangler says. "We're making history here. There are lots of people who would like to know everything they can about this experience. It could lead to other kinds of discoveries."

"It's like being dropped into a bottle of soda," I say.

Riley smiles at me.

"Yeah, just like she said."

The other children chatter excitedly.

"My head doesn't hurt at all!" he continues. "Just like you said, Donovan."

Spangler taps on his tablet, and suddenly Riley's eyes open wide with surprise.

"I hear a voice!"

I hear one too. It's telling me to take the shot, but both Spangler and Doyle are watching me like hawks. Fathom takes a step closer to me, presumably to have a better position if he has to attack me.

"What does the voice say, Riley?" one of the scientists probes.

"It's whispering to me, asking me if I want it to do anything. I swear it's coming from the pool underneath us. Who is it, Lyric?"

Everyone turns to me.

"A friend of mine named Ghost believed that the voice

belongs to the Alpha god, the Great Abyss," I say, feeling like a phony. I'm the last person in the world who should be explaining the religion.

Cole is the next to get his glove, then Tess, Emma, Jane, Finn, Alexa, Dallas, Priscilla, Pierre, Harrison, and Geno. Spangler hands each kid one with a smile. They help one another put them on, and once each glove is in place and snaps shut, the children's eyes shine like supernovas. They celebrate and chatter incessantly about how it feels or how their brains don't hurt or what they want to do with this incredible power they have just been given. Each time I hear a glove snap shut, I die a little more, knowing that another life is forever changed. Chloe is the last one to get a glove, and she holds it out in front of her hands and studies it closely.

"Doesn't Samuel get one?" she asks, looking to the boy in the wheelchair.

"I'm not sure that Samuel could make it work, Chloe," Spangler explains.

Chloe frowns.

"That's not fair. If he can't have one, then I want to give him mine," she argues.

"Chloe, now honey, I don't think you understand."

Harrison steps forward and pulls Spangler out of the conversation. He has a million questions about the carvings and the metal and how it works. Meanwhile, Chloe looks at me with her sad, tired face. She doesn't understand that Samuel is a broken kid who serves no purpose to Spangler other than to keep me satisfied.

When all the children have their gloves, the pool is opened and the kids are ushered to its side. The scientists lug their instruments and cameras over and set them up to eagerly watch what happens next. I guess that's my cue to start.

"All right, I'm going to be honest. I'm not much of a teacher, but I think that starting small and simple is the best strategy."

"That means you kids can't throw me in the pool on the first day!" Spangler says.

The children laugh at his joke. They believe that my attempt to kill him was just a stunt.

"The gloves were invented by—"

"Oracles, Lyric. We call them Oracles. We've trademarked the name," Spangler insists.

"They were invented by the Nix, a clan in the Alpha Nation that is known for their work in science and math. The gloves were meant to help the Rusalka with their headaches, because the Rusalka were once part of the Alpha Nation as well. Now, before you start thinking the Nix were being nice, the Rusalka were practically slaves. Their clan did all the hard work, and if they had headaches, everything slowed down, so these gloves—"

"Oracles!" Spangler says.

"These Oracles were supposed to be medicine. Now, like lots of medicines, they had a side effect. When the Rusalka put them on, they found not only that their headaches were gone, but also that they could manipulate water. No one really knows why."

"Was it just the Rusalka?" Breanne asks.

"No, some Alpha could use them. Ghost had one, and his girlfriend Luna. There was a boy named Thrill. I have a friend named Arcade who is a Triton, and she wears one."

"Where is she?" Riley asks.

I turn to Spangler, and every eye follows.

"She'll be here soon," he promises.

"Great! So, the Rusalka were suddenly very powerful, and they realized they didn't have to be slaves anymore. Long story short, the Alpha refused to let them live in freedom, so the Rusalka declared war on the rest of the empire, and here we are now."

"So, the Rusalka aren't actually evil?" a blond teen asks from the back. I think her name is Sophie.

The rest of the kids have the same confused expression on their faces.

"Thank you for the history lesson, Lyric. Maybe we should move on to your demonstration," Spangler insists.

I shrug and lift my hand high over my head. The glove goes off like a bottle rocket, and the children watch me in stunned silence. I hear my mother telling me to take the shot, but Doyle is right. It's not going to work, at least not today. I need to make a plan, and until I do, there are just too many moving parts. I need to wait for my moment, just like I did when the silver bowl wouldn't go through the slot. Someone will make a mistake. I just have to be ready.

For the next few minutes, I use the pool water to create a number of different objects, from spears to tridents to enormous fists. Anything my imagination can conceive becomes a living sculpture of liquid.

"Anything you can imagine, you can make, but I suggest you stick with things you've seen in real life. If you understand how long something is or what it's actually made of, then it's easier to mold that shape. I know what a hammer looks like. I know how heavy it is. I can use that information to make a larger version. I know a sword is long and pointy—you get what I'm saying. Stick with real-world stuff today. Tomorrow we'll get creative."

A blast of liquid springs out of the pool and morphs into the shape of an anaconda. It wraps around Riley and lifts him off the ground. The children gasp.

"It's okay. I won't hurt him," I say, looking little Chloe directly in the eye. "I promise I will never hurt any of you."

"It's cool," Riley says, and his grin is bigger than ever. "But you're getting my tracksuit wet!"

I set him down, and he leads the applause.

"Water is liquid, but it can be solid, too. You can pack it together to make it dense. You can thin it out to make rain. It's up to you. So, everyone, let's aim your gloves at the pool," I say.

"I guess you don't actually have to point it at the water, but it helps me to focus if I do. Good. All right, now concentrate on the surface, and let's see if you can affect it. Try to make a little ripple. It doesn't have to be big. It can be a tiny thing, like you dropped a stone into a still pond. You've seen a ripple a million times."

"I've got it," Riley says as he closes his eyes tight.

I turn to Spangler. He smiles and nods approvingly. I want him to think he's tamed me, at least until I can get off his leash.

"All right, now, here's where things get tricky," I say, turning my attention back to Riley. "It's not your imagination that makes the ripple. It's your spirit."

"I'm confused."

"I'm talking about you—the big, awesome force that is Riley. The stomping giant that hides in your heart. That's what fuels your Oracle. It's the same thing that makes that sarcastic grin."

The children laugh.

"So it's like the Force?" Cole shouts from the crowd.

Riley's face lights up, and he smiles at me. He's always smiling at me. Why?

"No, not the Force. This is about raw emotion, not calm meditation. The person who taught me to use this told me that if I wanted to make it work, I had to be a force of nature, like a hurricane, all turmoil and raw emotion."

"Show us," Finn begs.

I've got more than my fair share of raw emotion, and letting some go will do me good. Best of all, I know just who to unleash it on.

I turn to Fathom. He hovers in the shadows, watching my lesson and doing his best to keep his distance. I raise my fist and his eyes widen. When my entire arm explodes and light flies upward to illuminate the rafters, his mouth opens in shock.

"Watch and learn, kids," I shout, and at once all the water in the pool is in the air. It sails across the room until it is directly above Fathom, and then it swirls into a bubbling whirlpool, spinning faster and faster until his hair and clothes flap in an angry wind. Then I send it crashing down on him. He's caught in my churning heartbreak, and his body flails about as he struggles to free himself. He's not quick enough for my attack and his body slams into the floor over and over again, until he comes down in one bone-cracking slam. I direct the water back to the pool and watch Fathom struggle to stand, fighting with his lungs for a breath. He shoots me an angry and frustrated expression but I turn my back on him and face the children.

"Don't worry, kids. He's not hurt. In fact, Fathom can't feel anything. That's how he's made," I say.

I expected the kids to be shocked and afraid, the way they were when I attacked Spangler the day before, but they are smiling and eager, if a bit intimidated.

"I don't think I feel anything that powerful," Chloe says.

"My ability is fueled by loss and betrayal, something I'm sure all of you have experienced. But you don't have to feel pain to do what I can do. Happiness is just as good. Fear, anger, love—"

The word feels dry and tough in my mouth. I'd spit it out if I could, right here on the grass. I'd step on it and squish it into nothing. Fathom has recast its very meaning so that it feels unwelcome and foreign. I can recall the feelings, but they are covered in so much despair, like the sudden loss of a person. Like how I feel about Shadow. All I can do is mourn. Put it aside, Lyric. Lock it up in a box and shove it deep under the bed. Don't let him see what he's done to you. Don't turn and look. Don't give him the satisfaction of knowing he had power over you.

"Lyric? Are you all right?" Doyle asks.

"Sorry. I was saying you don't need to feel something that intense. It could be something as simple as a happy memory or the secret wild thing inside you."

"I'm lost," Harrison admits.

"Have you ever read *Where the Wild Things Are*?"

"Riley reads it to me," Chloe says, giving him a wink.

"Remember when Max wins the staring contest and the wild things bow down to him and make him their king, and then they do that crazy dance?"

"The wild rumpus," she says, standing tall and proud for knowing the answer.

"Is there a wild rumpus inside you?"

Doyle crosses the room and stands close.

"Maybe I can help," he says. "What is it that you want them to do? Give me the instructions, and I can help them understand."

"There aren't instructions," I snap. "This isn't a microwave. It's fueled by feelings, the more powerful the better. It doesn't have to be happiness. It can be aggression or arrogance or rebelliousness or even overconfidence. It's like punk rock. It's like a first kiss. It's like a fistfight. They need to tap into something that rocked their world. This stupid park you've created for them is—"

Doyle looks at me skeptically.

"He's doing it!" Priscilla cries. I turn to the pool and watch the water rippling back and forth until it becomes a violent wave that sloshes over the sides.

"I can't believe it," Riley says.

"You made it move! What did you think about?" I cry.

He gives me that grin again but keeps the answer to himself.

"Let's let someone else give it a shot," Doyle says.

"Riley, are you okay?" Chloe whimpers, then points to his face.

Blood is trickling out of his nose.

"Amy!" Spangler shouts, and from his mob of groupies comes everyone's favorite nurse, urging the boy to tilt his head back and pinch his nose. She leads him away while Spangler stares at me like I'm mold.

"It's okay. That happens to me sometimes too. He's not hurt."

Spangler punches a couple of buttons on his tablet.

"Is he sick?" Emma asks.

I shake my head, but to be honest, I don't know. These gloves could be killing us all.

"Let's take a break," Doyle says.

He takes my arm and walks me out of everyone's earshot.

"You're confusing and scaring them," he says. "They don't need to know the Rusalka were mistreated. You don't tell a soldier to empathize with the target. You tell them they eat babies and will kill us all in our sleep."

"I'm not trying to scare them. They need to understand what they're getting into and why they're fighting," I argue.

"That's not your job," he says with a sigh. "You've also got to get specific about how to make these things work."

"I can't be specific. I've tried to explain this the best I can. The glove is fueled by their spirits."

"We don't have time for spirits!" he says. "And what's this about the nosebleeds?"

"Hey, look!" someone shouts from the crowd.

Doyle and I turn toward them, only to see Chloe hovering near Samuel. She slips her glove onto his hand, and it clicks into place.

"Chloe, no!" Spangler shouts, but it's too late. Samuel's eyes glow and then dim.

"It wasn't fair he didn't have one," she tries to explain. "I want everyone to play."

Samuel lowers his head and looks at the glove on his hand, then looks up at me. For a moment, he seems like his old self again, but then it fades.

"That is a very big problem," Spangler says to me.

CHAPTER SEVENTEEN

WHEN I GET BACK TO MY ROOM, IT'S FULL OF new furniture—someone has even patched the holes in the wall. But Bex and my parents are gone. The soldier who escorted me has no idea where they are but uses his radio to find out, while I have a panic attack.

"They're okay, Lyric," Doyle says when he finally shows up. "Your dad is in the infirmary getting x-rays on his ribs. Bex is eating lunch with your mother. They're safe."

"Spangler is going to hurt them. He thinks I made Riley's nose bleed."

"I told him you didn't, and he believes me," he says.

He reaches out to take my hand, but I swat it away like it's the mouth of a rabid dog. "There won't be any repercussions, but what happened with the little girl has made him apoplectic. We don't have any more Oracles."

"Stop calling them that!" I snap. "It's not some fancy gadget you buy at the Apple store."

"I've offered a solution that he's going to consider. I hope it makes everyone happy. In the meantime, you're making your life harder every time you open your mouth. Stick with what you're supposed to do, and keep your opinions to yourself. Get smart, Lyric."

He turns to leave, but then stops.

"Tomorrow you're starting your combat training," he adds.

"I don't want your help."

"Spangler is going to drop you into a pack of Rusalka and heaven knows what else. You're going to need to know how to fight and defend yourself."

"I'm from Coney Island. I know about fighting."

"Your first class is after you train the kids. If you don't show up, I'll have you dragged there," he threatens.

The next day, Calvin arrives to take me to the park. He's nervous and keeps reaching for his gun. His nose is still swollen.

"Hey, old friend," I say, enjoying the panic I create in him.

"Don't talk to me. Just keep moving," he orders.

In the park, the children gather around me, but they don't have the same excitement as yesterday. Riley's nosebleed shook them up, and now they have trepidation about me as a teacher. This is not good news, Doyle tells me.

"Where's Samuel?" I ask, scanning the room for his wheelchair.

"He's with the doctors," Spangler explains when he enters the room. He's busy tapping on his tablet and doesn't even look up. "Well, get started."

"Yesterday Riley had a nosebleed. Did it scare anyone?"

Chloe and little Geno raise their hands, and even Dallas admits her fear, but when Riley raises his, everyone explodes with laughter.

"There's no need to be afraid. The nosebleeds are normal," I say.

"They did some tests on me, and I'm superhealthy," Riley says. "In fact, they told me my brain is actually working better than it did before I put the Oracle on my hand. Apparently, it's making everything work better. By the end of the day, I'm going to be a genius."

The kids laugh again.

"If the bleeding was hurting you, then we'd stop what we're doing. Your health is my only priority," Spangler says robotically. He's still busy with his tapping.

"Keep in mind that the gloves weren't built with people like us in mind. They were designed for full-blooded Alphas —like Rusalka. We're only half Sirena, so maybe it's interfering with our bodies, but I haven't had any problems other than the bleeding. A lot of times I don't even know it's happening. Still, it can't hurt to be careful. If you get a nosebleed, then you should take a break. Deal?"

I feel like a liar. I don't know anything about the nosebleeds. For all I know, the glove could be giving me cancer or cooking my brains, but what I've said seems to calm their fears. It's a powerful reminder to me that I'm not dealing with adults. As gung ho as they are to fight the Rusalka, they are still children. Even the oldest ones are sheltered and naive.

We return to our work with the water. There is very little success. Dallas, Priscilla, Tess, and Emma can't make anything happen at all. Ryan tries again and again, and grows more and more frustrated with each attempt. A seven-year-old named Leo and his nine-year-old brother, William, are quickly bored with trying and drift off to play on the swing set. A redhead named Suzi, Breanne, and even Harrison and Finn, lose their tempers and tell me all of this is stupid. Only little Geno, who is about the same age as Chloe, manages to cause a wave in the pool. It elicits a victorious cheer from all the children, and those who wandered off come running back, begging the little boy to do his trick over and over again. Geno is so proud of himself, basking in the jealousy that even the older boys can't hide. It spurs them all to try even harder, and by the end of our class, half the children have nosebleeds. Frustrated, I have them change into their swimsuits and practice breathing underwater.

At the end of class, the kids say their goodbyes and file out of the park.

"What am I doing wrong?" Riley asks, unsatisfied with the waterspout he created earlier.

"Riley, you're the best in the class."

"I'm average," he says. "Donovan says we're running out of time. A bunch of cities had to be evacuated yesterday. We have to get out there and fight, Lyric."

I'm tempted to tell him the truth, that he's being used and he's probably going to die. I look over my shoulder. The scientists are packing up their cameras, and Spangler stands in the shadows with only his frustrated eyes illuminated. He taps on his tablet. Still, it's too risky.

"Could you show me again?" he begs.

"Follow me," I say, and I lead him to the edge of the pool. He stares down at the water with his glove alight and his face set and determined.

"What I'm trying to teach you is almost innate," I say. "It's like trying to tell someone how to paint or how to write a story. It's something that you automatically know how to do or, in your case, something we might have to trick you into understanding."

"How did you figure it out?"

I sit down on the edge of the pool and let my legs slide into the water. This is a question I haven't really asked myself, and it takes me a while to sort through all the possibilities until I find what feels right.

"I didn't know what my mother was, what I am, until I was fourteen. Until that time, I felt like the queen of Coney Island. I was young, alive, and filled with attitude. Once I found out the truth about her, I had to go into hiding. Not literally, but mentally. All those things I loved about myself—my clothes, my big mouth—everything had to be stuffed down inside me and hidden from everyone. The only way my family could be safe was for me to be small."

"That explains a lot."

"Meaning?"

He laughs.

"How do I put this and still make it sound like a compliment?" he asks as he sits down next to me. "The Lyric Walker I met was a hurricane who blew people away, and then one day she was a wet fart."

"That's lovely, kid. So we've met before?"

A frown flashes on his face but it quickly fades.

"Sorry. What I'm saying is I met you and you were amazing, but every time I saw you after, it was like a different person was walking around in your body. It was obvious something was different."

"And how many times did you see me?"

He turns pink and looks into the water. "You're hard to miss."

"Anyway, that hurricane, as you say, was still inside me and it got so that I resented having to hide it. I suppose that's the most powerful emotion of my life, this need to let it go, to be the person I was always meant to be. When I use the glove, I think about letting loose."

"How did you deal with that feeling before you got your Oracle?"

"Yoga," I say, suddenly realizing that it's true. I don't think I gave it much thought until just this moment, but yoga was the calming effect on my life. It helped quell the headaches and center me. I used it to channel all the bad mojo into something

I could manage. Suddenly I know how to help Riley and all the others.

For the next thirty minutes, I teach Riley a few poses. We work on downward dog and sun solstice and mountain, and even resting warrior. He finds it embarrassing at first. A lot of guys do, but then he starts to understand that it's hard and he's not as strong as he struts around thinking he is. When it's over, I can see he's found some respect for it and a little *Om*.

"Now let's try again. You've gotten all the clutter out of your head, so focus on that moment you used yesterday."

"My happy thought," he says.

"Good, so focus on the happy, Riley."

He closes his eyes, and there's that grin. I have to admit he's cute—naive, sheltered, dumb—but very cute. Bex would dig him. He's a fixer-upper, and maybe someday when Shadow's death is not looming over her, she might want to give him a chance.

The pool starts to churn into a bubbling soup. It's unruly at first, much like the things I made when Arcade started coaching me, but then it takes form. I'm expecting some kind of weapon. That's what I usually create, but this is something entirely different, and it takes me a while to realize it's a soda bottle. It spins and spins in place, finally slowing so that the end is aimed right at me; then the water falls back into the pool with a splash.

"Big moment," he says, getting to his feet.

I look up into his face and he's giving me that grin, and

it's charming, cocky, and confident. Now I remember him. I kissed him during a game of spin the bottle three years ago.

"I better get going," he says. He strolls off through the double doors without another word.

Fathom enters and approaches, and suddenly my nice little surprise melts into anger.

"I have been sent to train you to fight, Lyric Walker," he says.

"No!" I cry.

"The one called Doyle insisted," he says.

Fathom takes off his jumpsuit, revealing a pair of tight swimming trunks.

"We will train in the pool," he says, leaping into the water with a splash. I look down at the clothes he left behind and scream. I'm not doing this. I refuse. I turn and walk, only to hear a *whoosh!* He soars over my head and lands in my path.

"I cannot let you die," he says.

"You pretty much killed me already, and the kids, too. If you hadn't given Spangler those gloves, he would never have been able to send us to face the Rusalka."

"You don't understand," he says.

"Then explain it to me! Tell me why you're helping him."

A couple of soldiers enter the park, walk toward us, and then stop to watch what we do.

"I do not wish to speak of it with others around. I will meet you here every day and I will teach you to survive."

"I don't want anything to do with you, Fathom. I don't

believe anything you do or say anymore. For all I know, you're here to kill me or teach me something that will get me killed. Do you understand me? That's how little I think of you now. We are not friends. Whatever we were or could be is dead. I don't want to be your selfsame or your girl-friend. I don't even want to be your friend. I want to be a stranger. I want to forget what we did so I can share that with someone who deserves it!"

He takes a deep breath and drops his eyes.

"I will respect any request you have, but I will not let you die. When I am confident you can fight, I will take myself out of your life," he says, then leaps back into the pool. I watch him swimming below, seeing how the water bends and twists his image into something I don't recognize.

"Ms. Walker, this is part of the deal!" Spangler shouts from across the room. His tablet glows at his hand. He's got a weapon too, and I know he's not afraid to use it to kill every-one I love if I don't give him what he wants.

For the next two hours, Fathom silently teaches me to fight, and for two hours, I punch and kick him with every bro-kenhearted fiber of my being.

CHAPTER EIGHTEEN

ODDLY ENOUGH, MY LIFE STARTS TO TAKE ON A ROU-
tine. I spend half my days helping my mother
take care of my father's injuries and letting Bex
bitterly complain about Fathom's "dumb face." In some ways
it feels like we're all back in our apartment in Coney Island.

Everyone is slowly getting stronger. Bex and I put on
weight, and our bruises fade. Her old self is returning as well.
One day I come back to the room and find she's cut up one of
the jumpsuits into something that borders on scandalous. She
even yanked the White Tower logo off the chest and threw it
in the trash. I ask her if she can do the same to all of mine.

My father is obsessed with getting back to his former self,
and my mother and I take turns scolding him for overexert-
ing himself with sit-ups, pushups, and jogging in place. He says
he's going stir-crazy and needs to do something. He wants to
be ready in case there's a chance to escape. He doesn't want to
be the one who holds everyone back. I worry he's making his
injuries worse.

My mother frets about us all, sliding back into her role as Summer Walker, hot neighborhood mom, but I catch her doing exercises as well. She lifts the sofa over her head and does pushups for hours.

The other half of my day is spent with the children, four hours of training with the gloves, then two hours of fight training with Fathom. Spangler hovers over it all. He pushes me to get closer to the kids, so I eat meals with them. I agree to lunch in their own fancy cafeteria, complete with a salad bar, an ice cream machine, and a taco buffet. A chef will make them coal-oven pizzas that look a lot like New York–style thin-crusts but for some reason aren't as good. Huge television screens play prerecorded cartoons and MTV all day. The children sometimes gather around, asking questions about the Alpha like they are characters in comic books or Greek mythology. They have an endless desire to know more about their Alpha families.

"What does a Selkie look like, Lyric?" Geno asks. He's been in this camp for almost three years. He has no memories of Coney Island or the arrival of the Alpha.

"They're big. Even the teenagers are almost seven feet tall, and they have spikes on their shoulders."

"I saw a Ceto once," Tess says.

"They're probably the most dangerous of the Alpha. They're electrified, like an eel, and one touch can kill a person," I explain.

I realize I'm telling ghost stories around a campfire.

"Donovan says there are hundreds of different kinds of Alpha. And there's something that eats your brain," Georgia says.

"He told me the same thing," William says.

"He showed us a news story where thousands of them came out of the water," Leo says. "If they come at me, I'm going to stomp them with my feet."

"Who is that boy who meets with you? Is he your boyfriend?" Priscilla asks.

Suddenly, all eyes are on Riley, but he's staring at his shoes.

"He's a Triton, and his name is Fathom. He's a prince, and his father is the prime."

"He's the king's son?" Chloe asks. "Is he bad too?"

I realize I don't know the answer to that anymore.

"He's not like his father," I say. It's the kindest thing I can muster.

"When I see the prime, I'm going to punch him in the face," Leo says.

Riley gives me a shy smile. He's got it bad for me and if we weren't locked up in this madhouse, I would probably enjoy it. He's got the worst timing in the world. A crush is just stupid right now.

But all these kids are stupid. They don't have a clue. To combat their naiveté, I push harder in our training sessions, trying to teach them to think of themselves as giants or dragons or whatever fierce beast they can imagine, though I've found that if I meet with each one of them individually, I have better luck with yoga. Within a week, ten of the kids can command the water nearly as well as I can.

Geno is my prize pupil by far. Despite his age, he's capable of complicated creations, and for such a little boy, he's not easily shaken or distracted. Doyle is pleased with him as well and tells me he will most likely lead the charge when we deploy. The very thought fills me with dread, and my instinct is to focus on the older kids, work on their abilities until they surpass his. I'm sure it hurts his feelings, but I'm doing it for his own good. None of these kids are meant for fighting, no matter what age, but I'm not going to help the littlest one lead the war.

Riley is ever present, hovering and joking and flirting, always showing off his growing control. I don't want to encourage him, but I do find myself smiling when he's around. He's thoughtful and kind with the little ones, and I suppose it's nice to have someone in this world who still thinks I'm hot. Or maybe it's nice to be around a boy who is allowed to like me, who doesn't have some weird tradition that keeps us apart, who isn't a liar. Riley and I are a lot alike, from the same neighborhood, with the same weird genetics, too, with the same secrets. But mostly, and I know this is selfish, what I like about him is that he's so obvious. He's into me, and he lets me know and I don't have to have a degree in Triton facial expressions to decipher what he's thinking. He reminds me of Shadow in a way—always there, dependable, fun.

There are moments when I see him in the park or pass him

in the hall and I get a little thrill when his whole face brightens. If we were a couple of kids hanging out on the beach, he would be a more-than-suitable rebound boyfriend, but now, in here, I feel shut down, like my heart is dead. Fathom ruined me for any future boys. I'm smooshed, and my feelings are unreliable. I can't trust anything. It's also hard to get excited about someone when you know his future is bleak.

"He says you're beautiful," Chloe whispers to me. "He tells me at night when he reads me bedtime stories."

"He tells you that so you will repeat it to me," I say.

"You think so?" she asks, suddenly angry with his manipulation.

"It's a boy trick," I say.

I rub my head beneath my hat, feeling the patchy hair slowly growing, and feeling self-conscious. I don't feel beautiful.

"I think *you're* beautiful," I tell Chloe.

"Yeah, I know," she says, then bursts into giggles, and I smile. I'm making a mini-me.

Chloe and I spend a lot of time together. I can't help but care for her, stepping in to act as the mom when her real mom is probably floating in a tank not four floors above us. I find myself prodding her to eat more vegetables at lunch. She draws me pictures where the two of us are walking on rainbows. I hang them in my room. She sits with me in the grass, and we talk about home and how much she misses it. I rub her temples when her migraines attack. One thing I've noticed is how she changes the subject every time I ask about her parents. All she will say is that her daddy is a hero and her mother is fighting the war. She tells me it's her turn to fight now, and she will, just as soon as she gets a glove.

"I'm glad you gave yours to Samuel," I say, but I leave out that I can't bear thinking about her on that beach, fighting things that will try to eat her.

"I know, but I don't get to have fun like everyone else. I asked Donovan for my own glove this morning. He said he would get me one tomorrow."

I hope it was an empty promise.

Fathom holds up his end of the deal and doesn't talk to me about anything other than fighting. He focuses on our training and pushes hard. He wants me to swing faster, kick with more intensity. Fighting underwater is so impossibly difficult, and he has no patience with my excuses. He slams into me, pushes me around, and knocks me over with his speed and strength. He shouts at me and criticizes every move I make. He shoots derisive looks my way, which just spark a fight when we get out of the pool.

"You can't come here and bark at me!" I shout.

Fathom springs out of the water, landing on the lawn in an effortless leap.

"You're not working hard enough. The Rusalka are fast and merciless, and you are like a sea turtle fighting the current."

"You and Arcade are clearly meant for each other!" I cry. "She was always telling me I was a loser too. I don't care if the two of you think I can do better. This is all you get!"

"Arcade would never be this lazy," he says.

I smack him so hard, it echoes off the rafters. Then I turn and stomp toward the door, mad at myself for needing to cry, but he's in front of me so fast, I feel the wind blow against my wet swimsuit.

"I'm trying to keep you alive," he says. "I can't lose you."

"You don't have me," I say bitterly, my eyes blinded by tears. "I always worried you would pick Arcade. In fact, I was prepared for it. Now I wish you had."

He looks stricken. Can't he see what he's done? This is us now: we're done, and it's underlined in red. It's what we're going to be from now on, and it's his fault.

"I don't want to be part of some stupid clichéd love triangle, anyway."

"What is a love triangle?" he asks.

"It's when one person treats two others like losers, and the losers love it," I say.

A soldier enters the room.

"Mr. Spangler would like to see you," he says to me.

"Lyric Walker, you must talk to me," he begs, but I turn and stalk out of the room.

Doyle is waiting outside Spangler's office when I arrive.

"He wants to see us both," he explains, but says he has no

idea why. He knocks on the door, and after a moment it opens and we enter.

Spangler is sitting at a fancy glass desk littered with electronic gadgets. He smiles and gestures for us to enter.

"Doyle, Lyric, I believe you both know Samuel."

Samuel Lir is sitting in his wheelchair off to the side, so I didn't spot him at first. When we turn to face him, he does something I never thought I'd see him do again. He stands. It's awkward and difficult, but he gets up and stays put. I cry out in both surprise and joy.

"Hello, Ly-ric," he says, knocking me out again. It's a miracle.

"How is this possible, Sammy?" I say.

He points to the glove. "I'm coming back, Lyric," he says. He turns to Spangler. "I'm tired."

"Of course you are," Spangler replies. He presses some buttons on his tablet, then helps Samuel back into his wheelchair. "You've had an exhausting day, and it's important to get some rest. We don't want anything slowing down your progress."

The door opens, and Rochelle and Terrance enter. Rochelle looks thin and tired, like they just took her out of her cell. Maybe they did.

"How?" I ask.

Terrance smiles at me with tears streaming from his eyes.

"I'm not going to question a miracle," he says. He and Rochelle wheel their son out of the room. On the way out, Sammy waves at me, then rubs his head, a joke about my hair.

"The Oracle is an amazing device," Spangler says once they're gone. "I have a theory about it. Would you like to hear it? I don't think it really moves the water. What I think it does is rewires your brain to force a leap forward in individual evolution. For Alpha, it adapted the Rusalka's mind so it could control its environment more efficiently. The insurmountable complications of living underwater forced their society to be a nomadic hunter-gatherer tribe. Being able to control what was once uncontrollable gave them a chance at a permanent home. For Samuel, it's taking on a different purpose: to allow him to walk and talk again. I've got the team working on it right now. If we can figure out how to adapt that technology for humans, the applications have limitless potential. A soldier could evolve into something bigger and stronger than the enemy. It could get an injured cop back on the streets. People could develop abilities we've never even imagined. It's mind-boggling. So, how about an update on the children?"

Doyle clears his throat.

"Lyric has been working with Fathom in the pool. Naturally, he's teaching her fighting techniques that I cannot. She's progressing as well as can be expected, but she could improve if you didn't turn off her connection to the water."

"Hmm. I'm not sure we're going to be able to arrange that at this time."

"The children continue to excel at their mixed martial-arts training, though based on sheer size and strength, few of them will pose any real threat to a Rusalka. They simply aren't strong enough. They'll have to rely on their Oracles when we deploy, another reason to turn on the connection permanently. The children could use the practice."

"Mmm-hmm," Spangler says absently. "Lyric, how goes it with your students?"

"Geno, Riley, and Georgia are the best," I say.

"And the others?"

"Twelve are very good. Of them, Finn, Ryan, and Harrison are on the verge of a breakthrough. That leaves sixteen who, as of right now, can barely make a ripple and will be killed the second they step on the beach. You might as well send a bunch of rabbits to fight in their place. Chloe doesn't have a glove, so sending her at all is a death sentence."

"Yes, Chloe needs a glove. The contract is for thirty-three soldiers, and I've got thirty-two gloves. I was going to take Samuel's from him before I saw his CAT scans. I am so glad I waited."

Doyle leans forward in his seat, his face choleric.

"You were going to amputate his hand?"

"Obviously I can't do that now. He's a walking medical miracle. My shareholders would have my head if I ever did something like that. That's not good business."

"It's always business with you," I hiss.

"She doesn't get it, does she, Doyle? Lyric, everything is about business, which leads me back to my problem. When it's a government contract, you really can't be short. I reached out to the client to explain, hoping there might be some wiggle room due to the unique situation and complexities of what we're doing, but negotiations fell apart. I have to give them what I promised."

Instinctively, I tuck my hand back behind me.

"Oh, not you, Lyric. You're number thirty-three and the best of the best. No, I've had to get creative."

There's a knock at the door, and when it opens, there's another wheelchair. This one has Arcade in it. Her head is tilted to the right and her eyes are rolling in her head. She's drugged and doesn't seem to know where she is, but she has a moment when she focuses on me. Her hands go up to strike, and that's when I realize one of them is missing and her arm is now wrapped in white gauze.

"Oh, no," I whisper, too horrified to scream.

"I will kill you slowly," she slurs as she swings wildly in the air.

"What have you done?" Doyle gasps.

"I need the two of you to understand the dire nature of what is happening, because things have gone from bad to worse. Rusalka have attacked lower Manhattan. They control everything south of Twenty-Third Street. It's pushed our time-table up. Chloe has her glove, and this time I made sure it went on her hand. I even locked it in place myself. She's ready to be trained. I know you're very close with her, Lyric, so I'm hoping you'll do your best to help her learn to use it. Delivery is in three days."

"Three days! They won't be ready!" Doyle cries, getting up from his chair so fast, it topples over. I'm too hypnotized by Arcade's stump to notice.

"The client paid for the product, and now it's time to ship it."

"The product," I say.

"You're sending those kids to their graves!" Doyle rages.

"I'm trying to save the world!" Spangler shouts. "That's our job, David. The Rusalka, the Alpha—whatever else is out there—they're coming for us. The kids are our only chance. You can cry in your bunk because they have to do the heavy lifting, but those are the cards we've been dealt. They're going, and when you're an old man sleeping in your bed and not worrying about mutated fish people coming to kill and maim your family, you'll see the price wasn't that high. Thirty-three children for the lives of millions, that's hardly a price at all!"

Spangler turns to me.

"Three days. Those kids can learn a lot from you in that amount of time. I suggest you get to work."

I wheel Arcade back to my room because the thought of leaving her with Amy is too frightening to imagine. I'm hoping my mother will know what to do, or my father, who was trained in first aid when he became a cop. Bex will be good for her too. Their friendship, if you can call it that, is complicated, but I do think they respect each other.

When I get her into the room, my mother lifts Arcade out of the chair and lays her on one of the beds. Bex rushes to get some cool washcloths, and my father checks her pulse.

"It's slow but not dangerous," he explains. "The sedatives they gave her are most likely the cause."

"He should know," Bex says, not having to explain who "he" is to me.

I nod, and suddenly my anger at Fathom is gone. Yes, he should see her. I go to the door and beg the guard to bring Fathom to my room. The guard is lazy but eventually relents and heads off as soon as a replacement comes to take his post. I wait outside until Fathom appears. His face has a tentative smile, and his eyes are hopeful. He thinks I've changed my mind about him.

"Arcade is hurt," I say.

"Arcade is a warrior," he says.

"Seriously," I say.

I lead him into the room and he hovers over her bed, lifting her wounded arm and studying the dressings where her hand once was. I brace myself for some nonsense about trophies won in war, that a wound is evidence of a fight, and that she will cherish this loss, but if he is thinking it, he keeps it to himself.

"Like all Triton, Arcade carved the cutting edges of her Kala with stones, from the time she was a small child until she had her first kill. Every edge is unique, the closest thing our people can produce to art. This wound has ruined her work. It is a terrible tragedy for her. Her designs were widely admired. When we were still living in the hunting grounds, she often told me she considered being a teacher, instructing young Triton in the forms their Kala can take. I encouraged her passion. I believe she would have been very good at it."

He stands over Arcade for a long moment before turning to me.

"Will you take care of her?" he asks.

"Shouldn't she be with you?"

He shakes his head. "Please do me a kindness and do not tell her I was here. She will be offended if she learns I was concerned. It will imply that I think she is weak."

"That's insane," my father says.

My mother shakes her head. "It's true. Triton do not nurse the wounded. It is insulting to the victim's strength and tenacity. If she wants him, she will ask, though I suspect she will not, out of pride."

"So that's it?" I cry. "You're going to go? And if she survives, then you two will go back to the normal routine, like nothing happened?"

"What would you have me do for her?" Fathom snaps.

"I don't know! Sit with her! Read to her. Sing her a song. She's your selfsame, isn't she?" I know it comes out spiteful. My bitterness is ever ready when he's near, but the actual words I'm saying are completely rational. Yes, I know that I'm a walking contradiction. A week ago I wanted to steal him away from her. I've envied her. Now she's seriously hurt and he should be with her. It's the kind, human, sane thing to do. Staying would prove to me that he's not soulless, but he can't bring himself to do it, for her or me. I'm starting to see that he isn't worthy of either of us.

Fathom goes to the door.

"Is this how you would have treated me if I was hurt?"

He stops, but he does not face me.

"I would have learned a new way with you," he says.

"You know, I used to think she was lucky!" I shout. "But now I'm thinking she's cursed!"

He turns. For a moment he looks as if I have stabbed him, but it vanishes just as quickly, and once again he is made of stone.

Then he leaves.

Bex and I move our beds so that we are on either side of Arcade. Mine is on the left, hers is on the right. We all lie in the dark, listening to the Triton girl's halted breathing, fearful of sleeping, in case she needs something. My parents whisper to each other in the adjacent room. My mother gets up and pours a glass of water, then paces the floor. I know she's watching over us, kneading the meat of her palm with her thumb as she does when she's nervous. Bex tosses and turns in her sheets.

It's torturous. The last thing I need is silence, because my mind fills the quiet with troubles. In three days, the children will be dropped onto a beach crawling with Rusalka, and they will die. Most likely, so will I. It was a miracle I survived that day on the beach, with the Rusalka leaping out of the waves with their hungry teeth, the prime and his insane wife trying to kill me, and the black tidal wave that nearly tore the world in two. Tens of thousands of people didn't share that miracle with me: Mr. Ervin, Gabriel, Luna, Thrill, Ghost, Surf, Mrs. Ramirez, Tammy, even Bex's stepfather, Russell—probably all dead, smashed to bits by the towering water, their bodies dragged out to sea. I don't suppose I'll get lucky again. I was so sure I would find a chink in the Tempest armor and get us all out of here, but the opportunity to find the EMP and escape never revealed itself.

What will it feel like to die? I wonder if it hurts. I wonder what happens next, or even if there is a next. The priests at church talked about heaven. They said all my friends and family who had already died would be waiting there for me. Everyone I ever knew—well, not Russell, but Shadow and the others. It would be nice to see them again. Then there's the Alpha belief—the return to the Great Abyss, the beginning and the end, the big nothing. It's hard to wrap my head around nothing. The concept of not existing, that all of this life and its troubles were pointless. It's depressing. I suppose it's why the Alpha live so fiercely. If this life is all there is, why not barrel through it?

I think of Chloe, with her sweet, hopeful eyes. I have grown to adore all the children, despite my best efforts, but she's special to me. She squirreled into my heart, with her stuffed bunny rabbit and her freckled nose. A whole life that should have been hers will probably be smashed into nothing.

And then there's Riley. I want him to live.

"Where are you going?" Bex whispers to me as I crawl out of bed.

"I'm going down to the park to train. I've got to save these kids," I tell her.

I find the guard outside my door. He looks surprised to see me this late.

"I need the team in the park," I explain.

"It's two in the morning," he argues.

"We're out of time. They can sleep if they live."

I work the kids the way Fathom works me, strictly and impatiently. They are not prepared for my change in attitude. A few cry. Tess actually curses me out, and the others stand by, bewildered, but it starts to get results. Finn makes a sudden and shocking improvement. He might even be better than me. Pierre and Harrison make great leaps too. Still, William, Dallas, Priscilla, the three sisters Tess, Emma, and Jane, and a few others are having troubles. Chloe, who I am particularly tough on, manages to do something remarkable, creating a butterfly from the pool water. It rises over the surface and flutters around the room, only to splash down like rain all around us.

• • •

"A butterfly?" Doyle says, unimpressed. "It sounds like you've got two problems, Lyric. You've got kids who aren't inspired and kids who are inspired by the wrong things."

I wave my arm around at his park, with its perfect trees and grass and the seesaw and tire swings.

"This place isn't helping them. You've built a fantasy world to keep them happy, and it's messing with their heads."

Spangler watches our argument.

"Please explain," he says, snatching his tablet and typing away furiously.

"This place is too safe and happy. It's phony, and to use these weapons, the kids need to feel something powerful and real and not . . . not sanitized. Georgia is one of the best we've got because her father's death gave her something to feel. It was raw and tragic, and she's channeled it into her ability. Listen, they're all going to come along, but we need more time to find the things that burn inside them."

"They need to feel something," Spangler says, letting me know he understands.

As he and Doyle leave, I see Fathom enter for our training session. I had completely forgotten about it, so focused was I on getting the kids ready. I honestly don't think I have it in me to be around him, even if he is trying to prepare me for war.

He walks over to the pool and undresses, and he's ready to leap in when I stop him.

"Not today," I say.

"There is not much time," he argues.

"I know. I . . . I just can't do this. I can't be around you. I don't understand how your mind works and . . . and when I look at you, I only think about our night and I don't want to think about that anymore. I'm so over all of this."

"Your anger with me is misplaced, Lyric Walker," he snaps.

"Your buddy Spangler cut Arcade's hand off, Fathom. He has tortured your people. He's tormented my family, and he's sending me to die. You're helping him. I think my anger is placed pretty well."

I hear the door bang open and watch Arcade stalk into the room. Two guards run after her with cattle prods. Bex is with them, as is my mother.

"Lyric, run!" Bex shouts.

I have to admit, I didn't see this coming. I knew she was angry with me, but I assumed we had mutual enemies.

"Arcade, I'm sorry," I say, but she doesn't listen. Instead, she leaps from one end of the room to the other, crashing down on top of me. I had no idea she could do something so incredible, and I'm completely unprepared. I tumble back into the grass and stare up at her growling face.

"You have insulted me, Lyric Walker."

"Arcade, stop," my mother demands. "I am a Daughter of Sirena and your elder. You will stop this fighting at once."

"My offense will be answered," Arcade cries.

Her Kala spring from her arms, and she cries out in pain. The damage to her hand is affecting their release, but now that they're out, she races at me, swinging her arms, trying to cut me in half.

"I have paid a high price since meeting you, bottom feeder. I promise you now that you will pay in kind."

"Arcade, stop it!" Bex shouts, but the Triton ignores her.

She springs into the air faster than I can react and comes down on me again. Her arms rise high, the edges of her blades locked on my neck, and then she brings them down. There is a crash and an explosion of sparks. Fathom has extended his own blades and has blocked her from chopping off my head.

"No," he says firmly. "I am responsible for your offense. I alone will bear your vengeance."

Arcade leaps to her feet. The fury is replaced by a cool contempt.

"Do you love this thing?" she asks him, waving at me.

He takes a deep breath and nods.

"How deeply?"

"We mated," he says.

"Lyric!" my mother cries angrily.

I'm too afraid of how Arcade is going to respond to be horrified, but she takes the news calmly.

"You are right, Fathom. It was you who have offended me. We are betrothed. We are selfsame."

"You don't love me," he says to her. "Both our hearts belong to others, Daughter of Triton. I ask for you to release me from the bonds of our parents so that we can find the happiness we both want."

"Wait! Don't include me in this," I snap, crawling to my feet. "I don't want him."

Arcade's blades slide back into her forearms.

"There is tradition, Fathom, Son of Triton," she argues. "The traditions of our empire and our clan that existed for thousands of years before the Alpha. We can't cast them off."

"The Triton are no more. What are the uses of traditions designed for a prince when there is no kingdom to rule? There is only now, and those who still live, and we can build a new way. You could be with him, Arcade."

"Who?"

"The one you love." He smiles. "I have eyes, you know."

I am so lost right now. All I know is that she doesn't look like she wants to kill me.

"I release you," he says.

"And I you," she whispers.

"Don't do this for me," I insist.

"I do not do anything for you, half-breed," Arcade snarls, and stalks past me. She bends and kneels before my mother.

"Forgive my insult, Daughter of Sirena," she begs.

My mother rests her hand on Arcade's head, then helps her stand.

"You have my respect, young one," she says.

Arcade allows the two guards to escort her back to the room, and soon she is gone.

"Um, what just happened?" Bex whispers.

"Lyric Walker, we need to have a talk," my mother growls from across the room.

Bex turns her head so my mother can't see her laughing at me.

"Please tell me I'm going to get to hear the two of you talk about how you 'mated,'" she whispers.

I wave my glove at her. "You're lucky they turned this off."

CHAPTER NINETEEN

I PRACTICE ON MY OWN. SPANGLER AGREES TO TURN OFF THE EMP, and I conjure the most violent creations ever, each one of them ripping him limb from limb in my imagination. There is so much anger and frustration in me, it fuels a surge in my control. Suddenly my ability multiplies tenfold. I experiment with different shapes, more shocking attacks. I can make a pretty wicked whip that can slice a tree in two. Arcade was right. I was holding back.

When the children file in, I'm expecting sleepy, but what I get is solemn. Tess, Emma, and Jane, already frail to begin with, look as if they might crumble under the weight of their own grief. William and Leo are distraught, as are Angela Benningford's children. Spangler stands with them and does his best to look concerned. When Riley spots me, he breaks off from the rest and hurries to my side. His eyes are red and bewildered.

"What happened?" I ask.

"Their human parents died from the sickness," he says.

"What?"

"Donovan says the doctors did all they could to save them. Lyric, I'm worried about my mom. She's been in the infirmary for almost two years. She could be next."

Spangler moves from child to child, giving them each his sad face and a hug, but his eyes are on mine daring me to react. These kids didn't lose their parents to a sickness. Spangler had them killed to give the children some raw emotion to fuel their weapons. It's so evil, it's staggering.

"This is a tragedy," he has the nerve to say. "And I'm afraid I only have more bad news. We've discovered that the illness your parents have contracted was created by the Rusalka. They brought the disease to the shore on purpose in hopes of infecting as many people as they could. They don't care about human life, kids. They don't understand what's important to us—family, compassion, and freedom, and they hate us for it. I want you to think about that when you're training with Lyric and David today. If you're feeling anger, heartbreak, and revenge, then use it. Let it power you."

Riley leads me over to the group and I step through the crowd to wrap my arms around as many of the kids as I can.

"I am so sorry," I say.

"We need to practice," Cole says through tears. "I'm going to make them pay for killing my dad."

His glove shines bright, as do all the others. They raise their hands and they radiate so intensely, I have to shield my eyes.

By the end of the session, every child manages to move the water, some with explosive and violent results. The loss has activated more than their power. It has ignited a call for vengeance, turning them all into killers. Spangler watches his handiwork with proud satisfaction.

"You're going to get justice for your families," he says as the children leave for the day. He pats each one on the back and tells them all to be brave. He tells them that only they can make sure no one died in vain.

Chloe hangs back for a moment and gives me a hug.

"If my mommy dies, will you take care of me?"

I kneel down so that my eyes are level with hers, then press my forehead against her own. Her skin is cool.

"Nothing is going to happen to your mommy. I promise," I whisper. "Go with the others. Get some rest."

Chloe runs off with her stuffed rabbit in hand, leaving Spangler and myself alone in the park. We stare hard at each other, the tension between us stretching taut to the point of snapping.

"Two days," he says to me, as if it justifies murder.

I hear the doors crash open and watch Doyle racing toward us. He tackles Spangler and knocks him to the ground. "You filthy—"

"I told you to get it done. You failed, so I took care of it."

Doyle clenches his fist, and for a few moments I'm sure he's going to slam it into Spangler's face, but he somehow finds the strength to hold back.

"I have to check on our client," Spangler says, when he gets to his feet.

We watch him leave, and once he's gone, Doyle turns to me, his face a dark soup of disgust and regret.

"Lyric, this thing between you and me stops now. I know you're angry, and I don't expect you to understand my point of view. I thought this would work. I thought I could save everybody, but I know when I am wrong. This ends today."

"What are you going to do?" I ask.

"I'm going to kill that monster."

Everything feels hot and red and sharp. I study Darren's face and then Calvin's as they escort me back to my room, wondering if they can read my mind. I'm sure everyone knows what Doyle and I are planning. Feeling a hint of the old madness I felt when I was locked in the cell. *They can see into your head. They will tell Spangler.* It's irrational, but I can't shake it.

"Lyric, what's wrong?" my father asks as he rises from the floor. He's been doing pushups again, and Mom has been scolding him.

"Spangler killed Tom Benningford."

"Angela's husband?" my father asks.

"And a few more of the human parents," I cry.

Arcade steps into the room. She eyes me warily, and I gasp.

"I didn't expect you to still be here," I say to her.

"Finish your story," she demands.

I shake off the awkwardness the best I can.

"Spangler decided the kids needed some kind of tragedy to motivate them, and it worked. They can all use the gloves now."

"Bastard," my mother says through gritted teeth.

"Doyle is going to stop him. He wants me to help," I whisper. I have no idea if we are being monitored, but it seems smart to listen to my paranoia and be careful.

"What are you going to do?" Bex says.

I walk over to the Japanese soaking tub and turn on both faucets. It causes a racket in the room so loud, I hope we can't be heard. Everyone gathers around while the sound drowns out our words.

"He wants me to bring all the kids back into the park for another training session tonight. He's going to turn off the security system. It connects a whole bunch of things — the cells, the tanks, and the EMP that blocks my connection to the water. Doyle says it takes five minutes to reboot the computer, and then everything gets locked up again, but the EMP has to be manually reset. The switch is outside. When he blows the system, he wants me to raise hell and destroy as much as I can on my way to the tanks. Then he wants me to open them all and free as many Alpha as possible while he destroys the EMP reset console."

"Lyric, this is dangerous," my father says, his voice struggling with being low. "Can you trust him? Doyle has betrayed you over and over again."

"I don't see any other way."

"You can't do this. It's one thing for him to play hero and another to use my daughter as part of the plan," he argues. "What happens when Spangler sends soldiers after the two of you?"

"He's going to kill Spangler."

Everyone is as quiet as if their words are locked inside a trunk at the bottom of the ocean. I sit down on the side of the tub and try to catch my breath, while fighting back a wave of nausea. My mother takes the space next to me and rubs my back with her hand.

"Doyle knows Spangler will come out there himself to reset the machine, and that's when he's going to do it."

"All right, how do we get you out of this?" Bex says.

I shake my head. "If there's a chance to get out of here, shouldn't I take it?"

"There's no going back afterward," Bex whispers. "I have nightmares about it every night."

"Bex, what are you talking about?" my father asks.

"I shot Russell," she says. Her expertly built walls crumble around her, and tears escape. Days before the Rusalka appeared in Coney Island, the same night that her stepfather helped a gang beat Shadow to death, Bex vanished with the "just in case" gun my father hid at the bottom of my backpack. Three days later she came back, but my family was knee-deep in the just-in-case we had always feared. There was no time to ask her what happened, and as days passed, I lost the courage. Maybe I didn't want the answer.

"I told him to meet me on the rooftop over the furniture store. I told him he could do whatever he wanted to me if he left Tammy alone."

"Rebecca," my father says, reaching for her, but she flinches.

"I let him kiss me, let him . . . I tried to be strong and make him think I was into it, but I started crying."

"Bex, no."

"But it only got him more excited. I realized he wasn't attracted to me at all. My tears were what did it for him. He was never going to stop, so I shot him."

"Honey," my mother gasps.

"The bullet missed, and the kickback made me drop the gun. When I knelt down to pick it up, he tackled me, and we fought for it. He told me he was going to do the same thing to Tammy that he did to Shadow, and he was going to make me watch. Then he was going to do it to me, and then . . . I still don't know how I got the gun back, but it was in my hand, and I pulled the trigger again. The bullet went right between his eyes, like in a cowboy movie. Smoke came out, and then he called me a bitch, and then that was it."

I leap up from my seat and rush to her, pulling her into my arms. She turns her face away and tries to free herself, but I hold on tight.

"Why didn't you tell me?" I ask.

"I didn't want to tell anyone," she whispers as she studies my father.

He shakes his head. He'll keep her secret.

"Bex, what happened to his body?" he asks.

"There was a gap between the furniture store and the apartments next door where the buildings had shifted. It was just big enough, so I rolled him over to the edge. No one would ever find him there, at least not until they demolished the buildings."

"The tidal wave made sure that would never happen," I say.

"And the gun?" my mom asks.

"I dropped the gun over the side."

"Russell killed Shadow. He did horrible things to you and Tammy," I remind her.

"But the most horrible thing he did was turn her into a murderer," my father says. "Killing changes a human being. I shot a man who was attacking people with a knife on the boardwalk, and it has never left me. I'm not saying I wouldn't do it again, or even that Spangler shouldn't be stopped, but there are repercussions to taking a man's life. Doyle is the soldier. He has been trained to kill. Let him do it."

"He can't do it by himself. What if he fails? There's only a couple days left," I say. "What if I wake up tomorrow and find out Spangler's killed more of the parents? I couldn't live with myself."

"If you kill Spangler, you might stop the children from being sent back to Coney Island," my mother says to me, then turns to my father. "It could save their lives."

"You must," Arcade says. "Look around you. Look at what he has created. He has to pay the price for this evil."

My mother takes my hands and kneels before me.

"Do it," she says.

"Summer!" my father cries.

"This place is death, and the people who work here feed off the corpse, Leonard. Spangler is the worst. If Lyric can stop him, she has to do it. She's the only one who can," my mother argues, then turns back to me. "Lyric, you are Sirena, my daughter, and the greatest regret of my life is teaching you to hide from it. Our clan is built on diplomacy, but your blood is made of countless warriors. You must fight like your grandparents and their parents before them. It is time for this camp to learn that you count yourself among them. If Doyle manages to turn that machine off, then I want you to hit this place hard and wipe it off the map."

CHAPTER TWENTY

I T ALL GOES DOWN AFTER DINNER. I MOVE FOOD AROUND ON my plate, unable to shake the thought that I'm about to help a man kill another. Spangler should die, but with each passing minute, I feel my role in it getting heavier and heavier.

Bex sits next to me. Her hand is on mine underneath the table. She has not abandoned me, though I know there have been times since we left Brooklyn when it made perfectly good sense to walk away. It was she, my besty, who steered me off a course of death. Sadly, I have found myself back on it.

My father is trying to be strong for me. My mother is resolute, revealing a side of herself that I never would have expected. And all around me are the children, eating their dinners, making ice cream sundaes, chattering away about the battle they are all so eager to join. I ache for what lies ahead if something isn't done to make sure they never get there. Spangler will drop us all into the middle of a bloodbath, but he can't if he is no longer breathing.

I give the people I love a quick glance. My mother nods.

My father does as well. Bex takes a deep breath and tries not to cry. I give her hand a squeeze, a little promise that I will not let this change me. I don't know if it's possible to keep my word, but I'm going to try.

"Have the kids meet me in the park," I tell Darren.

He calls over some guards, who offer to escort me, then calls Spangler on his radio.

"I love you," my mother says.

"We all do," my father adds.

I look to Bex.

"Good luck," she whispers.

"Do not fail," Arcade says. "And do not hold back."

Every step to the park feels like a trudge through cement. I waffle back and forth a hundred times on the plan, wanting to run back to my family and hide, then determined to help Doyle. All the while, my thoughts do a number on me. *Spangler is smarter than Doyle and me. The guards side with him. He has been one step ahead of us the whole time.* But then my anger takes charge. *He put you in a cage. He chopped off Arcade's hand. He's killing people.*

When I get to the catwalk, I'm sure we're making a mistake.

"Where's Doyle?" I ask the guards.

They call for him on their radios, but he doesn't respond.

I try to be cool about it, but the old panic returns. *Spangler knows the plan. He's already killed Doyle. He's up in my room slaughtering my friends and my parents. He's putting Arcade in the tank with the squid creature so he can watch her die.*

"Can you let Spangler know I need him to turn off the EMP? The kids can't practice with the Oracles when it's still on," I ask Darren just as the kids enter.

"You okay?" Riley asks, giving me a little nudge on the shoulder.

I nod, but I'm not really listening to anything he's saying.

Spangler enters with a bright smile.

"I love the dedication, kids," he says as he activates the machine that reveals the pool. "Show me what you can do! We don't have a lot of time left, so do your best."

My insides clench with how much I hate him. He needs to go away. I wasn't sure about it until right now. I'm going to help Doyle end this man.

The children line up to demonstrate the extent of their skills. Some are impressive, but all of them are good. Riley is still the best, then Geno and Georgia, but Cole, Breanne, Alexa, and Danny have all made dramatic overnight improvements. Tess, Emma, and Jane, as well as William, freshly wounded by the deaths of their parents, are not far behind. Even Chloe, with her tiny little body, makes a sword as big as a rowboat.

While the kids applaud, my eyes find Doyle on the catwalk high above. He paces, agitated. He checks his watch and disappears. The plan has started.

"Lyric, I did it," Chloe says proudly.

"That's great news," I say, leaning down to hold her hands. "Chloe, I want you to stay very close to Riley tonight. Can you promise me you'll do that?"

She nods.

"Good. Riley, don't let her out of your sight. Keep her close."

"Why? What's happening?"

"Lyric, you're not looking," Chloe scolds when she creates a dolphin that leaps into the sky.

"It's beautiful," I say, then scan the room for the other kids. I want to know where they are when the system crashes so I don't accidentally hurt anybody.

There's a piercing alarm, and lights go out. The ceiling glows with red emergency lights, and backup illumination appears above the exit doors. The children cry out, but Spangler and the guards urge them to stay calm.

"What's going on?" Breanne cries.

Spangler taps his screen, then does it again. He looks up at me, and suddenly his concerned face changes to one of understanding.

"This was a very dumb move, Lyric," Spangler says, then taps on his tablet and races off as soldiers rush into the room. Half attempt to corral the children, while the other half aim their guns at me.

"Lyric, what is happening?" Tess cries.

"Stick together!" I shout.

It's time to do my part. I power up my glove, and it burns brighter than I have ever seen it.

What would you have us do?

"Help me put a stop to this place," I whisper back.

The pool comes alive, bubbling and spilling over its sides. The water reaches up and snatches the armed guards nearby, violently jerking them off the ground like dolls and pulling them under. More soldiers charge through the doors, shouting orders, but I send a lightning-fast whip that smacks them across the room. With my path clear, I sprint forward, only to be clobbered from behind by a wall of salty liquid. I tumble to the grass, end over end, and land flat on my back. When my head stops ringing, I find Riley and his glove glowing in my face.

"I'm sorry. I don't know what's happening, but you can't—"

This is exactly what I feared. Riley and the other kids are siding with Spangler. I yank half the water out of the pool and throw it at Riley. He slides across the lawn as scales appear on forearms and neck, fiery red with confusion and anger.

"I'm sorry too," I say as I scamper back to my feet. "I'm bringing this place down right now. If you're smart, you won't try to stop me. Get away from here and take whoever you can with you."

"I thought you were one of us," he cries.

I dart through the double doors and into the hall as soldiers pop up in my way. I cause the pipes to burst on either side of them, and they fall over like chess pieces. I leap over their unconscious bodies and continue onward, racing up a flight of stairs to the cells, just like Doyle and I planned.

Bullets skitter on the floor near my feet. I turn and bring geysers up to destroy the flooring behind me. I watch several men topple into the massive hole I've created. That will buy me a little time.

"Lyric?"

I turn to see familiar faces. These are the parents of the children I've been training. They are filthy and bewildered but free from their cells; shorting out the system has released them. They take tentative steps into the hall.

"There's a flight of steps behind that exit door!" I shout, pointing across the hall. "Take them up until you find the surface. Get as far away as you can. I want to help you all, but there are so many others to save. Run. Don't stop!"

At the end of the hall is another door, and I slam through it to find another flight of steps. Once I reach the top, I'm in an identical situation as on the floor below—faced with dozens of scrawny, starving people who are afraid of what has happened. I tell them pretty much what I told the others, but this time a group of heavily armed soldiers storms into the hall. They open fire. People scream and fall to the ground. I see blood, but I can't tell who it belongs to. The water in the pipes along the ceiling shouts to me, and I free it. It's boiling hot and it burns the guards, but it avoids the prisoners completely. The soldiers scream, trying to get away from the attack. One hits the ground near me, and his rifle falls out of his hands. I snatch it off the floor and shove it into the hands of a tiny Asian woman who looks like she's been locked up for years. I don't stop to ask her if she knows how to use the weapon. If not, I hope she's a fast learner.

I race onward, up another stairwell, into a hallway where I find the elevator. I also find Fathom blocking my way.

"Lyric Walker, whatever you are doing must stop," he says.

I could stand here and let him try to explain why he's done me wrong. I could give him a chance to persuade me that Spangler's plans are good for us all, but I'm sort of sick of this kid's face. I have never turned my power on another person the way I do Fathom. Water hits him from every side, like four tractor-trailers crashing through an intersection and he's caught in the middle. It sends him crashing through the adjacent wall and out of my path.

I jam the elevator button, but nothing happens. I jam it again and notice the sensor pad. I'm so stupid! I need a passkey!

I use some water on the floor to help me pry the doors open and look down into the blackness of the elevator shaft. Up is no more inviting. There's just no way I can climb it. I'm sure I'd fall to my death the second I tried. I'm going to have to get creative. I'm unsure how far the shaft goes down, but if there's water at the bottom, I need it. I extend my hand into the void and bear down with my mind. What was it the preacher said about this valley? The mountains block the moisture. It's the driest place in the country. Still, there has to be some, maybe down in the bedrock below us, hundreds of feet deep. I feel some wetness on my lip. The nosebleed has started, and I'm beginning to feel a dull headache from trying so hard. Things are getting a little fuzzy, and then —

We are here, Lyric.

"Come," I whisper.

There's a rumbling from far below, an explosion, and *whoosh!* I watch the liquid blast up through the shaft, filling the space and rising higher. My hand gets whipped upward from the gushing water. I've made my own elevator.

I have no idea why I hold my breath. Maybe it's an old habit dying hard, but I do, and then I leap. The current rockets my body upward, higher and higher. My scales appear, and my gills take over for my lungs. The whole experience is . . . magical. I'm about to reach the very top floor, and with a sweep of my arm, the doors fly off. It's pretty badass, if I do say so myself. They crash into the laboratory, and water spills onto the floor, flooding everything. Unfortunately, I go with it. It's not the most elegant entrance. I flop around like a crab in a net, but it certainly gets everyone's attention. Spangler's science staff stands around me, gaping and dumbfounded. That is, until I stand, and they fall over themselves to get out of my way.

"How do you let them out of the tanks?" I shout. No one answers. I should have grabbed one of those nerds and forced them to help me.

"Lyric!"

I turn, half expecting Fathom, only to find Riley stepping out of my water elevator. He's dripping wet, breathless, and his eyes are wild and troubled. He's also got his weapon ready.

"Riley, please don't try to stop me," I beg. "I only have a little time to get this done."

"Get what done? What is this place?" he asks, staring hard at the tanks.

"This is where they keep the Alpha parents," I explain.

"You lie!" he shouts angrily.

"Riley, Tempest is the lie. Everything Spangler and Doyle and the guards have told you about this place is a lie. Your human parents aren't sick. They've been prisoners locked up in this building, and your Alpha parents are in these tanks."

"That's not true!" he shouts.

Water seeps out of the elevator and wraps itself around a chair. Suddenly, it's off the floor and sailing right at my head. I manage to command it to slam into a wall before it clobbers me, but it was close.

"It is! I've seen it all. I was locked away myself. Spangler only let me out when I promised to train you with the gloves."

Another chair soars across the room. A leg clips me in the side, and my ribs burn.

"Riley, I don't want to fight you, but I will, and I'm a lot better with this thing than you are, so do yourself a favor and just look around!" I scream.

He stops his assault and does as I ask, his head whipping from one end of the room to the other. Suddenly, he's running at me and I'm sure he's going to attack again, but then he sails past me to one of the tanks. It has an unconscious Selkie floating in it, most likely unaware of what is happening around him. Riley stumbles to the next tank and the next, and I hear him gasp when he comes across one filled with Rusalka hands. He turns and sees another with human body parts, and finally he comes across a Sirena whose chest cavity has been opened wide so that we can see her beating heart.

"My father? Is he here too?"

I nod.

"You can help me rescue him and all the others."

"What's real?" he shouts. "Is the plague real?"

"No!" I shout to him as I plant myself in front of a computer. I search the screen, looking for a button that might say OPEN TANKS or STOP BEING EVIL. I quickly realize I'm wasting my time. I press a few buttons, hoping to get lucky, but nothing happens. All I know about computers is how to make a Vine.

"Then the parents didn't die?"

"He killed them!" I shout. "He needs all of you to be as good with the gloves as you can be, and giving you something traumatic and worth fighting for did the trick."

"Coney Island?"

"That's real. He's sending you to fight the Rusalka, but none of you are ready. Riley, I know you have a million questions, but right now we have a very limited amount of time. We have to get these people out of these tanks."

I hear a crash and then the sound of sloshing water. I turn to find one of the tanks has cracked, and a man tumbles out onto the floor. Riley scoops him up and pats his face, trying to wake him up.

"Dad, I need you to get up and walk."

I wasn't prepared for the Alpha to be drugged, but there's no going back now. I turn and find a Ceto sinking in its tank. A sign has been taped onto the glass that reads CETO NAME: BUMPER.

"Bumper!" I cry, remembering her from school. I concentrate on the water behind the glass. There's a crack and then another gush of water onto the floor. Bumper falls out with it and flops about as she morphs into her more human form. I take her squishy hand and lock eyes with hers. She recognizes me.

"It appears that I have missed some important events," she says.

"Riley, get to work on the others!" I shout.

He's reluctant to leave his father, but he does what I tell him. Soon another tank is shattering next to us, releasing a Sirena. I do the same to Nathan, the pufferfish man. When he spills out of the tank, he nearly knocks me down.

Riley rushes to another tank and is about to break it when I stop him. Inside is the squid creature Spangler warned me about. Its hundreds of tentacles slam against its tank. I don't believe much of what Spangler has said, but when it comes to this thing, I think he was telling the truth.

"Not this one. And skip the Rusalka, too."

"What about these people who are torn open?" Riley cries.

I shake my head, though it hurts my heart.

"We can't help them. If we open their tanks, they could die. It might be cruel to leave them here, but if they're alive, they still have a chance at rescue."

"Why didn't you tell me, Lyric?"

"Spangler threatened the people I love, Riley," I explain as I free an adult Triton I've never seen before.

"Is Uncle David part of this?"

I groan. "Yes! *Doyle* is part of this. He still might be, but right now he's trying to do the right thing."

The lights dim and flicker.

"What was that?" Riley asks.

"I don't know, but it would suck if that's the system rebooting," I say. "Listen, we need to break open all these tanks at once, but again, keep the ugly ones in time-out."

"I don't know if I can," Riley says.

I take his hand, and we turn our gloves on the tanks. I watch them rattle and shake. There's an ear-jamming crash and then the sound of gallons of water spilling everywhere. It rushes at us, and I'm so focused on freeing everyone, I'm not ready for it. Both of us are pulled under and slammed around. I bang the back of my head on something, and the pain is searing. All the time, Riley holds my hand. He never lets me go, and eventually he gets me to my feet.

"Are you all right?" he asks.

"I'll survive," I say.

"What now?"

"The rest is up to Doyle," I explain.

"Lyric?" Spangler's voice broadcasts through speakers mounted in the corners of the ceiling. I hear it echo outside, too, and in the halls. It's everywhere. "Lyric, it's Donovan. David and I are outside, and we need to have a chat."

"Riley, stay here and help everyone you can," I say.

"No way!" he cries. "I'm not letting you go out there alone, not after what you told me about him."

"*Lyyyyrrrriiccc*," Spangler sings. "Come on out."

"Riley, please," I say. "These are our people, and they need you more than I do right now."

I walk past all the tanks to the elevator. The water has sunk back down, but it's a simple thing to recall it. I leap into the shaft, and it rises to catch me. I go down one floor, force the doors open, and then race down a hall until I find an emergency exit door. I push it open and find myself outside in the chilly Texas night. My wet skin and clothes make it even worse, but I have to keep going. I race around the building's perimeter with only the moon to light my way until I find Spangler and Doyle. Both men are aiming guns at each other.

"Lyric, it's over," Spangler says.

"All the Alpha and the human parents are free. Soon the kids will know about your lies," Doyle says to him.

Spangler smiles like he's being patient with a small child.

"That's going to be tedious to clean up, but it's not

unmanageable. I'm willing to let this go, but you have to power down now, Lyric. I'm going to reset the EMP's console, and then we're all going to go back inside and go to bed. We have a big mission soon."

"Put the gun down, Spangler. I'm not going to tell you again," Doyle demands.

"I've got this," I say. I call two waterspouts from deep in the earth. They shoot out of the ground and collect in a puddle at Spangler's feet.

"I have to say I'm impressed by this act of teamwork. The thing is, we're all on the same team. It's true, Lyric. Down deep, both you and David understand what's at stake. We're all trying to save the world."

What happens next, I might truly never understand. It all seems to happen at once, yet I witness everything as if it is its own exclusive event. Spangler spins and slams his free hand on a button inside the door of the electrical shed, and all at once I don't feel the connection anymore. Doyle fires his gun. Spangler's eyes roll into the back of his head, and he falls to the ground. He stares up at the stars and dies.

"It's over," Doyle says.

There's another gunshot, and Doyle falls. His body lies next to Spangler's, and the two of them leave this world together. I turn to find a wheelchair rolling into the light. Calvin is pushing it along, and in the seat is Governor Bachman, her hand wrapped around a pistol. Her body leans sharply to the left, as if her spine has been cracked and put back together by a child.

Her face is marred by a jagged purple scar that cuts a wide canal from the corner of her mouth up to her dead white eye. Despite it all, she's got the whitest teeth I've ever seen.

I can't believe she's alive. When the Rusalka arrived on our shore, the Navy sent ships to intercept them, but the creatures used their gloves to lift a battleship out of the water and hurl it onshore. Bachman was in its path. The fact that she's breathing is a miracle.

Her eyes hold me in place and burn with hostility. Her hands tremble as they lift a red, white, and blue megaphone to her mouth. Then an ear-piercing feedback whine stabs my ears, and a series of ugly barks and mumbling moans flies into the desert. I have no idea what she actually said, but the tone is crystal clear. She hates me.

She gestures to the guard, and Calvin jumps into action, walking over to Spangler's body and taking his tablet. He hands it to the governor, who trades him the gun. She taps on the screen and hands it back to Calvin.

"'I'm the client,'" he reads. "'If you understand that, then we can move on. We've got a lot of packing to do.'"

CHAPTER TWENTY-ONE

I SIT IN THE CAFETERIA, SHAKING UNCONTROLLABLY. RILEY sits next to me, with my hand in his. He's trying to comfort me, but I need more than a hand to feel better now.

The governor sits at our table in her chair while Calvin empties the contents of a plastic bag into a cup. It's a murky green substance that smells both sweet and foul at the same time. Calvin inserts a straw, and she slurps it. Most of it dribbles down her chin, and Calvin is there to wipe her clean after every attempt. All the while, she taps on her machine.

"Everyone was captured and placed back into holding cells for their safekeeping," Calvin explains.

"What about my family and friends?" I ask.

Bachman shakes her head.

"She still needs you to live up to your commitment and suspects that taking them from you would only cause delays," Calvin says. "The Rusalka attacks have escalated, and we no longer have time for a battle of wills. We're leaving today."

"Today?" Riley cries.

"What do you mean 'escalated'?" I demand.

Bachman presses some buttons and then spins her tablet so we can see. What appears are images of the prime walking onshore while hundreds, maybe even thousands, of Rusalka swarm behind him.

"I don't know what to believe," Riley says, exasperated. "Who is telling the truth? Is any of this real? Are we really under attack?"

Calvin nods. "The governor and I, along with several of our intelligence agents, will escort you to the front, where you will be placed under the command of Major Tom Kita of Marine Special Operations Forces."

"What about the others? What about our families?" Riley cries.

Calvin takes Bachman's tablet after she taps into it, then reads her response.

"'Your parents, along with Lyric's, will accompany you. As will Ms. Conrad, the Triton prince, and the Triton girl. Everyone else stays.'"

"No way!" Riley shouts. "Everyone goes free."

"Here is the deal on the table," Calvin says. "You fight. You kill the monsters. Your Alpha and human parents go free. Everyone else stays. If you tell the other children any of this, we will kill all of the human parents. They are expensive to the bottom line of this company anyway."

"We can't win!" I say.

Bachman taps on her tablet.

"'I know,'" Calvin reads. "'You are grotesque to me and

the rest of America, but you may kill a few of them before they kill you.'"

I stand up and lean over Bachman. "What did you do with Doyle?"

She shifts uncomfortably.

"If you bury him—all of him—then I'll go," I say. "He was a soldier. He deserves a burial."

She shrugs.

"You got it," Calvin says.

"I've got your back," Riley says as they escort us to our rooms.

I lean in and kiss him. Maybe it's inappropriate. Maybe it's sending the wrong signals. Maybe I'm not thinking straight and I'm scared and in the middle of a nervous breakdown. Or maybe I just want to kiss somebody who wants to kiss me, somebody who's not in a loser triangle. It's a nice kiss. It doesn't pull me into an undertow, but it's got potential. It's probably the last one I'll ever have.

The story Calvin tells the children is that Mr. Spangler and Mr. Doyle have the sickness and, during the crisis, Riley and I raced to get them to the infirmary. Only a moron would believe that story. It makes zero sense, but the kids don't question it. Their blind acceptance makes me fear for them all the more.

We gather in the park. The children, Riley's family, my own, Bex, and Arcade. Fathom hovers in the shadows.

Everyone is looking at me. I suspect they are holding their breath until I give them permission to breathe.

"You need to say something to them," Riley whispers to me. "They're all afraid."

"They should be afraid," I whisper back.

"They don't need to know that," he says. "Give them some hope. Who knows what could happen? You survived the first attack, didn't you? You didn't think you'd survive this place, but you did. Miracles happen. I just had one happen to me."

He gives me that smile again, and I take it.

"You're that boy who pushes people to do things they're not comfortable with, right?"

He nods earnestly. "Talk to them."

I turn and look out on their faces. They stare back at me, waiting for some kind of guidance, but I have no idea what to say. I bet my dad would nail a speech like the one they need. Even Bex would be good at it. But it's me.

Breathe, Lyric.

"Today is the day," I stammer. "We've been training for it and now it's here, and we're going to save the world. I'm not going to lie and I'm not going to candy-coat it like Spangler and Doyle did. Some of us may die today. We are children going off to face monsters. There are only thirty-three of us. There are thousands of them. We are saddled with human feelings like mercy and fear and kindness. They make us weak. Our enemies aren't burdened with things like that. They only know revenge and bloodlust.

"So why send us? The answer is simple. We are special. We can do things that a normal person cannot, and we're fighting something the world cannot deal with on its own. So it's up to us. That's a lot to put on our shoulders. But like I said, we're special. We can breathe underwater. We have weapons that can break the ocean apart. And we've been trained to fight. But that's not why we're going to win. We're going to beat those things because we have each other. Look around you. Look into the faces of your friends. We aren't just a group of people thrown together to fight for a good cause. We're family. In fact, we are related by blood now. We are our own Alpha clan."

"The Sons and Daughters of Lyric," my mother shouts. The kids clap and cheer but I'm too embarrassed.

"We're going to stick together today and that's how we'll beat them, because our enemy may know how to do terrible things but it doesn't feel like we do. It doesn't know what it's like to be part of a family. It doesn't know that we will fight and die to protect one another.

"Stay close to one another and stay close to me. Keep your eyes out for those around you. Make sure that if they fall, you pick them up. And stay close to me," I say as Chloe steps forward to take my hand. "I will keep my eye on each and every one of you. You are my family now, and in my family if you want to pick a fight with one of us, you have to fight us all."

"We're going to win because they have to fight us all," Riley shouts.

When everyone is packed and ready, we head outside to the airstrip, where a plane is waiting for us. My father hobbles along, a reminder that he is still not one hundred percent, but standing tall, nonetheless.

Waiting for us are Terrance, Rochelle, and Samuel Lir. Gone is his wheelchair. Samuel has two walking canes now. He smiles at me, and I smile back, even though Bachman isn't going to let him leave. The Lirs are too valuable to White Tower. I worry he will never escape this place. I promise myself that when this is done, I will come back and rescue everyone.

"He's feeding himself," Terrance says to me.

"It's an amazing thing," I say sincerely. "They'll take him apart if they get the chance."

He nods grimly. "Come back for us."

Chloe joins me at the airstrip. She's in a jumpsuit with her glove polished and a pack on her back.

"Where's Mr. Fluffer?" I ask when I notice the bunny is not in her hands.

She smiles.

"I don't need him anymore. I have you."

"It's cold in New York right now," a guard shouts as he hands out hats and gloves. He gives everyone a jacket with the White Tower logo. It has an American flag patch on the shoulder and the words PROPERTY OF THE UNITED STATES OF AMERICA stenciled on the back. "Put everything on, and keep it on."

Bex stands next to me, holding my hand. Riley is nearby,

waiting in his jumpsuit. His mother and father look bewildered. He holds his mother's thin hand like it's the only thing keeping her standing.

Calvin wheels Bachman into the crowd of children. Word spreads about her injuries, a fairy tale about how she was hurt fighting the Rusalka. They gape at her disfiguring scars. They can't help themselves.

"All right, let's do this," Darren says. He stands by the steps to the plane and helps the children climb them, one by one. Riley's father gives the guard a shove when the guard tries to help his wife. Darren's eyes alight with fear from his strength. I smile. I like Riley's dad a lot. I do the same to the toady when it's time to get Dad on board, though I doubt my skinny arms give him much pause.

The inside of the plane is not what I was expecting. Whenever I've seen movies set on planes, there are flight attendants and overhead space and little trays for drinks. This plane is stripped down like it's designed for flying packages more than people. My mother sits with my dad, and I take a seat behind them with Bex. Riley sits across the row from us and gives me a fist bump. It's so corny, but I grin.

Bex shakes her head and rolls her eyes.

"Your next boyfriend can't have fins," she whispers.

"None of my boyfriends have ever had fins. Besides, I'm giving up on boys. It's you and me, Conrad," I tease. "If we survive, I'm thinking we move in together and be crazy cat ladies."

"Deal." She sighs.

Arcade boards, followed by Fathom. They are silent and pass us on their way to the back. She doesn't look at me at all, and when he passes, my face burns and I look to the floor. I notice Riley watching, but he plays it cool and doesn't say anything, even when I crane my neck to take a peek at them. Arcade finds a seat first and Fathom tries to sit next to her, but she shoots him a look and he's smart enough to sit a few rows farther back.

Fathom closes his eyes and leans into his headrest. He looks nervous and lonely. Despite everything he has done, part of me wants to walk back there and hold his hand during takeoff, but a bigger part tells the first part that it's stupid. Soon enough, both parts resume hating him.

Bex takes my hand when they close the airplane door.

"Have you ever been on a plane before?" she asks.

I laugh, remembering how cheaply we used to live back in Coney Island. A plane ride was much too fancy, and we never went anywhere on vacation anyway.

I shake my head.

"With our luck, this thing will crash," she whispers.

"Oh, now, we're not going to get that lucky," I say when the engines rumble so loud, I can feel them in my legs. "We'll get there. Coney Island is worse than a plane crash."

We descend into JFK five hours later, and I am startled to see snow flurries. Bex is as troubled by it as I am. It's a painful reminder of how long we have been away from our home and how long we have been locked in the camp.

We touch down, then taxi to a small hangar on the far side of the airport. Outside the window, I see something disturbing. There are soldiers everywhere, real ones, in the hangar, guarding the tarmac and waiting for us. Military vehicles are parked all over. Planes have been pushed together in an awkward jumble to get them out of the way. I've never been to JFK but I know this isn't right. Looks like the airport is now the property of the United States military.

The pilot parks the plane and then opens the cabin door. A blast of early-winter air dances down the aisle, and I zip up my jumpsuit. We're definitely going to need those hats and gloves.

A huge green bus waits for us at the bottom of the steps. Its driver is a tall, broad-chested soldier who can't be more than a couple of years older than me. His face is set and serious but slightly confused. I have a feeling he didn't know he was going to chauffer the "terrorist" and a bunch of children around today. When they bring Bachman down the steps, he can't hide his shock.

"Yeah, the freaks have landed," I say to him.

We board his bus, and he drives us south on the Belt Parkway. The whole road is ours. Never in my life have I seen an empty street in New York City, especially at this time of day. There should be bumper-to-bumper deadlock, cars creeping along like snails, but today it's barren and lonely. A few military jeeps drive on the other side, but other than that, nothing—all the way through Queens and into Brooklyn. It's sobering. Even the children who haven't seen their hometown in years appear to know this is wrong. They press their faces against the windows and stare out at a dead city.

The drive to Coney Island takes about half an hour. We pull off at the Cropsey Avenue exit, several exits before the beach. These roads are as barren of cars as the highway but overflowing with rubbish and devastated by monstrous potholes. We bounce up and down as the driver weaves around craters. I look out the window and see a burned-out car sitting on its side like roadkill.

It's all a maze to me, the way he backtracks and makes turn after turn to avoid roadblocks, downed power lines, and abandoned cars. I recognize only little things—a storefront, a street corner where we used to meet, but it doesn't look like my home. Everywhere, I see a brown stain that runs parallel on all the buildings, marking how high the water was after the tidal wave came. It's above the second-story windows here, and we're still nearly two miles from the beach.

The homes we pass look empty and deserted. Some have burned to the ground. Big letter B's are painted on the walls with numbers—some kind of code—B2, B5, B7.

"What's with the numbers?" I call out to the driver.

"That's how many bodies were found inside," he says, his eyes meeting mine in his rearview mirror. He blames me for this.

Bachman sits at the front in a special space for wheelchairs. She turns her head and flashes me the same look the soldier did.

Eventually, the driver takes us as far as he can. He explains that the roads beyond are for emergency vehicles only. We're walking the rest of the way.

"We're not an emergency vehicle?" my father asks.

"Roads are dedicated to vehicles in retreat from the battle zones, sir," the soldier explains.

As we step off into the road, I hear rapid-fire pops that come in short bursts, pause, and then repeat. There's a huge explosion, and the guns resume again. Bex and my father give me wary looks, but the children seem fine. Doyle told me he taught them how to use firearms, so maybe they're used to the noise they make. It's not like I haven't heard gunshots before, just not so many.

Waiting for us is a tall African American soldier, maybe in his early thirties, with dark, tired eyes that look like they haven't seen a lot of sleep lately. He's wearing sandy-colored camouflage and heavy boots and has an M-16 in his hands. He tells us his name is Jackson, but I can't be certain if that's his first or last.

Calvin wheels Governor Bachman forward.

"Are you authorized to sign for this delivery?" Calvin asks.

"Are you from White Tower? What happened to Spangler?"

"He's pursuing other opportunities," Calvin says. "Allow me to introduce you to former New York State governor and now acting CEO of White Tower Pauline Bachman. If you would be so kind as to sign this acceptance form, we can transfer ownership to you."

He hands Jackson the tablet, but the soldier doesn't take it. Instead, he shoots Calvin a dismissive look that sours even more on its way to Bachman.

"These are babies," he says, gesturing to my team.

"You're mistaken," Calvin says, pushing the tablet at Jackson again. "These are thirty-three human-Alpha hybrids who can breathe underwater. They are trained in combat and equipped with fully functioning Oracles."

"What?" Jackson balks.

Calvin reaches over and snatches Tess by the wrist, waving her glove in front of Jackson.

"The devices that allow them to control water, sir. They are also armed with handguns and ammunition. Ms. Bachman is so pleased with the relationship that White Tower has with the U.S. military, she is also throwing in four full-blooded Alphas, two Tritons, and two Sirena at no extra charge. We appreciate your patronage. All you need to do is sign the screen with your finger."

Jackson studies us once more, and looks confused and irritated by this unwelcome surprise. He sees what I've seen all along. We're a bunch of children sent to war. He lifts his radio to his mouth and walks a few yards away, telling someone more important than himself what White Tower has tried to dump in his lap. After a moment, he returns. I can also see he has no choice. He signs Bachman's tablet.

As he finishes, Calvin steps forward with a metal box and places it on the ground at Jackson's feet.

"This is a portable EMP. It's set on a timer right now that will shut off in fifteen minutes. Only then will their weapons activate."

"Long enough for you to get far, far away from me," I say.

Bachman locks her eyes on mine. She wears what might be an obviously triumphant smile if her features weren't so mangled.

"Fourteen minutes, Governor," I whisper to her. "And then I can throw another battleship at you."

She blanches, then gestures for Calvin to wheel her back to the bus. It's heartbreaking, but she won. I'm here with the kids in the most dangerous town on earth, and she gets to go back to her mad scientists' lab. She still has the parents and the Alpha and the Lirs. She's still the boss. Doyle was right. White Tower replaced Spangler with someone worse.

"I'm coming back for you, Governor!" I shout to her.

Neither Calvin nor Bachman acknowledges my threat. They get on the bus with the rest of their White Tower guards, and soon they are gone.

"We're going to the beach!" Jackson shouts in a thick southern drawl I didn't notice until now. "Keep your eyes open. Sea monsters are not the only problem we have around here. There are still a handful of locals living in the demilitarized zone. They're die-hards who would rather face the risk of being eaten by Rusalka than leave their homes. They are heavily armed and can get violent if they feel threatened. If we encounter one, please let me handle it. You should also keep an eye out for stray dogs. Packs of them wander the streets, and they're hungry. Most of them aren't very nice. But our biggest concern at this moment is the roamers."

"Roamers?" Riley asks.

"The creatures sent a wave at us this morning. When that happens, you can bet a few of them are in it. They get behind our fortifications and cause trouble. They pop up everywhere."

I look around and then to my mother and father.

"We're not all Alpha," I say. "My father is injured, and we've got people here who aren't trained to fight. Is there a safe place they should go?"

"Command wants everyone, so everyone is coming. Do your best to keep up," he says sympathetically.

"Mom, help Dad, and Dad, you let her," I scold. "Bex—"

"She will be my responsibility," Arcade says, stepping forward.

"Thank you," I say.

She shrugs.

I grab Chloe by the hand. "You're with me."

"All right, let's move—" Jackson's voice is drowned by gunfire nearby and what sounds like a shrieking.

"Rusalka!" Fathom shouts.

The children reach into their pockets and remove their

handguns. They load them quickly and then grab the free hand of someone smaller. They're calm. Doyle did a good job with them.

"Run!" Jackson commands, and he takes off at a sprint, pointing his rifle down every intersection we pass. At one street corner, I see a Rusalka running in our direction, snarling and growling like a lion. Jackson fires again and again, going through two or three dozen rounds. Finally, Georgia joins the firefight and the creature falls to the ground dead.

"It takes a lot to put one down!" Jackson shouts to us as he continues running. "Everyone needs to be watching. If you spot a roamer, I need you to shout it loudly and clearly and then get out of my way. I can't have you between me and them, understand?"

Georgia nods.

"Good shot, by the way," he admits to her.

We climb over piles of trash and broken bicycles. This can't be good for my father's ribs, but he doesn't complain. My mother helps him when he will let her. We race down a new street until we reach a place in the road where a yellow school bus has crashed. To me it looks like the soldiers have used a welding torch to cut a path right through its belly. It still requires a few awkward steps, but we get through. I help Chloe over every obstacle.

"Are you okay?" I ask Chloe.

Her eyes show panic, but she nods bravely.

On the next block, there are houses shoved off their

foundations, now sitting squarely in the street. On the side of the road is a car from the Cyclone. Its blue paint is a shocking hue in this cold and gray world. I spot bicycles and baby carriages hanging in tree limbs high above the ground. Toys and books and photo albums lay strewn in the gutter. A discarded birthday hat is impaled on a twig, fluttering in the frosty breeze. There are empty lots where only the basement remains, filled to the top with murky, fuel-tainted muck. Everywhere I look, I see the death-count numbers. B8. B3. B5. B12. Some are painted on the sidewalk or a street lamp because the house that once stood there is gone.

We turn down a side road to get around the debris, and that's when I see the fate of the Wonder Wheel. It lies flat on its back, having crushed several brownstones and a post office when it fell. It looks like a bully shoved it to the ground. The Wheel was a huge landmark, part of the neighborhood's history. I used to use it to navigate the streets when I was a kid. It always pointed me south, toward the beach. The wave not only toppled it but dragged the whole thing right through the neighborhood. It's far from where it once stood. I can't even see the water from here.

We're joined by two more soldiers, who keep up with Jackson's sprint. One has a bulky bandage on his hand. The other has a fresh wound on his cheek.

"Are these them?" they shout to us in disbelief.

"That's what showed up," Jackson shouts back.

The other soldiers curse in frustration.

"Rusalka are flooding the beach. We've got a squadron handling it and bombers on the way," the soldier with the bandage explains. "Command is pinned down in that abandoned building."

A few blocks ahead, we come across a dozen more soldiers running perpendicular to us. Their gunshots ring through the air. I can't see what they're firing at, but it causes Jackson to tense up. He drags us off the road behind a burned-out semi-trailer. While we wait, he calls out to someone on his radio. The voice on the other end tells him to hold his position. Moments later, I watch four fighter jets scream overhead, low enough to clip the tops of apartment buildings.

"Cover your ears!" Jackson orders.

The air rumbles and builds into a shocking catastrophe. It jostles my bones and organs.

"The bombers have just knocked a hole through the Rusalka, but we have to act fast. There are a few buildings about a quarter mile from here that the waves haven't destroyed yet. They're as close to the frontline as I can get you, and it's where Major Kita is waiting for us. We need to get there and help. Are you kids up to this?"

"We are," Priscilla says.

I turn and see that all the kids are nodding. Their faces are firm and serious. Each has taken a handgun from their packs. It's unsettling, especially the little ones.

Jackson is off like a dart, and the children follow him into the battle zone. Gunfire comes from every direction. Bullets tear through the air and crash into the ground. Rusalka spring up everywhere we go, seemingly out of thin air, before the kids turn their guns on them. I watch one Rusalka fall, get up, fall again, then leap back to its feet as if the bullets were mere annoyances. No wonder the military has such a tough time with them. They won't stay down.

Another Rusalka leaps into our path. Jackson raises his gun, but the monster swipes it out of his grip. Jackson falls backwards, scampering for some kind of footing, but the beast stalks him. He takes a look at us, then stops. There's a crackling sound near my ear; then a geyser rises up from beneath the monster, sending the ugly thing flailing into the air. It slams to the ground in an unnatural position.

I turn and realize that Chloe's glove is glowing and bright. She's smiling proudly.

"Good girl," I say, then turn to help Jackson stand. By the time he's upright, there are thirty more Rusalka in our way.

Arcade and Fathom sprint ahead, faster and more agile than any human could hope to be. Their Kala pop out of their arms and flash in the gray sky. They bring them down on the monsters' heads. Fathom tears into their bellies, spilling black blood into the street. Arcade goes for their limbs, and blood falls like rain. My mother hurries to join them, delivering punches that cripple Rusalka where they stand. She's fast and vicious, breaking the creatures in half. My father swings at the beasts with a metal pipe he found in the road. All the while, the soldiers keep up their assault, firing at anything that gets close.

Jackson takes my arm. He points toward the beach amid the gun smoke and fires.

"It's there!"

A building rises into view, not far from where the boardwalk once stood. I recognize it immediately as the remains of Childs Restaurant, an abandoned eyesore that's been standing for longer than I've been alive. I've walked past it a million times, not giving it much attention. Now that my life depends on reaching it, I notice its bizarre architecture with its arches and crenelations. I can't believe that of all the buildings in this town, it counts itself among the survivors and that it's the site of the military's line in the sand.

Jackson urges us onward so I snatch Chloe, and we dash through the sand until we reach the building, then race through an open door. Everyone follows.

The inside of the old restaurant is a beehive of activity. Soldiers work on laptops plugged into generators. Maps of the coastline and sonar images of the ocean floor are tacked to the walls, each marked with red circles and lines. Almost everyone is shouting into a radio or calling someone on a phone. There are cases of ammunition on one side of the room and canoes and kayaks stacked near the doors.

"What are those for?" I ask Jackson.

"Getaway cars," he says.

This was once a fancy eatery with tiled floors, marble columns, and tin ceilings; now armed soldiers hover at every window, some with rifles, others with rocket launchers. They are all trained on the shoreline. They fire over and over again. I peer out of one window and see the beach beyond. It's swarming with Rusalka and soldiers, all in a struggle for control of the shore. The more Rusalka die, the more crawl out of the sea, clambering over the bodies of their dead brothers and sisters.

I turn away, too terrified to look any longer. It's insane for us to be this close. I gather the children to me, preparing to make a run for it at any moment.

"Major Kita, the White Tower team has arrived," Jackson explains as he approaches an older, graying soldier in camo gear. Kita is trim and clean-cut, Japanese American, and, based on how the others treat him, the man in charge. His chest full of medals is another clue.

Kita turns and studies us, unable to hide his confusion and irritation. We're just as much an unwelcome surprise to him as we were to Jackson when we arrived.

"You're Lyric Walker," he says, stepping to face me.

"I am."

"Can all the children do what you can?"

"No," I confess. "But all of them have some ability."

"I appreciate the honesty, so let's keep running down that road. Can I trust you?"

"You can trust that I'm going to do everything I can to keep these kids alive. If we survive, we're all going to walk away, and if you try to stop us, you'll regret it."

It sounds so badass, I just hope my face matches the words.

"If we survive this, I'll buy you all bus tickets out of town myself," he promises. "You kids ready to clock in?"

I nod.

"Find a window and help a soldier!" he shouts to us. The children look to me for approval, and I nod. They each race to follow their orders, turning on their gloves and blasting Rusalka from the safety of the building. Riley shouts out suggestions and cheers the team every time a monster is killed.

"Incredible," Kita says. "If we can get your team out into the drink, we might be able to fight them back."

He pulls out one of the maps on a table and points at a huge mass of shadows in the water.

"The Rusalka are hunkered down about a mile off the coast. We've failed to make an impression on them, and they keep returning to the beach day after day."

My mother and father join us to look at the maps.

"We want to drop you here," he says, pointing to a small span of ocean. "The idea is that you will push them toward the shore."

"You want to squeeze them," my father says.

Kita nods. "I was told you kids can breathe underwater?"

"We can also die under there. What's this big black blob over here? Is that more Rusalka?" I ask, pointing to a mass on the maps.

A soldier enters the restaurant carrying something that looks like a huge mop. It's as big as a golden retriever and made entirely of slimy, wet tentacles. Bex squeals with revulsion, and I gasp. It's one of the squid creatures from Spangler's tanks.

"Sir, we found another one of these things down on the beach."

"Oh no," my mother gasps. I turn and see terror all over her face. It's mirrored by Riley's father, John, by Arcade, and even by Fathom's expressions.

"That's what that blob on the map is made of," Kita says. "Ugly things, and fast as lightning. They've got a spike buried in there that latches on to the back of your head—"

"How many of these have you found?" Fathom interrupts.

"Ten," Jackson says. "We sent five to White Tower to study; the rest we left to rot."

"Spangler had them in the tanks," I explain.

"You need to leave this place," Fathom says.

Everyone turns to him in surprise.

"That creature is death, and even the bravest of my people are smart enough to keep their distance. This one has led the way for many more."

"I don't know if you noticed that beach out there," Kita says, "but I've got bigger problems to deal with than a bunch of fat squids. I've got monsters throwing tidal waves at the shore and eating my dead soldiers. It takes ten bullets to slow one of them down, and ten more to kill it. These ugly things go down with one shot, and they're as dumb as dogs. They're not a problem."

"You need to listen to us, Major. He's right. This thing is called an Undine, and it is the real threat. This is just a baby," my mother says, pointing at the dead mass of arms. "It's one of ten million born on the same day."

"Ten million?" Bex cries.

"Three days later, its mother gives birth to another ten million."

"That's not possible," Jackson says. "We would have noticed these creatures if there were that many. One of them would have washed up onshore or gotten caught in a fishing net."

"Undine have a way of keeping their own populations under control. When one is born, its hunger is insatiable. To survive, it turns on its brothers and sisters and eats them. One Undine can devour a hundred others in a single day, and normally it's the feeding frenzy that keeps their numbers low."

"Understood. So why is this a problem for us?" Kita asks.

"Undine babies rarely escape the birthing cave," John adds. "If one is here, it's because they are all being led here."

"By what?" my father asks.

"The mother," my mom says. "And trust me, the mother isn't dumb. She's as intelligent as any one of us."

"Well, what does she want?" Jackson begs.

"Food," Fathom says. "The prime has told her that there is plenty to eat here."

He turns on his heel and rushes for the door.

"Where's he going?" Jackson shouts.

I look to Arcade, fully expecting her to chase after him, but she shakes her head and lets him go. I throw up my hands and run after him myself.

"So we're here and now you're leaving?" I shout after him, once I get outside.

"I have to tell them," he says, turning back to me.

I scowl. "You've got some serious daddy issues. Fine, go to your father, but if I have to kill you, then don't be surprised when I do."

"I'm not going to warn my father. I'm going to warn the other Alpha about the Undine. My uncle Braken and cousin Flyer wait with what is left of our people. Thousands strong. Ghost and Surf are among them. They must know that you have returned and a more dire enemy approaches."

"Me?"

He takes a step toward me, but I flinch.

"You. My people cannot defeat the Rusalka on our own. We need you."

"I don't understand what you're talking about," I say, my voice rising in anger.

"Hey, you two, if you want to stay alive, you need to get off the beach!" a soldier shouts as he runs past us. "The Rusalka are hungry today."

Fathom ignores him.

"There has been much I wished to explain to you, Lyric Walker, but you would not listen. Are you willing to hear me now?"

"If it makes sense, yes!" I cry.

"When we parted in the water, after the first attack, I went in search of Alpha survivors," he says. "The Great Abyss had taken many, so I asked him to give me fortune in finding the rest. He was kind, and I discovered them before they went too far out to sea, where I would never find them. It took much convincing on my part to get them to stay. My father's shame damaged my standings, and my dismissal of my royal obligations did not help. Most refused to listen to me, but my uncle and cousin demanded I be heard. I told them that there were good humans, people on the surface who were honorable and worthy, and that I was in love with one."

I have to catch my breath.

"That probably didn't help," I say.

"No, it did not, but Ghost came to your defense."

"Ghost? He hates me!"

"He is well respected among my people, and he was able to sway them to resume our fight. After a vote, they agreed, even though they believed we would be slaughtered. It was Ghost who gave us hope of victory. He believed that you would be captured eventually and taken to Tempest, where the children of Alpha were held. He also believed that those children would be able to hear the Voice the same as you. Rescuing you and the children could help us stop our enemies and give safety to the surface world. I returned to the beach, collecting as many gloves as I could among the dead, then gave myself to the soldiers. As Ghost predicted, they delivered me to Tempest, but you were not there. You had managed to elude capture, so I met with the ones they called

Doyle and Spangler. I gave them the gloves and encouraged them to find you.

"I don't think you understand what the word *rescue* means," I snap. "You kept me from destroying that place, Fathom. I could have brought it all down on Spangler's head. We could have gotten the children out and their parents, too. Don't you realize what you did? There are Alpha back there in those tanks who would be free today if you had not gotten in my way."

"Escape was never a question, Lyric Walker. For our plan to work you needed to train the children to use the Voice, and I needed to train you to stay alive."

"Are you listening to yourself?" I cry. "Fathom, those kids back there aren't warriors, and no amount of preparation is going to help. They're babies and you may have killed them all."

"No!" he shouts angrily. "They are not babies, Lyric Walker. They are hope. They can save us all, and you will lead them."

"I'm seventeen!"

He takes another step toward me, grabbing my shoulders in his strong hands and giving me a shake.

"I will hear no more of how you are small. I will not listen to any further nonsense about your weakness. They are lies you tell yourself that no one else believes. I love you with every drop of my blood, and I know any chance of winning your affection is slim, but I cannot walk away without saying this to you. It is time to stop acting delicate. You are not fooling me. I see what you are."

"And what's that?" I shout, pulling myself away.

"You are a raging sea!" he bellows.

He takes a few breaths to calm himself, then looks out to the ocean.

"Yes, I manipulated you to get you here. I prevented you from escaping and blocked your plans, but the world needs you. The safest place the children can be is a step behind you," he says, then turns back to me. "There are thousands of Alpha waiting for battle, men and women who have proved their courage countless times, and all of them have pledged to follow you into the Great Abyss. You are the only chance we have. Ghost knows this. My people know this. I know it."

"Aaargh!" I cry. "I can't stand any more of this Triton craziness. Are you telling me you put me in danger because you love me?"

"I did not put you into danger; you are already in danger. I brought you here to fight because I know you are capable of destroying what the rest of us cannot. This is not Triton craziness. This is how I love you. The soft-handed humans may believe their women need to be protected. They teach you to hide and lock yourselves away. If that is what you want, you will find plenty who will happily underestimate you. My love expects you to be what you are—no more and no less."

Fathom takes off the boots that White Tower gave him.

He rolls up the bottoms of his jumpsuit and lets his blades slice through his shirtsleeves.

"Stay alive, Lyric Walker," he says; then, with a blast of wind, he speeds toward the shore, sending sand up in his wake. He cuts Rusalka down in his path but does not slow. Into the water he leaps, disappearing in the frothy waves.

"You do the same," I whisper.

CHAPTER TWENTY-TWO

SOMETIME AFTER DUSK, THE RUSALKA MAKE A SUDDEN retreat. One moment they are fighting; the next they march back into the sea. Some of the children celebrate, but Kita tells us that this always happens before they send another wave. His words are followed by screaming sirens. I order the children to the windows and tell them to push back any waves away from the resturant. There's an eerie silence, then the trembling of glass in window frames. A massive crash hits the beach, like a giant punched the side of the building. It knocks a few people down, and dust trickles from the rafters. We wait in silence for a second strike, but it doesn't happen, and Kita tells us to relax.

"They must not have as many gloves as we thought," I tell him.

"What makes you think so?"

"They could easily knock this building down with a little combined effort," I explain. "We are able to push their attack aside."

"The prime has these animals spread out up and down the East Coast," he tells me. "Maybe he's a little thin."

"Thin is good," Jackson says, then turns to me. "Do you think your team could make a wave for us?"

I look out at the kids, huddled together for warmth.

"I don't know," I confess.

There is a flurry of activity and noise on the beach. I watch heavy machines roll along the sand, creating huge dunes between the water and the building. Inside, soldiers shout orders at one another and plead for assistance on radios and telephones.

My father is eager to help. He divides the team into two groups, urging one half to try to get some sleep while the others continue to watch the windows. I think sleep is wishful thinking, but to be honest, I really don't have a better plan. When I was in kindergarten, the teacher used to make us take naps to keep us busy. Maybe it will work for them.

Riley looks tired, but he stays alert and positive. He does his best to keep everyone's spirits high. He tells the little ones that they are brave and the older ones that they're amazing. He's so good with them. He seems to know what to say and who needs a little attention. Everyone brightens when he's near. It's almost magical. I wish I had a little of his charm. It seems like I did once upon a time, but it's hard to remember that Lyric Walker.

"You need a pep talk?" he asks me.

I shake my head, even though I really do. I just don't think lover boy wants to listen to me flail back and forth about Fathom. His words echo in my ears. He's made me redefine everything I thought I knew. The hatred I have clung to so tightly has come undone and flaps in the wind like a filthy sheet. I have no idea how I feel.

He gives me a curious look.

"You think I don't want to hear about it?" he says knowingly.

I blush. "You read minds too?"

"I read faces," he says. "I'll listen, but I doubt I'll be very objective."

"Who asked for objectivity?" I laugh.

"I've been wondering how I can compete with a guy like him. It's odd to have superpowers and still feel insecure. So I'm just going to say this. You're funny and you're hot. I like you."

"Short and sweet," I say.

"That's how I roll," he says, then wanders off to talk with Harrison and Ryan.

Chloe lies next to me on the floor, her head resting on my leg as she sleeps. I watch out a window and listen to the crashing of waves. Coney Island's electricity was knocked out by the first tidal wave and was never reconnected. For the first time in my life, the light pollution that kept the sky a dim yellow is replaced by galactic majesty. I see stars! It's every bit as beautiful as the Texas version.

It's almost amazing enough to make me forget the dramatic temperature drop that came when the sun went down. The wind is bitter and biting, and when it blows through the open windows, it howls in my ears. There's not much in the way of blankets, and though the White Tower jumpsuits and jackets are padded, the children and I are freezing. For all of Doyle's training, he didn't prepare them for a frosty night by the ocean. Jackson hands out little red packs filled with something that feels like sand. When you shake them, they get hot, so I tell everyone to shove them in their boots and gloves. Finn puts one under his cap. It's silly, but he says he feels better.

"You need a break?" my mother asks, gesturing to Chloe.

I look down at my sleeping sidekick and nod. My mother cradles her up in her arms, careful not to wake her.

"How is Dad?" I ask.

"Stubborn," she says. "We need to get him out of here. This was not a good place to bring him or Bex."

"I'll talk to Jackson," I say. "They didn't give us much of a choice when we arrived."

She takes the little girl away. I stretch out my legs and try to rub the feeling back into them, only to find that Arcade is standing over me. She looks restless and frustrated, basically how she looks all the time. I feel the pull of her missing hand, but I keep my eyes on her face.

"I know you hate waiting," I say as sympathetically as I can. "I think we should let Kita come up with a plan."

"The soldiers are fighting bravely. That is good enough for me," she says as she kneels down next to me. With her back against the wall, she stares in the opposite direction as me. It's uncomfortably close. Maybe not if she were Bex or, well, anyone else for that matter, but it's an invasion of my personal space for someone who recently tried to kill me.

"My problem is with you," she says.

"Are you going to kill me?" I ask.

Arcade shakes her head, but in the dark I can't see if her face is as sincere as the gesture.

"What's the Alpha punishment for a person who tries to steal your boyfriend?"

"Death."

"Then you *are* going to kill me? Should I have been more specific? Are you going to kill me sometime in the future?"

"I seek to understand you," Arcade whispers to me.

"I'm not sure I can help you with that," I tell her. "I don't understand myself most of the time."

"You have rejected him?"

I look out the window to the ocean and wonder if Fathom found his friends.

"I did," I say.

"I freed him of his obligations to me. The two of you are free to mate."

"Ugh. What is it with you people and that word?" I grumble. "Do you really want to talk about this?"

She nods.

"He lied to me," I explain.

"He told you of his plan?"

"Yes, after he manipulated me and used me to help him fight his war, he told me his plan," I say.

She sits for a long moment as if flipping my side of the story over and over, studying angles and colors she didn't see before.

"Yes, I didn't see it in that way. I doubt he did either," she says. "Our people are not known for avoiding conflicts."

"I get that," I confess, "but there's other stuff too, Arcade. It's . . . I don't know how much drama I want in my life. Fathom and I are like fire and gasoline. We're intense, and we burn really hot, but we're dangerous. I keep getting scorched. I feel reckless when he's near me, and I do things I wouldn't normally do."

"The mating?"

"Aaargh," I say. "Keep it down? My dad is right there. You're going to ruin his life. It's . . . I knew he was with you, and I didn't care. I don't do things like that, not since Stevie Brinks in the third grade."

"Who?"

I wave her off. "Never mind. It goes against the girl code."

"You are a liar and a coward," she says matter-of-factly.

"Um, okay. I thought we were making a little progress—"

"You love him, Lyric Walker, so do not lie. I don't know what this word 'drama' is, but it sounds like something you have invented because you are afraid to feel what you do. Love, like war, is supposed to be overwhelming."

"When did you turn into a therapist?"

"I know these things. I am a liar and a coward as well. When Fathom and I were children, our fathers committed us to each other. Such arrangements are rare and frequently lead to unhappy unions, but there are greater matters than happiness when it comes to leading an empire. Fathom, for his part, did his best to make our responsibility joyful. We have a deep bond."

"Until I came along and ruined it," I say, my way of apologizing again.

"You ruined nothing," Arcade says. "I ruined it."

I peer through the darkness, trying to read her face.

"So you are in love with someone else?"

"The humans named him Flyer," she whispers.

"Fathom's cousin? Does Flyer know?" I ask.

She looks offended. "Absolutely not!"

"Fathom knew," I remind her.

"It appears I have not hidden my feelings as well as I had hoped."

"Fathom says he's out there," I say, pointing toward the ocean.

She turns and cranes her neck for a better view, as if she might catch a glimpse of him.

"If you love this other guy, why did you threaten to kill me?" I ask.

"You broke the girl code," she says.

"Wait, you actually know what that means?"

"Bex Conrad explained it to me in the desert. You violated many of its rules. She was quite incensed."

"So she trash-talked me?"

"I do not know that term. I do know I was angry. You meddled in my relationship and used your disapproval of it as an excuse. That's against the code."

I can't help but laugh.

"I am sorry I broke the code," I say, throwing my hands up in surrender.

"We have a peculiar friendship, Lyric Walker," Arcade says.

"I thought we were bitter enemies," I say, so shocked, I can barely get the words out of my mouth.

"I kill my enemies," she says. "I will not deny that there are certain things about you that I find trying and—"

"Let's not ruin this special moment," Bex interrupts as she crawls over to join us.

"Sorry if we woke you," I say.

"It's hard to sleep when everyone's talking about mating." She giggles.

"Oh, that's war, Conrad. Now I'm going to have to say the word you can't stand."

"Don't do it, Walker!"

"*Moist.*"

"Aaargh," she growls, holding her hands to her ears.

"Are all humans mentally ill?" Arcade asks.

• • •

I'm woken by the sound of helicopter blades whipping the air outside the windows. It's jarring. The last time I saw helicopters, they had White Tower logos on them, but these are military choppers designed to carry a dozen people. They land in the sand behind the building.

"What's that about?" I ask when Jackson rushes into the room.

"That's your ride," he explains. "We're going with Kita's plan. Gather a team of ten and assemble the rest on the beach. We're taking the prime out today," Jackson insists. "Hurry, Lyric. We have to get you into the air before they launch another attack."

I turn to the children and order them to gather. Chloe takes my hand, and we follow everyone onto the beach. With the team spread out before me, I mentally try to organize who should go with me and who should stay behind to fight the Rusalka stampede. It's hard trying to find the right balance.

Kita meets us on the beach, flanked by a dozen soldiers trying to get his attention. He's shouting at someone on the phone, demanding more artillery.

He hangs up and turns to face us. "The Rusalka moved closer to shore last night, as did the Undine. They're trying to give us a one-two punch, hurt us with the angler people, then kill us with the squids. We have to act now if we're going to have any chance at all," Kita says. "The plan is to take out the first punch and deal with the second when it arrives. We're going to do it by putting the squeeze on the Rusalka, dropping you and your team in the ocean behind them. You're going to drive them forward to the shore, where the rest of your team and my soldiers will take them apart. You attack from your end, and we'll attack from ours. It's a classic vise move."

"We're going into the water?" Tess asks.

"You can do this, kid," he says confidently, then turns to me. "You need strong swimmers and good fighters, and do any of you have experience with concussion bombs?"

I almost laugh at his question until I notice that all the children raise their hands.

"Good. You're leaving in five minutes!"

I look out over all the faces and feel dread creeping up my throat. I try to remember what Fathom said to me. These kids are our only hope, but all I can see is how young they look.

Riley steps forward as if he's able to hear my uncertainty.

"Tess and Emma, Harrison, Finn, Jonas, Georgia, Eric, Ryan—"

"I am going," Arcade interrupts.

"That make sense to you?" Riley asks me.

I nod, though I'm not even sure what just happened.

"Yes, that's fine," I stammer.

"Good! When we get into the water, we need to focus on the Rusalka who are wearing Oracles. If we can stop them first, the rest will be easier to beat," Riley says. "You are going to have to kill them. Can you do that?"

Everyone nods.

"Good, because if you don't, they will kill you. Arcade, will you lead the attack?"

She nods like the answer is obvious.

"Keep an eye on yourselves and the rest of the team. Remember, we stick together," he says.

"Lyric, get your team into the helicopter!" Jackson shouts to us.

"I need you here with the other team," I tell Riley.

He shakes his head emphatically. "Finn will stay and direct everyone."

He gestures for the kids to board the chopper. I watch them trudge through the sand, eager to join the fray.

My mother and father look on, with Bex at their side.

"Jackson is having us taken to a safer spot," my dad says.

Riley is still hovering. "Give me your gun," I say.

He takes it out of his pocket and hands it to me. I put it in my father's hand.

"Make sure you get there," I say to him.

He nods and slips the weapon into his jacket.

"Don't die," Bex demands. "'Cause there's going to be a lot of cats at our place, and I can't take care of them all."

I press my forehead to hers. "I'll come back. I won't abandon you, again. I love you, Bex. We're sisters now."

She pulls back and stares at me for a long moment as if locking what I've said into some sort of puzzle, one she's never been able to solve until just now.

"Sisters," she says in agreement.

I give my parents hugs and promise to be safe. Jackson shouts for me to board again. This time he's angry.

"I've gotta go," I say apologetically, and I turn and run to the helicopter.

Chloe runs to the helicopter as I step inside and find a seat.

"I don't want to be separated," she says.

"I'm giving you a very special job, Chloe. I need you to look after my family," I say, pointing to where they stand. "You need to make sure the soldiers get them to safety, and I want you to go with them."

Bex rushes forward and takes the girl's hand.

"We'll stick together," Bex says.

"I'll come back, Chloe. I promise."

Jackson closes the door, and I wave to everyone. The pilot flips switches and pulls back on the throttle. A moment later we rise into the air, and I watch everyone grow smaller. Chloe's sad face shrinks into the scenery.

Jackson sits in the front with the pilot and shouts information about our mission into the speakers in our helmets.

"Each one of you is going to detonate a concussion bomb when you reach the drop zone," he says.

"Heads-up: I sort of skipped concussion bombs in public school," I confess.

"I'll show you," Riley offers.

"They're simple. Don't worry," Jackson assures me. "They don't do much more than make a lot of noise, but try not to get too close, because they will rattle your brain. Loud noises spook them so it should send the Rusalka swimming for the beach. They told me you can breathe underwater?"

I nod.

"Can you talk?"

I shake my head.

"That's unfortunate," Jackson shouts. "Stay close together, then."

The beach disappears into the horizon, replaced by a threatening purple sky. The water below looks like a vast black drain. The children see it the way I do, suddenly losing their eagerness to fight. They are silent and wary, watching the waves with anxious eyes. I know Riley would like me to say something to inspire them, but I'm not feeling all that inspiring right now. Fathom says I'm a raging sea. Right now I feel like I'm going to pee my pants.

About a mile offshore, the helicopter slows and Jackson reaches back and opens the door.

"We're here!"

We take off our helmets, then our boots.

"Good luck!" the pilot shouts to us.

"Wait! Aren't you going any lower?" I say, looking out at the water. It's a good fifty feet below.

"A Rusalka can jump out of the water pretty high," he says. "This is about as low as we dare."

Before I can argue, Arcade pushes past me and leaps out of the chopper. I watch her body plummet and then disappear into the waves. If I do the same thing, I'm going to smack into the water. It's going to feel like pavement.

"You're not afraid of heights, are you, Lyric?" Georgia teases.

"It's really what's at the bottom that bothers me," I say.

"You're so funny," she says as she powers up her glove. A moment later a spout of water rises up until it's parallel with the helicopter. Georgia jumps out into it, and I watch her body sink down into the ocean below. It's a pretty cool trick. Eric and Ryan are next, then Emma, Tess, Harrison, and Jonas, until it's just Riley and me.

"Let's go, Walker!" Jackson shouts as he shoves a canvas bag into my hands. Inside are ten metal canisters as big as softballs. Each has a single red button on its side. "Here are the explosives. Get as close to those ugly things as you can and push the button. After that, just hold your ears."

My heart is racing. My head feels like it might pop off. This is so stupid. I am not a soldier. Can't anyone see that? Why is Jackson shouting for me to jump?

Riley reaches over and gives my shoulder a squeeze.

"You can do this," he promises, offering me his hand.

Fathom would probably think I was being weak, but I take it nonetheless, and together Riley and I leap out into nothing. When we hit the spout, my whole body locks up. The water is icy cold and it steals my breath, even as my gills appear to take over the job of breathing. We drop downward until we splash into the murky ocean unharmed. Riley is still holding my hand. The scales on his face and hands are silver and blue. He's beautiful.

He says something to me, but it comes out as bubbles and nonsense. He's grinning. I think he's flirting with me. I think he's telling me I'm beautiful too.

Arcade finds us and points us toward the others. Once we are gathered, I hand out the bombs. Arcade gestures for us to follow her and takes off swimming. Her speed is incredible. Like the rest of my team, I have to depend on the glove to propel me forward, but once we get going, we take off like a shot.

The team slices through the water using the dim light from the surface to keep us together. It isn't long before Arcade comes to a halt. She points first at our concussion bombs, then just ahead of us. She makes a monster face. It's ridiculous, but it gets the point across. The Rusalka are near.

I press the button on my canister, then use my glove to send it torpedoing in the direction Arcade has pointed. I watch it zip away into the darkness, then watch my team mimic my actions. Eight more bombs shoot ahead and vanish into the pitch-black. I turn to Riley to see if he might be able to tell me how long it will take before the explosion, only to be knocked backwards by an ear-shattering boom.

It jars every bone in my body and knocks me about. I spin in a dozen directions, so that I can't tell which way is up. When I finally right myself, I search for my team. Most of them flailed out of control as well, but none of us have been injured.

Arcade waves at us frantically and swims furiously toward the explosion. The Rusalka are on the move, racing toward the shore. Kita's plan is working! Arcade doesn't hesitate. She charges after the creatures, slashing their backs and their legs with her blades. They scream in agony, and black blood pours out of them. It makes the water smell coppery, and I nearly gag knowing it is in my lungs. I shake it off. I can be sick about this later. Right now I have a job to do.

I wave to the team, showing them how to pull debris off the ocean floor. I mix it into sharp shapes, then fire it into the fleeing Rusalka. The children give chase, each one mimicking my trick, launching spears into the fleeing beasts.

Our attacks have ferocity. The children channel whatever it is they've bottled up since they were taken to Tempest. Most of what they still believe about their mothers and fathers is a lie, but they have a cause I will not steal from them. Whatever gives them the courage to fight is good enough today. I have my own passion to fuel me. I fire one deadly rocket after another, watching them cut the Rusalka down.

"Show me which ones have the gloves," I beg the water.

Magically, I can sense them all, as if we are linked together. They are spread out so many miles away, but there are a hundred close enough to be targets. If I can destroy them, the soldiers and my team waiting on the beach might actually have a chance. I reach out, concentrating on what is in the water. There is so much debris at the bottom, remains of Coney

Island dragged out when the water crushed it to death. There are nails and pieces of glass and car parts and jagged planks of wood. I stop and focus on it all, pulling up as much as I can. It swirls around me in a whirlpool of filth, and the water seizes each deadly piece, turning it toward the fleeing mob and shooting it in one massive assault.

I watch the pieces zip forward, catching monsters in the back. Bodies heave, then sink; and glowing blue gloves fall like stars into the deep. The kids are following my lead, creating their own shrapnel attacks. There's too much agitation in the water to know how many we have killed.

Suddenly, the chase comes to a screeching halt. We've reached the beach. It's up to the soldiers and Finn's team to do their part.

Riley swims close and grabs my arm. He points toward the surface. There's a rush, and suddenly he and I are soaring out of the water and into open air, riding the crest of a spout. The other children do the same, and soon we are all looking out over the battle zone. Despite the carnage we inflicted, there are still so many Rusalka that they have melted into a single black and purple mass tumbling onto the shore. The soldiers spray them with gunfire. Finn shouts orders at the children, and several rockets crash into the water, ripping dozens of our enemies apart in fiery explosions.

But in this grotesque mess are five Rusalka who survived my attacks and have gloves like mine. I can see their glow from high above, and each monster is slobbering with fury. Together they lift their gloves skyward, and I hear a sound like the earth has cracked in two. Riley and I turn to find a swell rising higher and higher in the distance. It grows into a tower of liquid that is ten feet, twenty feet, fifty feet. It's twice as big as the one that destroyed my home, and it's coming right for us. It will kill everything when it arrives, charging through our numbers and crushing our bodies. It's an act of desperation. These creatures are willing to be torn limb from limb if they can take us with them.

"I will stop this," Arcade shouts, leaping off of Harrison's spout. He tries to hold on to her, but she wrenches free and leaps down into the throng of Rusalka in a falling arc, She swings wildly, dismembering everything nearby. I have never seen such violence. She is killing and killing and killing, moving closer and closer to the last five who can destroy us all. I hope the Great Abyss has answered her prayers today, but she may not reach them in time.

"We have to push it back!" I shout to the children. The power needed to make it happen is all-consuming. We tumble out of the sky and land in the shallows. I feel my ankle wrench, and a burn rolls up my leg. I may have broken it. Emma and Harrison look hurt as well. I can deal with it later, if I live.

"Hold hands!" I shout.

The children link to one another, and the wave trembles.

It knows we're in its path of destruction and we plan on stopping it.

"You are all giants!" I shout at the children. "You are all five hundred feet tall. You have to believe me. We can stop this, but you have to believe that you are a force of nature."

"I believe it!" Riley shouts, and then each of the children says the same.

"All right, bear down," I instruct. "Don't let it move forward another inch."

There are ten of us against an angry ocean, and the nosebleeds begin. Harrison is first, then Tess. I'm too exhausted to know if it's happening to me. Georgia is shaking like she's having a seizure, and the others are screaming from the intensity.

"They're breaking through!" someone shouts.

I turn my head to see Rusalka storming onto the beach. Breanne is attacked and cut open. She falls to the ground, clenching her belly. Without her defenses, a dozen more Rusalka charge forward. They cut down Suzi, and a boy named Tucker, and Priscilla, leaving them bloody and in shock. Tucker can't stop looking at the wound on his arm. He's set upon by others. I hear his screams over the gunfire. The Rusalka leap forward, cutting five soldiers in half. One snatches up a loose rifle and accidentally shoots itself in the face.

And our luck runs out. One of the Rusalka turns to find out what drove them to shore and realizes we are in the water behind him. He lunges forward and digs his claws into Jonas's leg. The boy cries out and falls backwards into the water. Losing his connection causes the rest of us to lurch with pain.

Another Rusalka leaps to slice me open, but I kick it in the face and it tumbles back. Five more follow. Riley manages to punch one before it can hurt him, and Emma turns her glove on the creature, crushing it between two spouts of water. Unfortunately her diversion weakens our hold even further. The energy needed to hold back the wave feels like it is ripping me apart, and I know if it's this bad for me, it's hurting the others even more. This is how it felt that day on the beach when I failed everyone. I fought and fought, but it was pointless. Everything was destroyed anyway.

Everything.

"Let go!" I shout to the team.

"We can't!" Harrison cries.

"Let it go. Turn your attention on our people. Get them out of the water before they are swept away."

I call names out to the sea, asking it to keep everyone safe. When I say Arcade's name, a wave shoots her into the sky. I see it happening to everyone on the beach. Kita, Jackson, all the soldiers and children. They are all hurtled skyward when we let the water go.

Riley and I shoot into the sky as well, just as the monstrous wave stampedes beneath our feet. It crushes everything that dares stand in its way, even the Rusalka who created it. It swallows them up and chews them apart, and I feel my connection to their gloves snuffed out.

The wave rolls up the beach, smashing into Childs Restaurant, knocking it off its foundation. It continues onward, bulldozing everything in its path. The destruction from this wave will wipe out neighborhoods that survived the first. I hope the die-hards who would not leave have a chance to escape. My mind searches the water for my parents and Bex and Chloe, but they aren't out there. I hope Jackson fulfilled his promise. I hope they're on their way to safety.

When the ocean has had its way with the land, when it is just a simmering boil of hostility, I nudge it back to where it belongs. The other children help me until we can see the beach once more. There is nothing left, no debris, no weapons, no evidence that this place was once a neighborhood.

We ease everyone back to the ground and gather in the wet sand. Arcade waits for me. She points at a jagged cut on my thigh. A Rusalka must have slashed me and I didn't notice. I'm so full of adrenaline right now, I can't even feel it.

The children cry at their losses. There were thirty-three of us when we arrived. We lost nine in the fight. I stretch out and find their bodies. There is no life in any of them. We lost Breanne, Jonas, Emma, Tess, Leo, Georgia, Pierre, Tucker, and Danny.

"Look!" Finn shouts.

There's a splash, and then something lands at our feet. I almost fall backwards in fear. Another Rusalka has arrived. Its yellow eyes study us for a moment, and its forked tongue licks the air. It barks and howls at us in its ugly language, but I can't begin to understand what it wants.

"He is not here!" Arcade shouts at it.

The Rusalka stomps its feet and growls angrily.

"Then he is a coward. I demand he retreat. His invasion has failed," Arcade shouts.

The creature lets out a defiant huff and springs back into the water, disappearing from view.

"He is coming," Arcade says.

"Who?" Cole asks.

"The prime. I will fight in Fathom's place," Arcade says, then stares at me with serious eyes. "I will not allow interference."

"This is my fight too!" I shout.

I see the tips of tridents and swords rising out of the surf. All along the shore as far as I can see, they come, hundreds of Rusalka marching in our direction. Unlike the others, they wear the same armor that the other Alpha have been known to wear. It's made of shells and bones and claws. In their midst is the prime and his pregnant wife, Minerva. They each bear smiles a million times more terrifying than their monster army. Once they are in position, they all stop and stand tall before us.

"Where is the traitor?" the prime says, his eyes gleaming with hate.

"Ever the coward," Minerva hisses.

"No mind. He will learn the new way of things when we root him out," the prime says. "As for the rest, you may kneel and beg for a quick death."

"That is merciful," Minerva says with all sincerity.

"You are no prime," Arcade cries. "The Alpha Nation is dead and scattered, all thanks to you. You are the leader of memories, not First Men."

"I think this child has lost her ability to see," Minerva says. "Isn't the empire standing before you? Only a small portion of it, of course, but it grows with each passing day. The Alpha live on."

Arcade looks up and down the beach at the beasts.

"What did you have to say to get them to bend their knees to you?"

"I simply offered them what they have been asking for all along—a place in my kingdom, a voice in my ear," the prime answers. "I gave them the freedoms that my former advisers refused to allow, and apologized for the disrespect. I appointed several of them to be advisers and then welcomed the rest into my royal guard. Don't they look fierce in their armor? They will play an integral part in our glorious future."

"Imagine the lives you could have saved if you had just given them a hug earlier," I say.

"I see the mutant has survived," the prime snarls, then turns back to Arcade. "Throwing your lot in with the human filth too, Arcade?"

"Kill her, lover!" Minerva shrieks. She's so angry, her body shakes. "Kill them both!"

The prime's blades spring from his forearms with a deadly *shhhkkkt*.

"Yes, I think that would be fun," he says, then crouches as if he's preparing to lunge at me.

The air fills with a pounding rhythm. It begins with a low, plucking tone but grows louder until the air around my head is shaking with a thrum.

Behind the wall of Rusalka, I see a second set of weapons rise. Along the beach for a mile in both directions come the Alpha—Nix, Sirena, Ceto, Triton, and Selkie. At the center is Fathom, dressed in his own armor. Next to him is a boy roughly his own age with long brown hair and an older man with a shaved head and a pointy goatee. I've seen them before. They are Flyer and Braken.

The Rusalka part for them, and Fathom walks toward the beach. He looks to me and then Arcade, and nods respectfully.

"You have done well," he says.

"Glad you could make it before the party is over," I say.

"Father, I come to you with an offer of peace," he says to the prime. "Return to the hunting grounds. Rebuild the empire in whatever form you choose. I will not try to stop you as long as you leave the surface world alone."

"Is that your offer, little minnow?" Minerva mocks. "Shall we retreat now?"

"It is not retreat, Minerva. It is a fair offer to my father!" Fathom shouts at her.

"Yes, I am your father!" the prime rages. "And you should be proud of me, boy. I have taken our people back to a more glorious time, when we took what we wanted—food, weapons, slaves, and territories. The surface world is no different. It is ours for the taking."

"You are insane!" Arcade shouts.

"The only madness here is the way we live," the prime cries. "I am setting things back to the way they were always meant to be."

"And look at the price!" Fathom shouts. "Look at the death!"

"And from it, birth," Minerva says, rubbing her pregnant tummy. "I will raise the heir in the old traditions. He will bathe in blood and treasure. The surface is his dowry."

"Father, hear me. Consider peace," Fathom says.

"I desire war."

"Is that your final word?" Fathom asks, releasing his Kala.

"It is, pup. Do you wish to challenge it?"

"I must." Fathom lunges at his father, roaring with war. The prime blocks his attack and sends his son tumbling to the ground. He leaps to strike as well, but Fathom rolls out of the way and springs to his feet right off his back. Father and son trade blows that would kill an ordinary person.

"You have taken our great people and turned them into

scavengers, and now you have thrown in with the very beasts that killed so many of us. You are the king of the dead," Fathom says.

"King nonetheless," his father roars as he lands a savage hand to his son's face. Fathom's cheek opens, and blood pours down his neck.

"This was how it was always going to end, traitor!" Minerva screeches. "The old heir must be removed to make room for the new one."

The prime leaps onto his son, pressing his forearm against Fathom's face. If he releases his blades, they will slice off his son's head.

"It's over, son!" he shouts. "I have beaten you. I'm sorry to see you go. I would have liked to watch your face when the humans surrender."

There's a *shkkkkkt!*

I scream.

The prime chuckles, and blood leaks out of his mouth.

"Finally, son, you understand what you are. You are Alpha. Take what you want. It is yours."

He closes his eyes, and Fathom forces the body off of him. He pulls his own blade out of his father's throat.

"I will earn what is mine," he says.

Minerva backs into the water one step at a time. I expect her to say something insane, but she doesn't. Instead, she sinks beneath the waves and is gone. The Rusalka follow, and soon their weapons disappear as well. The Alpha part and allow them to retreat; then they step out of the water to gather on the shore. There are thousands of them.

"I was told there would be a battle here, Fathom," Flyer says.

"It appears the raging sea got here before we could," Fathom explains, flashing me a smile.

Ghost joins us. He's a happy sight, despite his grotesque appearance.

"It is good to see you, blob fish," Ghost calls out to me. "I hear you have become quite average with your glove."

I bristle at his insult, then remember he was the one who convinced the others that I could save everyone. I almost bust him but let him have his pride.

"Is it over, nephew?" Braken asks Fathom.

"Hopefully Minerva will take her foul brood to some dark corner of the ocean," Fathom says. He kneels before his father, and I see that, despite the madness, Fathom still loved him.

"Flyer?" Arcade says. She steps to him tentatively.

He smiles as wide as the sky, then sees her hand. He gives it a serious look.

"Did you do this to impress me?" he jokes.

She smiles. I didn't think she could. I didn't think her face made that shape.

"We have much to discuss," she says to him.

He cocks an eyebrow. "We do?"

"We do."

Suddenly the ocean grows still. There is no tide, no waves —just eerie silence.

"Talking will have to wait," Ghost says, pointing out to the water.

It's then that it begins to churn and bubble. There's an explosion, and something crashes onto the shore at our feet. It's as big as a dog and made up entirely of tentacles. It charges right at me, using all of its hyperactive legs to drag itself forward.

"Undine!" Fathom shouts.

"Run!" I shout to the team, and everyone races inland.

The air fills with the shrill cries of the Undine. I don't know which scares me more, the sound they make or how many I think there are behind us. I take a peek back and hate myself for it. I didn't need to see the entire beach blanketed in sticky tentacles.

"We can't outrun them!" Arcade shouts. "We have to fight."

"Minerva has set them upon us. They will kill everything they touch!" Flyer shouts as he grabs Arcade by her good hand and pulls her onward.

The creatures spring into our numbers, attempting to cling to heads. One lands on the back of an older Triton, and I hear the sickening sound of its spike plunging into flesh. The Triton lets out a horrible cry and falls to the ground. I want to stop and help, but Riley snatches my arm and keeps me running.

In the distance, I spot the wrecked bus we walked through to get here. Soldiers are running through it in our direction. I shout and wave at them, hoping they'll see what's happening and run for their lives.

"They're coming!" I shout to the soldiers. "Turn back!"

"Kid, you're about two months late for that announcement!" one of them shouts back.

"Not the Rusalka," I cry. "Something worse!"

One of the soldiers hoists his rocket launcher to his shoulder, aims, and fires. I watch the rocket's wobbly path as it slams into the endless sea of tentacles. Fire and smoke rise from the charred carcasses, and bodies fly. The other soldier shouts at his radio for more troops when an Undine crashes into him. It's then that I see the horrible spike they hide. It's red and coarse, like coral, and it jabs into the back of the soldier's skull. He screams, but the pain isn't the worst thing that happens to him. Within seconds, the spike is sucking out everything inside him—blood and bone—until he's nothing more than a bag of skin discarded onto the sand. The monster rolls onto the ground like it's stuffed from a Thanksgiving dinner.

I hear a pop, and watch a black streak of smoke fly across the sky. Whatever the soldiers fired lands on the ground not far from us and explodes with a massive boom. I can feel the shock wave. The effect is devastating and grotesque. One rocket blasted a whole twenty yards in diameter, turning the octopus creatures into glop. I cheer when two more streak above, shaking the air as they go.

"The human weapons will not stop them," Braken barks at us. "Distance is the only thing that will save us."

My team makes its way around a semi truck just as four jets roar overhead. Each one drops a bomb, and a moment later it feels like I'm in the middle of an earthquake. My eardrums ring, and I'm thrown to the ground. Fathom falls as well. One horrible explosion follows another, shaking my bones. While the world is being ripped in two, I watch hundreds of soldiers racing past us, guns ready and aimed at the shoreline. They storm the beach and fire, their bullets tearing into the octopus creatures one by one.

Riley gets me to my feet, only for us to hear a horrible scream. I turn and look, spotting a soldier flailing about, trying to remove an Undine that has locked onto his head. It ends in the same nightmarish way as the last.

In the chaos I hear someone calling my name. Chloe races out of nowhere.

"Chloe, what are you doing here?"

"I didn't want to go with them. I want to be with you!" she shouts.

I scoop her up in my arms.

"Hold on," I beg her, and then we're running again.

Soldiers race in the opposite direction. I watch one pull the pin from a hand grenade and hurl it as far as he can. It explodes, causing an orchestra of shrieks. Riley waves them on, giving the children time to catch up with us. An Undine lands on Priscilla's head. She screams, but before it can drive its spike into her neck, Harrison grabs it and hefts it back into the horde.

"They're flanking us!" a soldier shouts, pointing to the left, where I can see a wave of Undine scurrying ahead. To the right of us, they are doing the same thing. In seconds the beasts have completely surrounded us and are pressing in to finish the job.

An Undine leaps at us and locks onto Suzie's head. She cries out in pain, and I realize it has her now. Another one comes and grabs Ryan, and Eric next, and they are gone.

One crashes into my head, knocking me to the ground. I can feel it squirming around, its suckers gluing to my skin as it gets in the right position. I hear Chloe screaming and can feel Riley doing his best to pull it off. Fathom shouts my name, urging me to free myself, but it's got me like a vise. I hear a sucking sound and then a crack, followed by several more, and a pain shoots into my skull. Suddenly the creature's tentacles release me and it scurries away.

Riley helps me to my feet.

"What happened?" I say, reaching around to the back of my head.

Riley smiles. "The staples stopped it."

I reach up and touch the wound and the clumsy staples Nurse Amy inserted to close it. I guess I owe her one.

An Undine crashes into Riley and latches tight to his head.

I scream and try to help pull it off him as the red spike rears back to impale his spine. There's a slice, and I see that Fathom has used his blades to cut the foul thing in half.

"We're not going to make it!" someone shouts, and I brace for another attack, only the Undine have stopped their assault. Instead, they sit patiently, waiting quietly.

The sky fills with the loudest, shrillest roar I have ever heard. I look toward the ocean and see something that, despite all the impossible things I have seen, just should not be frickin' possible. A tentacle as large as a plane rises out of the water. It's almost as tall as an apartment building.

"The mother is here," Arcade says.

CHAPTER TWENTY-THREE

WHEN IT SLAMS ONTO THE GROUND, IT CAUSES A shock wave that blasts us off our feet. As I stagger to stand, I help Chloe do the same.

"Hey, kiddo, talk to me," I cry.

She's groggy, but she mumbles that she's okay.

Riley lies next to us, unconscious. In fact, all the children are down. Only Fathom and the rest of the Alpha seem to have suffered the calamity well. I move to see about the others, only the tiniest step kills me. I look down to see my ankle swelling. It's almost twice its normal size.

Fathom puts his arm around my waist, and I drape one around his shoulder.

"You did well," he says. It sounds a bit like surrender.

Another tentacle rises out of the water, then another, and another. Ten, twenty, a hundred more, join them, and together they drag a monstrosity onto the shore. I've never seen anything this big, short of a shopping center. It probably stands as tall as the Cyclone once did, and as wide as a city block, and it's made up of legs and blubber.

I lift my hand and power my glove. I aim it toward the beast, but it seems silly and pointless, like I'm a mosquito trying to knock down a full-grown man. Still, I have to try. I focus, urging the water to push the monster back, but nothing works. Even when I bear down with every ounce of concentration I can muster, when heat sears my frontal lobe and blood pours freely from my nose, there is nothing I can conjure to stop it. I'm so tired, so broken, even holding my hand up feels like more than I can handle.

"Fight, Lyric!" I shout at myself. "You're a wild thing. You're a giant. You're a raging sea!"

But my words are hollow. The monster towers over me, moving a fifty feet every second. The next tentacle falls hard and sends another shock wave into the ground.

We need to be stronger than the others, the water whispers. I'm so confused, I almost think it's a hallucination, but the voice returns. *We need you to be more.*

"How?" I cry.

The water guides my thoughts until it finds the severed hand of a Rusalka. It's encased in a glove.

There, the voice urges.

I will it to me. There's a tiny splash, and it flies out of the water, crashing in the sand at my feet. There's a click, and the metal slides off the dead flesh. I pick it up and realize it will fit my other hand.

The Undine mother continues her approach. I don't know if this is a good idea. One glove might be frying my brain.

Two might kill me, but I don't have any choice. I slip it on and it clicks itself shut; then both my hands glow like suns, and—wow.

I am an erupting volcano, an avalanche, a supernova.

The voice in my head is no longer a whisper. It's a shout, and it's coming from everywhere—the sky, the wind, and the ocean. I can hear it in my blood and the blood of my friends. I can hear a storm in the ocean hundreds of miles away. I can hear the moisture in the air. It sings to me. It twists around me in beautiful colors and arcs, slipping through my clothes and fingers.

A figure steps out of the water and approaches me. At first I cannot make out her face, but she feels familiar. She's tall and thin and wearing . . . a tube top?

"Tammy?"

She takes a drag of her cigarette.

Take care of my girl, she says, before shifting to Deshane, then just as quickly to Gabriel.

I was wrong about you, he says as he runs his hand though his bushy black hair. Suddenly, he transforms into Mr. Ervin, then Donovan Spangler. He gives himself a shake like a dog caught in the rain, and Mrs. Novakova is suddenly in front of me.

Nope, she says in her thick European accent. She morphs into David Doyle. Doyle looks down at himself as if unsure of whether or not he likes what he's seeing. He sips from his coffee mug. *I did what I thought was right, Lyric. Please forgive me.*

"I do," I say.

I watch him make one final change into a round-faced Latino boy with shaggy brown hair—a face I remember and love very, very much. He smiles at me, holds up his smartphone, and presses the record button.

"Shadow?"

I have to document this. His voice feels distant, yet right in my ears. *No one is going to believe what you're doing!*

"Am I dead?" I ask. Did the second glove really kill me?

He laughs.

No, you're not dead. You are still kicking it.

"Is this real?"

He shrugs and looks around. *Feels real to me.*

"But . . . how are you here?"

Damn, Lyric, what's with all the questions? I am here because you need me to be here. I'm what makes sense to you right now, a friendly face, you know?

"So you're not really Shadow?"

I'm sort of everything. You'll understand one day.

"Like God?"

He sighs. *How about you just stick with Shadow? How's Bex?*

"She misses you."

She admitted that? Things have changed.

I turn and look at my surroundings. The baby Undine surround me. The mama is on her way. My friends are struggling to survive. Chloe is in danger. But all of it is frozen and still.

"How is this happening?"

Here's the thing, Lyric. Right now the gloves are giving your brain a reboot, so you're kind of in a time-out. When it's done, you're going to be Lyric 2.0, a brand-new version.

"How new?" I worry.

New new. *You'll probably like it.*

"Probably?"

He smiles. *Probably, but you'll need it. It's just going to get harder from here, especially when you get to the big twist.*

"What big twist?"

They're not what you think they are. Actually, they're not what they think they are. But, that's all the spoilers you get. Well, friend, we're almost done. I love you. Give my girl a hug for me. I miss her a lot. Tell her that Duck guy was a douche.

"Wait! Do you know what is going to happen next? Am I going to survive?"

He shrugs. *I can't wait to find out.*

There's a *whoosh*, and I'm yanked back to the here and now, watching a tentacle crash down from the sky, ready to crush us all. I reach up and touch it, and it freezes in midair, then shrivels and blackens and turns to dust. I realize that I just drained all the water out of it with a simple touch.

"Woah," I say.

"Lyric!" Riley cries as he staggers to his feet. There's blood leaking from a wound on his arm, and I know I can make it stop, so I do. I caress his hand, willing the blood to do as I ask, because the blood is made of water, as is every part of his body. I suddenly realize that the nosebleeds were just my growing control. My blood was trying to help.

"How did you do that?" he asks.

"It's complicated. Riley, get the others to safety. I'm going to end this right now," I say as I focus the blood in my own body to repair my busted ankle.

"Lyric, you can't fight that thing by yourself!" he cries.

"Actually, I can."

I wave my hand over all the baby Undine, and like their mother's tentacle, they shrivel and die.

"Lyric Walker?" Fathom says.

"Stay with my people," I tell him.

I run through the Undine as they turn to dust around me. When I hit the shoreline, I dive in headfirst, feeling my gills and scales form. My gloves pulse with energy here in the depths. I feel even more control than I ever thought possible. I can sense things from miles away. I can feel a hurricane brewing, hear the currents racing past the continent, hear whale song hundreds of miles away. I can tell where the Rusalka are hiding and know that I could destroy them with just a thought. I decide to let them live. Let them crawl under rocks to escape me. The Undine mother is my only concern.

I shoot straight up out of the water, riding a spout that

reaches fifty feet into the air. Once there, I let the moisture around me take over, and it keeps me suspended. The Undine mother knows something has happened that has tilted the scales, and I can smell its fear. It howls and wriggles with indignant anger.

There's a shriek that forces my hands to my ears, an ancient cry that rips open the sky. The mother's limbs swat like lightning, and one connects with me. I crash into the water, and the beast plunges down after me. It hits me again, and I'm flung onto the beach. I stagger to my feet, and it barrels over me, knocking me aside as it charges inland.

"No!" I shout, and a blast of energy shoots from my fingertips into the beast's hide. A massive bubble inflates on its side. It grows and grows, and the monster shrieks and flails. Its limbs shrivel and break off as if I'm turning it to stone, and finally, with one horrible scream, it pops. The Undine explodes. A moment later, a horde of its babies appear and encircle their mother as she crumbles to dust. They are silent for a long moment, then turn and slither back toward the shoreline. Soon, they have all vanished into the surf.

I feel a sudden wooziness, and I'm unable to stand. I hit the sand face-first. There's a click, and I feel both gloves slide off my hands. They clang as they hit the ground. With them goes the last ounce of my strength. I can't hear the voices. I don't feel the water any longer.

I hear a splash and feel clawed hands on me. They drag me to my feet. I'm still dazed but able to make out three figures.

Two are Rusalka. The third is Minerva, her face alive with sadistic joy.

"Bring her," she says to the beasts.

"Where are you taking me?" I say as they drag me into the surf.

"It's time for you to meet the Great Abyss," she says.

The water is cold and black, and then there is nothing.

ACKNOWLEDGMENTS

Lots of people kept me afloat while I wrote this book. My editor, Sarah Landis, managed to help me with this baby while having one of her own. My wife and super agent, Alison Fargis, does more than a wife or an agent should have to do for a husband and a client. All the merfolk at Houghton Mifflin Harcourt put a million little notes into bottles and sent them out to sea. I have been overwhelmed by what came back. My friend Meredith Franco Meyers was a tireless supporter, and Joe Deasy—thanks for always understanding the plot and the subtext.

Thanks to friends and family, near and far.

And most of all, thanks to my little minnow, Finn.